A Merry Pair

Also by Sarah Madeline

A Fowl Match

A Merry Pair

SARAH MADELINE

ISBN 979-8-9928360-1-1

First edition: 2025

For those who dream about snowy fields and twinkling lights year-round. Go sit by the fire, make a mug of hot chocolate, throw on some festive socks, and grab a cozy blanket. It's time!

Thornwood Valley

Green House

Thornwood Valley Park

NSSG

The Laundry Basket

The Olive Bean

The Post Office

The Hoarder Emporium

The Chop Shop

Bobbie's Freeze

The Cozy Cottage Retirement Home

The Valley Harvest

Parking

Cats & Novels

Dr. Paula Newma

Thornwood Cabins

Hiking Trails

Chicken Coop

Valley Pond

Annie's Diner

The String
Cheese

Chloe's Closet

Rooster's

The Cozy Cabin Inn

Fix-Its

Dan's Auto

Stop and Fill

Suds in the Bucket

The Rhett Family
Farm

The Clearys

Liam — Sophia

Mason · Jackie · Ryder · Hannah · Joe · Charlotte · Mateo

Emma · Logan · Baby

The Watsons

Alex — Beth

Owen · Paula · Olive · Oakley · Jamal

Octavia

Chapter 1

OLIVE

Coffee shoots toward me in a steady stream, hitting me before I have time to react. "Ouch!" I cry out, feeling the burn as it splashes against my neck. Stepping back from the machine, I rub the sore spot with my fingers. "What did I do to you?" I ask while pointing to the espresso maker. I already know an angry red mark is forming on my neck.

Yes. I'm completely aware I'm talking to an inanimate object, albeit an insensitive one. No one's here to witness this travesty (fortunately for me). But no one's here to help me (unfortunately for me).

My once white T-shirt and brown apron are now covered in a wet mark. It seeps into the cotton fabric, creating a thick layer. I don't think the toughest stain remover could get this baby out.

Great. Just what I needed.

I need to think of the positives. At least my apron's brown, and my shirt is heavyweight cotton, or else my skin would be screaming there as well. I don't smell bad. My new coffee-cologne is a little sweet and rich, with a hint of hazelnut. I'm giving off a cozy aroma.

It would've made things easier if I'd known how my day was going to start. I was not expecting this to happen. But there's no way to foresee the future or dodge those little complications. Unless, of course, you're a psychic. But I'm definitely not one.

It would be great if I were.

Only a few moments ago, I was having a wonderful Friday morning. Everything was going smoothly. I woke up with ample time to get a shower and air dry my hair. I even had enough time to crochet some retro daisy granny squares while watching an episode of a crime documentary (that may have freaked me out a lot). That went downhill the second I tried to make myself an espresso shot. I needed a pick-me-up—some energy for the morning rush—while pastries were baking in the oven.

Coffee continues to spray, not aiming for the cup whatsoever. I swear under my breath. I open the cabinet doors under the counter and shut the valve to the water line off. I pull the plug on the espresso machine. Putting my hands on my hips, I contemplate my options. Option one: go back to bed. Option two: fix it somehow. The former is tempting, but the latter is the *sensible* option.

I open in thirty minutes. If I don't have any espresso, the townies are going to be cranky. They survive on a coffee IV injected into their bloodstream. Delivering the bad news will be the icing on the cake of my disaster. Today will be declared "The Day Olive Sent Thornwood Valley into Chaos" in an article written on the town's social page. A headache starts to form at my temple just at the thought of it.

I fiddle with the machine some more.

Please work.

Just what I assumed. I have no clue how to fix it. There's nothing apparent—at least to me—that looks broken. The group head looks normal; the portafilter looks fine. I stick to making coffee and baked goods—not fixing appliances. I swipe the screen on my phone and send a quick text to my best guy friend, Mason, hoping he will be able to do something. *Anything.* I need some good karma, quickly.

Olive

> Please help me. The coffee machine is broken. I'm desperate. Melting Face Emoji.

I head into the back room, grabbing a mop bucket, cleaner, and a few rags. I wipe down the cabinet and machine, then swipe the mop across the floor, ringing it out after every few passes. Leaning against the counter, I brace my hands on either side and let out a long sigh. My eyes linger on the door, silently willing Mason to walk through.

Within minutes, he enters, wearing a pair of dark jeans and a sherpa lined coat. "Hey," Mason says. He might as well be wearing a suit of armor since he's come to my rescue and all.

A cool gust blows snow through the swinging door. As he reaches to hang his coat, the bottom of his owl tattoo peaks from under the sleeve of his black T-shirt. He blows out a winded breath. "I came as fast as I could. Did it burn you?" A look of concern forms across his features. He walks behind the counter and reaches out, fingers brushing against the mark on my neck. His cool touch sizzles against my irritated skin.

"I'm used to getting burned by coffee. It will go away with a little bit of aloe."

Hopefully, because it probably looks like a hickey right about now. Another thing to fuel a new article. This headline would be something like "Olive's New Relationship" or "Who's Olive's Mystery Man?"

"Don't lie to me." His eyebrows shoot up.

"I'm not lying. I'm fine. I was trying to make an espresso, and it started spraying from the sides all over me. That's how I entered a wet T-shirt contest." I motion to the brown stain covering my clothes.

A smile lifts the corner of his lips. "Let me see what I can do." He scratches his beard in concentration.

"I turned the water line off and unplugged it."

"Good." He takes the glasses off the top of his head and puts them on his nose. He grabs the portafilter and examines it. A line forms between his brows.

"Can you fix it?" My eyes widen in panic.

I can't afford a new machine. Splurging on it in the first place was a risk. I knew it would be an investment, but the townies grew to love the new coffee varieties. A lot of folks here are what you call set-in-the-old-ways or highly-resistant-to-change kind of people. It was hard enough to get them to try the colorful, caramel drizzled, sprinkle-covered concoctions with whipped cream. They've learned to adapt.

"I'm not sure yet. I'll try to figure it out." His voice is deep in reply.

I put my thumbs in my pockets and rock on my feet. "Thanks for coming so fast."

The corners of his lips tip upward as he stares at the machine. Not looking away he replies, "Anything for you."

He's got his concentration-face on, so I take it as my cue to run away and change my clothes while I have the chance.

I jog up the narrow stairs to my apartment. I weave around a few straggler skeins of yarn on the floor, as if I'm in an obstacle course. Peeling off my stained clothes as I go, adding them to the dirty clothes pile on my bathroom floor.

I'll get it later.

Using a damp cloth, I wipe away my coffee covered skin. I hiss from the sting of the cold towel and smear some aloe on it. It's soothing, immediately relieving some of the ache. A light discomfort is still there, but it's enough to ignore. I shrug into a clean shirt and apron. By the time I make it back to Mason, he's leaning against the counter.

"All fixed."

"That fast? You're incredible!" My day is saved.

"It was nothing." He points to the machine. "It needed a new O-ring. I found one in the drawer with the manual. They should be replaced every year or so in the group head. The old one wasn't sealing anymore when you put on the portafilter. That's why it was spraying everywhere."

Pressing my palm to my forehead, I say, "I should've read the directions. I never do."

"I know. I remember when you put together the desk in your office."

I giggle. "The drawers were upside down. You had to tear the whole thing apart and rebuild it for me."

"And the time you built the swivel chair." He nods to the door behind the counter in my office.

My eyes widen as I realize he's right. "Twice. I've only not read the directions *two* times."

"The nightstand?" He raises a questioning brow.

I place my hands on my hips, standing my ground. "Okay! Fine. *Three* times. I swear, that's it."

He directs a sly grin my way and leans back further, bracing against the counter. "What about the corner bookshelf?"

Crap.

"I forgot about that one." *Honestly, I did.*

"I can keep going, but we'll be here all day." He lets out a deep chuckle.

"*Please* don't." I give him a pointed glare.

Okay, so maybe I have a problem with throwing any and all directions to the wind.

"There's never a dull moment with you, Firefly." The corner of his mouth turns up when he says my nickname.

"And you wouldn't have it any other way, Knight." The nickname I came up for him when we were younger is perfect. He's always coming to my rescue. I don't know what I would do without him. Better yet, I don't have to worry about that. He's never too far since his bar is right down the street.

"To be fair, I don't follow directions when baking," I say with a shrug. "But everything always turns out fine."

I've never had a catastrophic baking disaster. Well, maybe the occasional over-done pastry here and there. *I'm only human!*

"You were born with a spatula and a knack for baking. You couldn't make a bad pastry if you tried."

I blush. "You don't mean that."

7

He waves a hand. "Don't be so modest. We both know you're a great baker. The entire town of Thornwood Valley knows it. That's why there's already a line around the block."

What!

I look out the front glass window in disbelief. He's right. Townies are lined up on the sidewalk conversating. I didn't realize it was six o'clock already. Dan and Constance are first in line; she's badgering him for little tidbits of gossip to spread. I can see it from her hand motions and nodding. He looks exhausted, but he's always polite. Patience is something he's mastered; being the town's mechanic, it comes with the title. Constance, on the other hand, doesn't have an ounce of those qualities.

A chicken walks in front of the line of people. I think it might be Hennifer, but I can't tell from this distance. Every chicken in Mason's flock is named. They weren't always roaming the streets, but when they escaped their run, the townies adopted them and named them. They roam free during the day, and Mason pens them up at night.

He releases his grasp on the counter and heads towards the coat rack. "Looks like you have a busy morning. I better go, unless you need me to stay and help?"

I shake my head. "You've done more than enough this morning."

"Will I see you at dinner tomorrow night?" Mason questions as he puts his winter coat back on.

"I wouldn't miss our hectic joint family dinners for anything."

I grab the coffee pot from its warmer and pour the drip into a to-go cup. I hand him the coffee and a paper bag with some jelly filled donuts. He snatches both eagerly and walks backwards towards the door. "Good, because I couldn't get through them without you." He swings the bag. "Thanks for these." He pulls out a strawberry filled donut and doesn't hesitate in the slightest. He shoves half into his mouth. His eyes roll back, and he gives me a thumbs up.

I giggle as he opens the door, motioning everyone inside. Each townie greets him with a warm smile and chipper demeanor. Once they've entered, he waves on the way out. Constance is the first one in line.

Shocker.

"What can I get you this morning?" I ask her.

"Got any gossip for me? If not, I guess I'll settle for a single shot of espresso with milk and two pumps of hazelnut. Oh! And one of those chocolate chip pumpkin scones. They look delectable." She laughs to herself, covering her mouth.

Not today or any day, Constance.

I make the coffee and grab a scone. I hand them over the counter. "One scone and coffee. No gossip to report here."

Constance takes a sip of coffee. "What a bummer. How was your Thanksgiving, dear?"

"Wonderful. How was yours?" My answer is clipped. I'm not saying anything. I don't want to give her any information for an article. Hopefully she doesn't notice the coffee hickey on my neck. Or it'll be the next thing she latches onto. I already have at least three great article names for her to use.

"It was lovely. Chuck, Chelsea, and I had a wonderful dinner. We had turkey, stuffing, and mashed potatoes. All the fixings. Chelsea has a new boyfriend; she invited him for Christmas. I think this one will be a keeper. That daughter of mine goes through men like I post articles. A new one pops up every few days."

I can attest to that. I don't know where Chelsea finds them; there are not many *options* when it comes to men in town. But articles? Constance posts a few more than a new one every few days. It's more like one a day or more.

"Anything else about yours that was interesting?" she badgers once more.

I sigh. This woman is relentless when it comes to digging for information. "There's not much to tell. If there wasn't a line out the door, I'd tell you more." *I wouldn't tell you more if no one was here.*

"Oh, dear. You're right. I'll be on my way. I'll see you tomorrow." She takes a gulp of coffee and waves.

Can't wait! "Bye, tomorrow it is." I wave and sigh in relief.

She knows how to test my sanity.

10

Chapter 2

MASON

"Delivery!" Dustin shouts from the back entrance of Rooster's.

I flip the last chair upright and slide it under the hardwood table. Eighty chairs later and I still have to help Leo, the line cook, prep the kitchen. Count inventory and put away all the items from deliveries: straws, assorted beverages, napkins, etc. Then check in with Amelia, my bar manager/server/waitress; she holds a lot of titles. I'm grateful. Without her, I wouldn't have any free time. Before I hired her, it was hectic. It still is, but now it's manageable.

I walk between the tables and behind the bar. I push the back doors to the kitchen open with a swift shove. The smell of grease from the fryer wafts through the air. Leo waves from next to the flat top grill. "I thought you'd never be finished with those tables, boss."

"You and I both. It's been a long day already, and the night's just getting started. Saturdays are always the busiest day of the week." I chuckle.

"Hey, you two. Less talking, more working," Dustin says, pulling a dolly with three boxes stacked in the door. When it swings open, I hear the rooster crow from the chicken coop way behind the bar. He never did stick to only crowing in the morning. That's a myth—roosters crow at all hours of the day. He never shuts up.

"Listen here, Farmer, we don't have time for your antics. We run a tight ship," I joke. Dustin and I have been good friends for years. I met him while helping his grandparents with hay in the summer when we were younger. He came back to town a few years ago, and we reconnected. It's as if he wasn't gone for years. He's a good friend and someone I trust if I ever need help.

"That's a good one." He slides the top box on the stainless-steel counter.

"What do you have for me this time?"

"Garlic and herb, plain, and feta goat cheese." He pulls each out of the box. "And more cheese in the next. The bottom is, you guessed it, more cheese." He pulls the third box and sets it next to the other two.

"Thank you. Looks great," I say as I start packing the industrial fridge full of the items. "Goat cheese burger specials then?" I ask Leo.

"I can do that. It's been a while since we've made them." Leo nods and continues chopping lettuce at a rather fast speed. My fingers would've been gone by now if I chopped like that, but he does it with careful precision.

"Need any help before I go?" Dustin asks.

Help is something that would be amazing. I need to hire more employees, but I can't afford it at the moment. The tourists aren't in town right now, so the bar isn't as busy. There are always regulars who frequent the days I'm open: blue collar workers, shop owners, farmers, a few stragglers here and there. Our small town doesn't always bring as much business in the winter months. Once it starts to warm up, tourists filter in and stay at the Thornwood Cabins and The Cozy Cabin Inn. They travel here for the hiking trails, cabin getaways, and guided backpacking trips. Then there are more frequent customers, and I can pay my employees a seasonal bonus.

I also have less and less free time in the colder months. The bar is my home away from home—I spend more time here than at my house.

I shake my head. "No. I couldn't do that to you. You already have enough going on with the goats kidding."

"It's no problem. I can stay for a few hours at least." He shrugs. "The goats and I need a break. My grandpa's got it covered while I'm gone."

Well, if he insists.

13

"I wouldn't be opposed if you did stay. But he's gonna be pissed. Good luck with that."

"Good. It's settled. What do you need me to do?" He pushes the dolly to the storage closet. "And no, I don't care if he's pissed. There's no pleasing that man. He's grumpy."

"So that's where you got it from. I see now." I stack the cheese in the fridge. "I can help Leo with prep. Could you help Amelia with the front? We know how your cooking skills are."

"Firstly, I was only grumpy because I came back from New York after being laid off and had to become a farmer within hours. I got over it. So, no, I'm not so grumpy anymore. Secondly, no better than your cooking, asshole." Dustin's chuckle is deep and reverberating.

"Got me there. How are you and Vivi?" I continue packing the last few items in the fridge.

"She's wonderful. Being married is bliss. I don't know how I functioned without her. The A-frame is overflowing with plants. It's even worse than when you and Olive came over a few weeks ago. Every surface has a plant. Weirdly, I love it. Everywhere I look, I think of her." He pauses and laughs to himself. "Last night, she showed up with another cat. His name is Tuxedo. Cat's & Novels couldn't find a home for him, so she added him to the family and brought home a dozen books that are now stacked on the overflowing shelf in our room. I wouldn't have it any other way."

I smile. "That's great, man. I'm happy for you. I never imagined you as a cat dad, but now that you are, I can see it."

"Me neither." He shakes his head. "How's Olive?"

"She's good." *She's all I think about.*

"That's all?" He raises his eyebrows in question, not looking the least bit convinced with my dismissal.

"Yeah." I shut the fridge door and cross my arms.

Olive is my best friend. The person I call when I need advice and the one I hang out with every day. What I'm not going to tell Dustin is she's so much more to me than a friend. She's beautiful inside and out. When I'm having a shitty day and I see her red curls and warm smile as she skips in the door of my bar, all my worries melt away. Once she finds me, she sing-songs my nickname and laughs; it's like music to my ears. It's a daily ritual, and I'm captivated every time.

Dustin's voice halts my rampant thoughts. "When are you going to tell her?"

I look at the floor then up at the bright lights on the ceiling—anywhere to avoid his question. "What do you mean by that?" I know what he means. I just don't want to admit it out loud. If I do, it'll become real.

He gives me a knowing look. "You know what I mean."

"Never." That's the sad truth.

Never.

I stare at the floor for a beat and force my face to say, *This guy is not at all affected by his unrequited love for his best friend.* But I know he sees right through the facade.

The kitchen doors burst open. "Mason!" my sister Charlotte (Char) exclaims.

Her timing couldn't have been more impeccable. Thank God for sisters who save me from hard conversations.

She struts to the fridge next to me and says, "I need something for dinner. Can you hook a sister up? I don't feel like cooking tonight, and Mateo's still working." She puts her hands on her hips. "You two look like you're doing a whole lot of nothing."

Does everyone think I do nothing around here?

I silently thank her for distracting my mind.

Dustin clutches his stomach and laughs. He puts out his fist, and they fist bump. "Nice one, Char."

Is it gang up on Mason day? When and where was this decided? I obviously didn't get the memo.

"I was wondering where everyone was hiding." Hannah, my other sister, strolls in sipping on a glass of wine. That looks awfully like my inventory. I shake my head and laugh to myself. My sisters really make themselves at home.

"Where's the third musketeer?" Dustin raises a questioning brow.

"Jackie's staying with Mom and Dad. She's too boring to hang out with us anymore now that she's moved on to bigger and better places." Hannah swirls her wine and waves to Leo.

Char chimes in, leaning against the fridge, "We'll see her at dinner tomorrow. She's spending some time with them. Just because she moved, doesn't mean she forgot about us."

"Mhmm," Hannah replies and takes a gulp of wine.

Dustin gives me a *shit's-about-to-go-down* look and trails his gaze to the door. He pokes a thumb to the kitchen door and mumbles, "I'm gonna start setting up the tables with the napkin dispensers and salt and pepper shakers."

"About time," Char teases and says, "I'll help." She trails behind him and looks at Hannah motioning with her head for her to follow.

Hannah takes a sip of wine and rolls her eyes. "Coming." She slides her feet past me and waves as she pushes through the doors.

Poor Dustin. He's going to be in the middle of whatever conversation/argument they're going to have. But I'll admit, it's nice to have them stick around and help out tonight. It lessens the load of work on me. They don't ever say anything, but they know I need help. It means a lot to me.

As I grab a knife and begin to chop onions (a lot slower than Leo by the way), I can't help but think about Dustin's question.

When are you going to tell her?

Surprise. The answer is a final *never*.

I'm never going to tell her. How can I tell my best friend I've secretly been in love with her for years? Yeah—no—it's not happening.

Extra emphasis on *never*.

Chapter 3

MASON

Cleary and Watson Sunday dinners are non-negotiable. They started before I could walk or talk, and aren't going to end any time soon. It's become something I look forward to anyhow. Not to mention the free food and leftovers for the next few days.

That is reason enough.

If you give me a grill, I can make a mean steak or burger, but my baking skills are not up to par. I made a batch of chocolate chip cookies once. They turned into soup. So I appreciate any and all leftovers.

I know what you're thinking... I'll stick to burger specials, I promise. We don't offer soup cookies on the menu at Roosters. *Don't worry.* Anyway, that's why I hired Leo; he's good at what he does.

I trudge through the fluffy snow scattering over the path leading to the front door. Pennsylvania weather is unpredictable. One day it's warm; the next there's snow. I walk into Beth and Alex Watson's home with a fast gait. Eager for whatever the magnificent smell is to get in my stomach. Hints of bread and pumpkin fill my nostrils. Moose, my golden retriever and loyal companion, follows along beside me. His tail waggles back and forth. The muffled sound of laughter and conversation wafts from the living room and kitchen. My stomach rumbles so loudly; I swear it has its own personality. Moose high tails it to the living room and jumps on the couch with the guys. But I beeline it straight to the kitchen. I'm not sticking around to chat. I'll get roped into a heated argument over who's going to win the game because half of them are split on what teams they root for. Or they'll start trading drunken stories about stupid shit they've done. I won't make it out alive. I'll die of starvation.

My sisters, Hannah, Jackie, and Char are busy snacking on a fruit spread with Oakley. Olive, Paula, and Beth are making turkey sandwiches with leftovers from Thanksgiving. Olive won't waste anything; she's always revamping leftovers.

Having Olive Watson as a best friend comes with a lot of benefits. In the form of many things. Cookies. Pastries. Sourdough bread. You name it. She makes it all in The Olive Bean, her coffee shop. She's a literal baking goddess. One major perk of our friendship includes taste testing every recipe. And she makes something new at least twice a week.

"Hi, ladies." I grab a turkey sandwich and start chewing, trying to satisfy my grumbling stomach. *Now this is a blessing.* Something to be thankful for, since everyone is trying to list things they are grateful for around this time of year. I love a good post-Thanksgiving sandwich.

"Oh, nice of you to show up, Mason!" Char shakes her head and plops a strawberry from the tray.

"I had paperwork to do. I didn't realize it was getting so late." I take a bite of my sandwich.

"Do you ever take a break away from Rooster's?" Jackie asks.

"No. Even if I wanted to, I don't have the time," I say in between bites.

"That's crap. You can make the time," Hannah chides—she was always the most brutally honest one out of the three.

"Leave the poor man alone." Oakley, Olive's sister, points her finger to the three of them.

"Hey! They're right. He needs to take a vacation," Olive agrees.

"Thank you," the three of my sisters chide at the same time, looking smug.

Each of them is younger than me, yet they are all married. Being the oldest, I learned quickly to be protective. I gave each of their husbands a hard time at first, but now we get along great.

"I can't make the time. I've got too much to do. And anyway, Olive, I can't remember the last time you took a vacation," I retort.

"Guess what, Mason? She is! She's going to the cabins next weekend." Jackie winks at me and takes a grape from the fruit tray and throws it in her mouth.

Not now, Jackie.

I made the stupid mistake of telling my sister that I had a thing for Olive in high school. Do you think she ever lets that one down? No.

She told both of our other sisters. I never confirmed or denied anything. I've learned to keep my lips sealed around two of them—Hannah and Jackie. Char is better with secrets; she's the only one I confide in if there's something I know I don't want everyone else finding out about. Example A: talking about my crush on Olive.

Olive had a constant stream of boyfriends through the years, so there wasn't a point anyway. First there was Nick, *the biker*, then there was Austin, *the angsty singer*, and don't get me started on Chad, *the non-committer*. I was a friend to her when each one left. A best friend and still am. I wasn't going to be another man to disappoint her. She needed her friends. With our families being so close, a relationship between us wouldn't be ideal. It would be awkward if we broke up. It could jeopardize our friendship. I didn't want that. I still don't want that.

Nothing has changed over the years.

I can't help but gravitate towards any conversation Olive's in. The way her green eyes glimmer wherever she finds something interesting. The way her burgundy curls flow from the side of her face. The way her nose turns red when she's flustered. How her freckles dot her cheeks. I can think about her all I want, but we're just friends.

I never thought I'd still be single at thirty.

Here I am. Fantasizing about complications I don't need.

But I secretly want.

"Jackie, when are you leaving? Maine's a long drive," Oakley asks.

Jackie's eyes widen. "Are you counting down the minutes until we get out of your hair?"

"No! I was only asking—being polite." Under her breath, she mumbles, "Something you lack." She can't whisper to save her life. They all laugh, including Jackie.

"We'll miss you. I'm so glad you guys could drive out for Thanksgiving." Hannah puts her bowl in the sink and turns around to the counter.

"We'll miss you too. We'll be back for Christmas. And I'm sure you'll call me every day," Jackie says while grabbing more fruit.

"It's not the same. Why did you have to move?" Char's eyes look glossy.

"I know, but it was for Ryder's job. We've been over this. He couldn't pass up a position as a sawmill manager. Let's make the best of it and enjoy our time together," Jackie says, pulling Char into a hug. "Besides, Maine is growing on me. You should come and visit. I'm sure you'd love it. We've got a guest room and everything. And we're right by the beach."

"Sorry, I'm a little emotional right now." Char breathes out a sigh. "I will visit soon, I promise."

"What did I miss?" My mom walks in the kitchen and covers her mouth once she notices a tear rolling down Char's face. She always had the worst timing.

"We're embracing the moment, Sophia, and not worrying about when anyone's leaving," Beth, Olive's mom, says.

"That's a good thing. Let's enjoy it. Who wants to help me set the table?" my mom asks.

"Pass the stuffing please." Owen taps Olive's shoulder and mumbles between forkfuls of mashed potatoes.

"Can you chew with your mouth closed? I don't want to see your chewed-up food." Olive scowls at her brother. She passes the stuffing begrudgingly.

"Like this, Daddy?" Octavia chomps on her carrots, grinning. Her white teeth shine with orange pieces. "When am I going to get a sister?"

"Maybe sometime soon," Paula answers her daughter. "When Mommy isn't so busy. I'm the only doctor in town, and it's a lot of work."

Octavia claps and asks, "What will be the baby's name?"

Paula says, "We don't know yet. That will be something the three of us will figure out. But something starting with the letter 'O.'"

"Oh," Octavia sounds out. "Why?" she asks.

I laugh to myself. 'Why' is her favorite word right now.

"That's my fault." Beth clears her throat from the other end of the table while spearing a carrot on her plate. "Your daddy and aunts all have names starting with the letter 'O.' Owen, Oakley, and Olivia, but you know her as Olive. I thought it would make it better with organizing their things. And it was cute that they all matched."

"You are obsessed with organization," Oakley says.

"I second that," Olive says. "And it wasn't so cute when you embroidered all our backpacks with the letter 'O.' I'll never forget the day Oakley and I switched them. I was so mad when I pulled out her homework, not mine."

"I was there in Olive's class," I back up Olive's story, "fire was shooting from her eyes. Olive got up and stormed from the room. Miss. Jones wasn't so happy either when I followed her out of the classroom. We skipped school that day."

"You didn't. You two would never skip school." Beth gasps, covering her mouth.

If she only knew.

Olive gives me a knowing glance. "There are a lot of things you don't know, Mom. We hiked the woods behind the middle school looking for salamanders and hopped on the bus just in time like we were at school all day."

"Why didn't you just go to Oakley's classroom and switch backpacks?" Jackie questions, grabbing a dinner roll from the bread bowl.

Olive gives me a sly smile. "Now, where's the fun in that? I already made a scene."

"Why didn't the school call me?" Her eyes narrow. "Alex, dear, did they call you?"

Alex looks at his plate, studying his food like it's the most amazing thing he's ever seen. "It was a long time ago. I can't remember." He scratches his head.

Oh, they for sure called him. He's not going to admit it, though.

"We never swapped them again," Oakley says quickly, trying to get her dad out of trouble.

"I never had any issues," Owen states, unbothered.

Olive chimes in, "That's because your backpack was blue. Mom made yours special."

"Can you make me a backpack?" Octavia asks.

Beth answers, "Yes, dear, I would love to. As soon as I finish making Oakley's wedding dress." She's the town's seamstress and makes exceptionally detailed clothing.

"You're already making her dress? She's not even engaged." Olive gasps.

"Yes, I was excited. She will be soon enough. Right, Jamal?" Beth asks.

Oakley shrugs, and Jamal's forehead is glistening. *I wonder why he looks so nervous.* Jamal and Oakley have been together for a few years. He's talked about proposing to her for as long as I've known him.

Octavia grabs another carrot and chomps on it. Smiling wide again, distracting everyone. I chuckle; it's cute when she does it. I don't think Paula finds it very funny.

"We chew with our mouths closed, remember?" She demonstrates to Octavia and gives Owen and I the side eye.

I'm the *fun kind* of uncle. If that's what you'd call it. We're not related by blood, but we're about as close to family as it gets. I'm not going to be the bad guy and ruin all the fun. Octavia is at the age where she picks up on anything people say. That's why I try to watch my swearing around the kids. I don't need them repeating anything I say. Owen is the one who has the hardest time with that concept.

"They're calling for five inches of snow next weekend," Liam, my dad, announces, breaking everyone out of their side conversations.

"Oh shi—" Owen about proves my point, until he catches himself. "Oh *my*."

Paula's forehead creases, and she shakes her head with a half smile.

"Snow! Is Frosty the snowman going to be here?" Logan, Hannah and Joe's son, asks. He practically jumps out of his seat with excitement.

"Yes, and all of his friends!" Char beams, playing along. Logan, Octavia, and Emma (Jackie and Ryder's daughter) share a look of pure glee.

"Can we go play?" Octavia asks her mom.

"Of course, go ahead you three. Have fun." Paula nods. They scurry off to the living room faster than she could even finish her sentence. Not long after, Moose follows them, happily wagging his tail.

"Are you going to be okay driving into the mountains?" Oakley gives Olive a skeptical look.

"Who's driving into the mountains?" Alex asks, concern lacing his voice.

"Me, next weekend. I'll be fine." Olive shrugs. Pushing around the turkey on her plate with a fork.

"Maybe someone should go with you if you're insisting on going," Jackie chimes in. She's always the most logical one out of the bunch. Usually chiming in with unsolicited advice.

"I'm driving up Friday or Saturday depending on the snow. I don't mind if I'm stuck there. It's going to be clear enough by Sunday evening after the plow trucks make it through. I planned on leaving Monday morning anyway." Olive huffs.

"Maybe I should tag along with you," I whisper while tapping her shoulder.

Olive is stubborn. I know she wants to go on her own. But I worry about her. As any normal best friend would. The roads aren't so easy to navigate in snowy conditions, and I'd feel better about it if I went with her. There's no talking Olive out of something once her mind is set on it.

"No!" She tries and fails to whisper into my ear—it was more of a shout.

I put my hands up in surrender and rub my ear. "Ow. Okay. I got it. You can go alone, *Firefly*."

"Thank you, *Knight*. No need to bring out your war horse for this one. I'll be okay." She pats my shoulder and smiles softly.

I can't help but be protective. It's in my nature. I have three sisters.

Everyone continues talking about nothing and everything. Once dinner is finished, we all hang out in the family room with the Steelers game playing in the background. The room is filled with laughter and warmth. Everyone is fixated on the TV. When suddenly, Jamal is on one knee as a commercial rolls.

Shit.

30

Chapter 4

OLIVE

The room falls to a mere whisper while my heart pounds against my chest. The noise of its beating is loud in my ears. Goosebumps prickle along my arms.

My little sister is getting engaged.

Oakley and Jamal haven't said anything else yet, but I already know she'll say yes, and I know he'll say something that makes my heart melt. I can see it in the way she looks at Jamal. Love and joy written all over her features. Her face is bright and warm with emotion. And the way he looks at her. As if he's consumed with adoration. He's completely smitten. They're the definition of the perfect couple.

She puts a palm over her mouth in elation as Jamal starts to speak. His words are smooth. He doesn't have a speech written anywhere; it's not something he's spent hours practicing. It's coming straight from his heart. "Oakley Watson, you are my soulmate. I can't imagine my life without you. You are the light in an otherwise dark world. I still remember when we first met. It was the best day of my life. We were both waiting in the airport terminal. Our flights were delayed. You asked me for a pen. What a simple question it was. One flicker of a moment and I was entranced. Your beauty, your smile. If it wasn't for your tendency to misplace things, we would've never met. I was addicted after the first day. I knew you were the one I needed in my life no matter what. The one I was searching for. The love I have for you was instant. I love you, Oak. Will you marry me?"

"Jamal, I can't believe it! Yes!" she shouts. Tears stream down her face as she giggles with glee. "I love you too." Her voice is soft as he places the band on her left ring finger. Jovial sounds of clapping and happy tears fill the room. They hold each other at an arm's distance. Their gazes are locked, a silent exchange of love passes between them both, and they kiss. The kids jump up and down in excitement. Moose barks. Sophia begins taking pictures of the happy couple. Everyone revels in the moment.

It's contagious. I feel immense joy and excitement for them both. I'm so happy for my sister. She deserves a happily ever after. A partner to spend forever with. Someone to travel with her on a whim. And she found it with Jamal.

They were the last couple to get engaged from both the Cleary and Watson families. The rest are married, except for Mason and I.

I look across the room and see Sophia is whispering into Mason's ear. I can only imagine what she's saying. Something like: "When are you going to settle down? Start a family? You can't show up to another Christmas without anyone. Your window is closing. You've never brought anyone home." It could be a mixture of all or any of those.

I feel bad for him. I'm hoping Mom doesn't give me the same talk. Sophia and my mom are best friends. They are two peas in a pod. They share the same views; they want everyone to be in a happy relationship. Although the thought is nice, that's not the case for me. I *like* being alone. Mason *likes* being alone too—at least, I think he does. He's never mentioned otherwise. And we spend so much time together, but that kind of conversation hasn't really come up. It would've by now, right?

I'm all in with the things I do. I want to be certain the person I spend my life with is *the* one. I've made too many mistakes with relationships in the past. I'm not going to search for one. If it happens organically, then so be it. If it doesn't, so be it. I'm content. *For the most part.* Besides, I'm twenty-nine; I still have plenty of time.

Mason's eyes meet mine and widen. He mouths, "Help me."

I shrug. There's nothing I can do. I could stage a distraction or yell for Mason to come over. I'm not going to spoil the moment for Oakley. She looks immensely happy. Jamal does too. Both our families are oozing with merriment. I wouldn't trade this moment for anything. I'm so proud of the woman Oakley has become.

After some time, I walk up to the happy couple and congratulate them with everyone else around the room.

"Congratulations, I'm so happy for you both." I hug Jamal and Oakley. She pulls me into her arms, and I rub her back reassuringly while she cries. "You're gonna make me cry."

"I'm sorry—Olive," she says between cries. "I wasn't expecting him to propose today—I can't believe it."

My parents talk to Jamal while Oakley puts her shaky hand in mine. "Your ring's beautiful. It suits you," I say and give her hand a reassuring squeeze.

Her ring is simple and elegant. A gold band with a pear cut diamond. She always wears gold rings, dainty necklaces, and simple jewelry. The ring speaks volumes to Jamal; he notices every detail about Oakley. The ring is what she would've picked out herself.

"Isn't it?" She stares at it, tilting her hand. "I'm going to get married!" Her animated expression makes me smile.

I look up from her hand. "You are going to make a stunning bride."

She squeezes me into another hug. "I guess it's a good thing Mom started making me a dress. I'll need it."

"Sometimes her eagerness comes in handy," I admit.

"It does, but I'm sorry." Oakley tips her head.

"Why are you telling me sorry?"

"It's your turn now. She's going to come at you full force with future planning. You know, trying to find you a boyfriend."

I sigh. "Don't worry about me. I'll use my best avoidance tactics. Enjoy your day; today's about you and Jamal and the bright future you have together. I'm so proud of you, Oak."

"Thank you, Olive." I pull away and sit on the couch to let everyone else congratulate them.

Mason sits next to me. In his eyes, I see the same realization I feel within myself.

I need to accept my fate. Mason and I are the only single ones left to be tormented. We need to figure out a way to avoid our mothers.

That will *not* be an easy feat to conquer.

Chapter 5

OLIVE

"If you make me hang one more strand of lights on this ceiling, I'm going to vault myself off this ladder." Mason grits through his teeth. His clipped tone conveys his agitation.

"I love you, but you are being *so* dramatic." I hand him another strand of lights. "I'm either one hundred percent all in on Christmas cheer, or I'm the complete opposite—the Grinch. This year I'm feeling festive, and since it's December first, I'm making this month my personality. I'm in the mood to be cheerful."

Who am I kidding?

I'm a replica of an elf from the north pole. My ears might as well be pointed. I want to decorate everything, spread the cheer, and sing along to Christmas songs at the top of my lungs. There's no wavering. I'm not half-baking anything about the season this year.

Mason groans. "Oh, I *know.* It's Monday, and you're already this chipper."

"I can't help it. When a customer enters my coffee shop, I want it to look like Santa's factory blew up in here."

"I think we already achieved that." He grins.

He may be right. Garland hangs on the window frames, multi-colored strands drape across the ceiling, a full-out decorated tree sits in the corner, and snowflakes float everywhere. I want my customers to experience the snow without the chill. To sip on hot drinks while watching snowflakes through the large glass window. Or iced drinks. *To each their own.*

"Rockin' Around the Christmas Tree" by Brenda Lee plays through the speakers, coalescing with the smell of peppermint cookies—they are what I owe Mason for his help. It's not like I'm taking advantage of him; I'm *not* an opportunist. Let's just say I'm more of a 'you help me, I help you *extra'* kind of person. Mason isn't going to like the plans I have for Rooster's, but he *needs to* like them. I owe him a favor, and I'm repaying it. I just have to figure out when I'll have the time. I tap my chin in thought.

"Don't give me that look." He peels another strand of lights from my grasp. He stands on top of the ladder, eyebrows furrowed.

"What look?"

"Don't play coy with me. We've been friends since before we could crawl. I know you're scheming something fierce in that red head of yours." He glares at me, his chocolate brown gaze burns with suspicion. He's right. We've been friends for so long. Our mothers were inseparable in high school. After they got married, it was just expected that their kids would be best friends too.

"I'm not being coy. You'll find out what I'm planning later. You won't see it coming." Mentally, I'm rubbing my hands together.

"No. Do *not* plan anything for me, now or later. Or ever." He gives me a look of pure terror. It's amusing. I'm already imagining the bar with poinsettias, twinkling fairy lights, and cotton strung on fishing line along the ceiling to look like snow.

I don't think that's a fire hazard.

In my head I'm cackling at the prospect of what's to come.

The sound of a timer going off clears my thoughts. "I need to get those cookies out of the oven. Unless you want rocks for payment."

He hooks the strand of lights on the ceiling and looks down at me, eyes widening. "No! Go, save the cookies, please, I beg you!"

"Smart choice." My ponytail swooshes back and forth as I retreat. I swing the door to the kitchen open and peek inside the industrial oven. The radiating heat hits me in the face like a brick wall.

Once the cookies have been on the cooling rack for a few minutes, I plate a bunch to bring out to Mason. Not able to resist the temptation, I have one for myself. The gooey chocolate melts on my tongue, pairing with the crunch of peppermint pieces. It's a culinary masterpiece. Mason and I both moan out loud, unashamed over our obsession with food in general.

"Hi lovelies, what are you up to?" Constance's voice rings from the entryway. I jump in surprise.

"When did she get here?" I whisper to Mason.

"I don't know. I didn't even hear her come in." He continues to devour more cookies, having no care in the world about her sudden presence.

"We are decorating for the holidays," I mutter.

"Oh, dear—it looks as if you bought every decoration The Valley Harvest had in stock." Constance spins and stares at what we've decorated so far.

"That's because she did." Mason guffaws while chewing. I slap him playfully on the arm. He starts choking on the cookie while continuing to laugh.

I love instant karma.

I place my hands on my hips. "I'm feeling the holiday spirit, and no *Scrooge* who comes in here is going to tear me down."

"No, it looks very *festive*, Olive. I love it! It's a maximalist Christmas!" she insists.

Liar.

She adjusts her glasses, squinting at the new menu above the register. Analyzing it. Committing the words to memory in a way that reminds me of how a health inspector would search a restaurant. A swipe of a finger against a table looking for a spec of dirt. "And new drinks! These sound delightful!" Her tone reaches a higher pitch.

What does she want?

Constance is the leader of the Thornwood Valley's town gossip. She's one of three ladies in what they call the gossip mill. Bobbie and Annie are the other two, they own businesses in town, but Constance calls the shots and writes the articles. If she walks in the door at an unusual time, you know there's nothing innocent about it. No coincidences either. This isn't part of her normal routine. She's predictable. She sits outside Cat's & Novels in the warmer months in the morning; in the winter she has a permanent table at Annie's Diner. Dutifully the first in line every morning for coffee. She either wants a favor or to start something. It's most likely the latter, and I dread it.

"So, what brings you in, Constance? Isn't it a little late for you to still be in town?" It's seven o'clock in the evening, and she's normally nowhere to be found after five. I'm not complaining.

"I'm here to tell you the good news!" she announces, waving raised hands in excitement. Mason snorts and covers his face, stifling another chuckle.

Oh no. This isn't funny, Mason. I think to myself. I want to tell him, but I hold it in for once.

I nod my head, telling her to go on. But in my mind, I'm telling her to leave. *Please, enlighten me with the good news.*

She continues. "We are hosting the first ever Thornwood Valley, Christmas Cookie Bake-Off! I had to come and tell you in person before I sent out the email. I know you would love to be a part of it!"

The prospect of a cookie bake-off is exciting. There's never been an event in town I was looking forward to. Annie and I won the small business games two years ago, so that was a plus. They happen every year in spring to raise money for the businesses in town. I still didn't want to participate, but we both won a trip to the Thornwood Cabins. So it wasn't all bad.

"But there's one condition."

I knew it! There are always conditions when it comes to Constance. Stipulations, I'm always careful to pay close attention to, similar to reading the fine print in a contract. They always get you with the tiny words no one takes the time to read. Just like Constance always has ulterior motives and little tricks to catch you off guard.

"It's a couples bake-off. A test of relationships and your culinary skills. Isn't that the perfect duo?"

No. No, it's not. Do I look like I'm in a relationship?

She would know, I'm not anymore. I haven't been in a serious one for almost two years. Not since Chad—the worst ex-boyfriend I ever had in my life—left me in ruins. And that is saying something because none of my past relationships were real winners.

Why is she so conniving? She knows I can't resist anything to do with baking. She knows I'm *single.* And to top it off, she has the audacity to show up here like I can participate. Tempting me with the prospect of a baking competition. It's downright evil.

"I'm not in a—"

Mason cuts me off mid-sentence. "What Olive means to say is we would love to be a part of the cookie games—or whatever you want to call them."

So, this is when you decide to speak up. I glare at him.

I'm not liking this.

"I didn't realize you and Olive were in a relationship now. That's great news! Congratulations! We're calling it the Cookie Chronicles. Isn't that clever?"

"Thank you. We haven't been telling anyone yet, so can you keep this to yourself for now?" he explains.

"Sure. Your secret is safe with me. Expect an email tonight. Glad to hear the good news." She grins a devilish smile and leaves within seconds. Her ability to appear and disappear within a few minutes is quite impressive. Constance comes in blazing like a storm and leaves like one too. In and out in a flash. Nothing but damage in her wake.

"Don't kill me," Mason pleads.

"I'm getting ready to. Nice to know I'm in a relationship with you. Since when?" I cross my arms over my chest.

It's not that he isn't attractive or someone I wouldn't want to date. Mason is a good-looking man and has a huge heart. I've never thought about him that way; he's always been there. A friend. A shoulder to cry on. A person to annoy that doesn't mind when I do annoy them. Someone to laugh with. Someone to cry with. Did I mention he's exactly six feet and five inches? I could list the things

I look for in a man, and he checks them off. Tall, check. Tattoos, check. Handsome, check. Funny, extra check. Gallant, three more checks.

But I don't have time for commitments. I like having him as a friend.

"Let me explain," Mason pleads with me.

"I can't wait to hear it."

Let's take off a check for him telling Constance that we're dating.

"Look." Mason scratches the side of his face along his beard. "This was the perfect opportunity."

"What do you mean?" I cross my arms. *Perfect opportunity to what? Make me fume with anger?*

"I can't handle one more of our conjoined family Christmases or New Years being single. The incessant criticism is driving me insane." He crosses his arms. "My mom was on my case when Jamal and Oakley got engaged yesterday." He sighs.

I pace back and forth. "I don't know."

"We both get something we want. I get to be left alone. I can enjoy the holidays without added pressure. You get to be in the cookie competition. And you don't have to deal with our mothers trying to find you a boyfriend. We can pretend to date until the day after New Year's Day and go our separate ways after the holidays."

"It all seems like so much work." I don't have the time or energy for a relationship. My last one drained all my vigor.

"It won't change anything. We always hang out anyway. You might have to hold my hand occasionally. Or act extra interested in me. That shouldn't be so hard, right? Plus, it's only for a month."

I guess that doesn't sound too bad.

"You promise no matter what happens, this won't hurt our friendship?"

"I promise. That's the last thing I would want," he says this with so much conviction. I can't help but believe his words. I trust Mason, and if he thinks this won't change anything with our friendship, then I believe him.

I sigh in defeat. "Deal." I extend my hand to shake on it. "Fake boyfriend?"

He shakes my hand. "It's a deal, fake girlfriend."

What did I just sign myself up for?

Chapter 6

OLIVE

"Who ordered a caramel latte?" I shout over the chattering. Townies are crowded inside the coffee shop this morning. There's a line to the door. I yawn, waiting for someone to claim their drink, so I can get started on the next one.

I still can't get over yesterday. I keep replaying the moment Mason announced our fake relationship in my mind. It swirls in a never-ending loop. *It's a deal, fake girlfriend.*

I can't believe I agreed to this sham.

"Me!" Vivi (Violet), my bestie, shouts over the voices, breaking me from my thoughts. She grasps her to-go cup. "This place is a madhouse. It's only six in the morning."

"It's insane! I don't know what's going on. What are they all doing here so early? I thought yesterday was nuts. There are double the people today."

"They probably read the article on the Thornwood Valley Social."

"What article?"

"The one about you and Mason. You'll have to read it. It's very detailed."

Your secret is safe with me. How could I be so foolish? No one's secrets are safe with her. Even if it's a made-up one—one that I didn't think would become public right away—to appease our families and get to participate in The Cookie Chronicles. *What a goofy name for a competition by the way.*

"It's okay. It's like déjà vu. When Dustin and I became a couple, they posted about it before I got to tell you the news. It's okay you haven't told me yet. But I'm happy for you. It's about time you guys got together."

I stare at her dumbfounded. I lean in and whisper under my breath, "We're not dating. We're fake dating. Keep it on the down low."

"Oh—okay. Got it." She looks to be considering something but then says, "Any luck finding guys on that dating app?"

I sigh dramatically. "Does it look like I have any hot dates?"

"Um. No?"

"That was rhetorical, but the only three 'matches' were Jackson, your lovely cheating ex. Chad, my lovely 'non-committal' ex. And Harvey from Fix-Its. He's old enough to be my grandpa. He's also the best option out of the three. That's saying something. So, the dating pool isn't looking very promising."

"That's a shame. But it's not like you could go out with anyone regardless. You're fake dating Mason now. How long are you going to pretend?"

"Until New Year's Day."

"That long?"

"He wants our families off his back. All they do is nag. You know this. I'm also sick of them getting on my case too. So, for the holidays, we'll stick it out."

"This could get interesting." Vivi drums her fingers against her cup.

"What do you mean by that?"

"Nothing—look at the time." She looks at the non-existent watch on her wrist. "I would stay and help, but I need to open my shop."

"Fine. Be that way. See you, Vivi."

"Bye!" She pushes her way out, parting the line of people.

"Who's next in line?" I ask the crowd. A few people started to scatter everywhere. No one's standing single file anymore.

"Me, I'd love a peppermint mocha," says Marigold, Harvey's daughter who also runs Fix-Its.

"Coming right up!" I say while scooping some of the pre-ground espresso beans into the portafilter. "How's business?"

"It's been slow, but Dan keeps us busy with ordering car parts."

I tamp the coffee grounds and lock in the portafilter. I slide a cup under the machine and click the button to brew. "I noticed him walking over every day."

"Yeah, he's supposed to come today. We ordered a muffler for Constance's SUV, and it'll be delivered sometime this morning. He also needs a few more odds and ends." She smiles and tucks her thumbs into the pockets of her pink overalls.

I fill a small glass with chocolate peppermint syrup that I made the night before and mix the espresso shot in. "Are you guys friends?" I ask Marigold.

Normally, Dan doesn't say much. He comes every day to get coffee, but otherwise, I don't think I've ever had a full-blown conversation with him.

"I'm friends with everyone in town," Marigold's smile is sweet, "but other than talking about car parts and an occasional hi and hello, we don't delve into anything else—he's very nice, though." She fiddles with the end of her braided blonde hair.

I open the mini fridge, pour milk into a stainless cup, and begin steaming it. "You're right about one thing. He is. I saw the poor guy stuck in line with Constance a few days ago. She was badgering him. He just smiled and nodded." I pour the steamed milk into the espresso shot in the shape of a Christmas tree.

"Constance isn't too bad."

"You say that because you avoid the competitions. You don't see her in her true form. And you haven't been a part of her scheming yet. Just you wait." I laugh and set her mug on the counter.

There's no doubt in my mind Constance has something up her sleeve for Marigold. Constance seems to interject herself in everyone's business; no one is off-limits.

"That's true. I'll have to wait and see." She smiles and takes the glass. "Thank you, Olive."

"No problem."

I ring her out, and she sits at a table in the corner while the next customer comes to the counter. I take each order, and once they file out, I'm left alone again. I check my phone to see what this article has to say.

Thornwood Valley Social
A Thornwood Valley Friends to Lovers Story Unfolds

Olive, owner of The Olive Bean, and Mason, owner of Rooster's Bar, are now dating! It's my pleasure to announce the good news. Olive and Mason have been best friends for years, as the whole town knows. Our sources include (but are not limited to): Beth Watson and Sophia Cleary. We went straight to the source to learn the facts. "It must be true if you're telling me they signed up for the Cookie Chronicles. I see the way they look at each other," Beth said. The excitement she had over the phone was proof enough. Although, it's unlike me to only base my findings on one quote, so here's another: "This is exciting news! The last of my children to fall in love," Sophia said. They are also the last of the Clearys and Watsons to be in a relationship after Jamal proposed to Oakley. Read the last article for pictures of the happy couple and a full story. It's so wonderful that our town is connecting so many in the name of love. We'll keep you updated on everything as it unfolds in real time.

Constance Williams – Thornwood Valley Gossip Mill Executive

I roll my eyes as I finish reading the *lengthy* article of absolute nonsense.

Our moms gave Constance statements and fed into the story. They had no information whatsoever, and Constance is a keyboard warrior with any little tidbit.

It's infuriating.

A new message pops up on my screen, and I open it. It's my ex-boyfriend, Chad.

Ew. Why?

Chad

> Hey, babe. Thinking of you lately. I miss you.

The endearment, babe, doesn't settle well in my stomach. It's been two years. *Two years!* I'm not his babe. I'm not anyone's *babe*. And I'm not anyone's to miss.

Didn't he get the hint when I threw a cup of coffee over him? Did that interaction get wiped from his brain? I made it perfectly clear that he wasn't welcome here anymore and not welcome in my life either.

Get your coffee-covered-lying-face out of my shop and don't come back. Don't talk to me again.

I remember exactly what I told him the day that he showed up with his new girlfriend, Chelsea, kissing her at the counter in front of me while we were on a 'break.' Taking some time to separate and work on our own problems, so we could be better together. For Chad it was a green flag to move on.

Does he suddenly miss me? *No.*

As soon as he caught a drift of me with Mason, he texts me again out of thin air. It's highly unlikely. He misses his perfect version of me. The one that lives in his head. The Olive I was with him. His perfectly curated, quiet and reserved Olive. Not me. Not who I really am. Not us.

This weekend getaway can't come soon enough.

"Hey, honey." I jump at the sound of my mom's voice.

She popped up out of nowhere.

I place a palm over my heart. "Holy crap, Mom, you scared the soul from my body."

"I wasn't trying to sneak up on you. I dropped off a dress for a client and thought I'd come in to see my lovely daughter. And get one of your famous hot chocolates."

"What's with the statement in the article?" I cut to the chase right away. I grab a mug and pour the hot chocolate out of a thermos.

She blinks rapidly, looking surprised by my brazen question. "About that. I'm sorry. Constance called me and asked about you and Mason. I had no clue. It was my honest reaction. Sometimes I forget who she is. She makes you open up to her. You feel like you can tell her anything, and she'll keep it between you two. That's never the case. I messed up."

"It's okay. I get it." I slide her cup across the counter.

She wraps her hands around the mug. "So you and Mason are really together?"

"Yes, we are. It kind of just happened."

Just happened? That was really believable. Not.

"That makes my heart so warm. I'm so happy for you two."

"Thanks, Mom." She's making me feel really guilty. Mason and I are faking this, but it seems as though the whole town has seen it coming, like it was bound to happen at some point.

Why would they think that? Beats me.

She blows on the hot liquid and takes a sip. "This is delicious. Did you make it?" Her eyes twinkle with pride.

"Yes, no powdered mix around here. I made it this morning."

"I still don't get where you got your cooking skills from. I'm a mediocre cook at best, and your dad's a step above me." She shrugs.

"No clue, but I'm glad for wherever it came from." My heart swells with pride thinking about how much I love what I do. Making drinks and pastries was my calling, and I'm so glad my parents supported my dreams. I didn't have to live in their shadow and continue their businesses or their aspirations. They encouraged me to start on my own and do what I love. And I love them all the more for it.

"Me too." She smiles. "I better go. I have a backpack to make for Octavia. I'm really happy for you."

I swallow hard. "Thanks, Mom, see you later." I wave and sit on the bar stool behind the counter.

I'm really happy for you. Her words make my deception sting.

I don't know if it was a good idea to go along with this plan. Is a cookie competition really worth faking a relationship? Not really. But helping my best friend and avoiding our overbearing families? Yeah, that makes it worth it.

Chapter 7

MASON

The sun's glare illuminates the dusting of snow on the sidewalk as I walk to The Olive Bean. Almost every shop I pass has their signs flipped to open. Chloe's Closet, The String Cheese, Annie's Diner, and Bobbie's Freeze. A few of my chickens scavenge the snow looking for mealworms that the townies feed them during the day. I pass by The Chop Shop; the inside is bright through the small window. Chelsea is busy cutting someone's hair while a few people sit in front of the window, reading magazines. The Hoarder Emporium is bustling with music; inside, boxes cover the windows. Each is filled with nick knacks and trinkets. Through the front glass door of the post office, Laura's stacking packages. She waves as she notices me. I wave back with a smile and grasp the handle of The Olive Bean. Before I have the chance to open the door, the aroma of buttery pastries and toasted coffee fills my nose.

Hannah and Joe sit along the wall sipping hot drinks. A few more locals sit at the rest of the tables. The room is filled with laughter, and the Christmas decorations make the place feel like home.

"Good morning!" I say to Olive as I hang my coat. "Wow! It looks like The North Pole."

The ceiling and its falling snowflakes, the lights, the tree... everything about her store is screaming Christmas.

She looks up from filling the self-serve coffee bar with straws, and her eyes light. "Good morning, sunshine. About time you showed up." She slides more straws into a cup and says, "That was the goal."

I move to stand next to her and lean an elbow on the coffee bar. "Listen, if I'm not late somewhere, something's wrong." I chuckle and catch her gaze. "How did the news go with your mom?" I ask. "Well—if you had a chance to talk to her."

Olive fills me in on the conversation she had with her mom yesterday. I'm relieved to hear everything went well after the article was posted. I felt guilty for getting her into this predicament in the first place. I wanted to send her a text after I read it, but I figured it was better to have a conversation in person than over the phone.

After a few minutes of stocking sugar packets, she whispers, so no one else can hear, "It felt bad to lie to her." Olive's face falls with the confession.

"I know what you mean. It's gonna hurt them when we break the news. You know, when this *thing* ends," I say under my breath, so if anyone's eavesdropping, they don't know. But what I really want to say—I can't.

It'll hurt me too when this is over.

I look at her, *really* look at her. Searching for any hint she might feel the same thing I do. I don't find it, though. She appears as she normally does. Bubbly, happy, and eager to take on the world. Not a flicker of sadness changed her expression when I mentioned us parting after the holidays. I should know better. Nothing will change. It can't.

"Sophia was excited?" she asks, bringing me back to the present.

"Mom was floored. She hugged me so tight and went on and on about how amazing you are." I shake my head. "She also told me I better not mess this up."

It's too late for messing things up. We've already gone and done it.

"I am pretty amazing," she states with a sly smirk.

"You are," I say softly while falling into her gaze. I mean it with my whole being. I know it with every fiber in my body.

She organizes a few tea bags while saying, "I was just kidding with you."

"I know, but I meant it. You are." My lips curve into a sincere smile.

She looks down blushing crimson. For someone so confident, it's rare for her cheeks to pinken. I love when it happens. When her freckles become pronounced and highlight her face in a warm glow, she looks radiant. I'm the luckiest fool alive to be able to witness it. Even if it's fleeting, I'll cherish every second of it.

"Did you see Constance's post?" She grabs the few empty boxes on the bar.

I lean my chin on my palm. "The one about the Christmas party on the fourteenth?"

"Yes. Do you want to go together?"

"That would be nice," I reply and take the boxes from her, throwing them into the recycling bin.

"Thanks. You know as a *couple*." She winks.

"As a *couple*." I raise my eyebrows.

"Okay, good! Now it's settled. Can I offer you a coffee and something on the secret menu?" Her eyes dance with delight.

"Secret menu?" I reply and pretend to have no clue what it is.

"The one for special people only. You know, the ones named Mason." She tips her head to the door and winks as she grasps my hand.

"I'm all yours." I chuckle as she takes me with her.

Olive's smile is contagious as she flies through the kitchen. She skips through the cooling racks and to the sinks. While scrubbing her hands, she says, "This might be my best pastry yet. And you'll be the first to try it."

"How did I get so lucky?" I ask honestly.

"I guess happenstance." She shrugs and pulls out a tray on the closest cooling rack. She hands me a croissant in the shape of a Christmas tree with a piece of wax paper. "Tell me what you think and be honest. Don't sugar coat it."

"Delicious," I say after I finish a bite. "What is it?"

Her eyes light. "A Nutella stuffed croissant. I made the Nutella myself."

"Can I take a few more with me for later?"

She smiles so brightly. "You can take as many as you like. You don't have to ask. We've been over this."

Even if they were horrible (which is not the case), I would've told her I loved them just to see her smile. Everything I taste test for her becomes my new favorite thing. Anything she makes wins me over.

"I'm so glad you opened this place," I confess. "This town would've never known what they're missing."

"Awe, shucks." She waves me off. "Believe me, you taking over Jack's Bar from your parents was the best thing to happen. That name was cliché. When you renamed it to Rooster's after your chickens, it was worth it. You gave the place character. I don't know why your parents picked such a boring name. At least The Cozy Cabin Inn is a cute name."

"That was the deal. Mom named the Inn, and Dad named the bar after his middle name. You can see why." I take another bite of the pastry.

"Oh, that's right. I completely forgot." She starts to fill a bag with croissants and asks, "What made you want to take it over? I don't think I ever asked you."

I tap my foot in thought. "I don't know. It was engraved in me. After seeing both of our parents running businesses—Mom running the Inn, Dad running the bar, your mom as a seamstress, and your dad with the Christmas tree farm. It made me want to do something for myself."

I learned, with a bit of grit, you can do anything you put your mind to.

She nods and grabs another croissant. "I guess that's why I started this place as well. I didn't want to leave once we graduated, and I knew I loved baking and making coffee. The town needed a dedicated place for it. After watching our parents struggle to get by when we were younger... I sometimes wonder why I wanted to start it and stay if I was going to struggle too." Olive tilts her head to look at me.

I push my glasses to sit on the bridge of my nose. "I think seeing them struggle motivated us. They gave us everything they could at the time. Your mom made us clothes. Your dad always made sure we had a Christmas tree. My parents brought home food. The whole town pitched in to barter and trade and provide services. Thornwood Valley is full of people who care. No matter how much they meddle. Their hearts are always in the right place. We never felt as if we struggled. We had each other, and no material item could compare to that."

She folds the bag and hands it to me. "Wow, Mason. I never thought of it that way. But you're exactly right. I never wanted to leave our small town because I knew someone would always have my back. I knew if I was struggling, you or anyone in town would be there to help me. I'd do the same for you and them."

I nod in agreement. "And that's why I love living here."

I never thought about leaving Thornwood Valley for a second. Why would I want to leave a place that holds so many wonderful memories? Sure, things go wrong... I have bad days, but I'd have them anywhere I went. My family is here. My friends are here. *Olive* is here.

"Me too," she agrees. The bell rings from the front counter. "That's my cue. Someone must want coffee."

"I'll get out of your hair." I grin.

She shakes her head. "You're never a bother, Mason. I enjoy every moment you listen to my babbling." She skips to the front, her festive apron flipping from the motion. She sends me out the door with a coffee, a bag of Nutella filled croissants, and some donuts to give to Amelia and Leo.

How could I not be in love with my best friend?

It's a real problem. It gets harder every moment I spend with her.

Chapter 8

OLIVE

Peace. Serenity. Tranquility. This is what life should be like. This is what dreams are made of. I never want to leave. I can live out the rest of my days in bliss. Quiet, unbothered, unperturbed bliss.

The bubbles foam an inch thick over me. A glass of white wine sits on the wooden tray draping across the top of the bathtub. Shadows dance across the wall from the candlelight. Warm balsam and cedar fill my nostrils. All I'm missing are some cucumber slices over my eyes.

This is so refreshing. It's so quiet. The water is scolding against my body, and I love it. The hotter the water, the better in my opinion.

I close my eyes and try to focus on relaxing my muscles, easing the tension. I needed this. I've been running myself ragged for weeks. Starting my mornings at four to get ready for opening and ending my nights late. I've been so tired. I needed the time to reset my social battery too. The small town gossip can be exhausting after a while.

The only thing that would make this stay better is having someone to share it with. It seems silly to wish for it. I don't have the time for a relationship or commitment. But with simple, slow moments like this, I ache for the companionship of another.

I don't want to feel vulnerable again. When I was with Chad, I gave him every little piece of me. Heartbreak and confusion is what I received in return. Love felt like a weakness for me—maybe that's because I haven't found the right person to show me otherwise. I haven't found the kind of love that transcends you.

This is too much for me to be thinking about right now. I need to enjoy the moment. *Relax.*

Knock. Knock. I just about jump out of my skin.

What the heck was that?

A soft knock continues. *That better be a ghost.* If someone is knocking on the front door, they're going to reap the consequences of my wrath. If it's a ghost, they better leave me alone. I'm not in the mood. I stand in the tub as the water sloshes around me. I pull the plug and watch the water swirl down the drain. I grab a fluffy gray towel and drape it around my body. I pile my hair in another towel on top of my head. I mumble profanities under my breath and blow the candles out with a whoosh. The smell of smoke fills my nose. I take a deep breath in and out.

Who could be here right now? The weather isn't exactly ideal.

The trip here a few hours ago was a breeze. I made it just in time. I'm so glad I decided to drive out today instead of Saturday. If I waited until tomorrow, I don't know that I would've made it. The snow started falling as soon as I parked inside the attached garage. I've been watching the inches of snowflakes cover the ground already from my view in the bathtub. It covers the hillside, draping as soft as a blanket. Falling from the sky in big puffy globs.

My wet feet squish against the floor with each step. I feel like a penguin trudging along ice. Good thing I'm not prone to clumsiness like my best friend Vivi. She's always breaking things, tripping over flat ground, and falling into the arms of handsome farmers—now one is her husband. That reminds me: I need to text her back. I promised I'd let her know when I made it here safely. She's probably worried sick about me. *Oops.* The bathtub was calling as soon as I stepped through the door. Service is wonky out here anyway. I'm not sure if it would go through or not.

That realization doesn't sit well in my stomach with the idea of a stranger on the other side of the door.

The knocking on the door starts up again. *Definitely not a ghost.* I wish there were a peep hole in this door, so I could see who's out there. I pull back the corner of the curtain on the front facing window, but I can't see anyone. There aren't any tire tracks on the driveway. *Weird.* I can see footprints and what looks like prints from some kind of animal. Could be a coyote or a bobcat. Nevertheless, there isn't a clear view of the door, so I'll take my chances with the hope it's not a serial killer. I swipe a knife from the wooden block on the counter.

You can never be too careful. I've watched enough crime documentaries to know the consequences of being too trustworthy.

As I swing the door open, I grip the knife tightly against my palm. Ready to attack whoever is out there.

Not today, serial killer! You picked the wrong cabin.

I'm prepared to strike and defend myself. I'm not going to hide.

My wariness fades away when I see Mason standing there on the stoop. His cheeks sanguine against the frigid air. Moose sits beside him patiently, barely containing the urge to jump on me. I drop my shoulders; at least I'm not in imminent danger. I loosen the grip on the knife in my hand.

That doesn't mean I'm not frustrated.

My now *ex-best friend, ex-fake boyfriend,* Mason, looks at me in horror.

I wanted to be *alone* this weekend. He never listens. I shake my head in frustration and roll my eyes.

"*Holy shit!* Were you going to stab me?" His eyes widen when they land on the gigantic kitchen knife in my hand.

"No?" *Maybe.* I shrug. "I'm out here alone. I had no clue who was showing up at the door. What if you were a serial killer?"

He strolls past me into the kitchen with Moose on his heels. "You're right. You were smart to grab a knife. But I'm not a serial killer. It took you long enough to open the door. It's freezing out there."

"You're kidding me right now." I slam the front door. It closed a little harder than I was anticipating. *That should do the trick.*

"Calm down, Olive."

"Me?" I point to myself with my free hand, still holding the knife at my side.

"Is there someone else here I don't know about?"

"Very funny, Mason. What are you doing here?" I place my hands on my hips and straighten my spine.

"Straight to the point. Someone's mad." He strips his coat, hat, and boots in the kitchen. "Could you put the knife down?"

"Mad! Are you sure? Do I look mad?"

So maybe he has a point, I shouldn't be waving a knife around when I'm clearly angry. I slide the kitchen knife back in its place on the counter.

I'm fuming. All I wanted was one weekend of relaxation. I know I wished I had someone to share it with. I didn't mean it. I take it back.

"You look—interesting, Firefly."

"What? This?" I wave my arms, pointing at the towel stacked on my head and the other one around my body. "It's not like you haven't seen me with a towel on before."

"Not that. Your face is turning beet red. The Olive monster is about to attack." He plops on the small leather sofa. "Wow, this couch is small."

I look heavenward to try and calm myself. "Why weren't there tire tracks? There weren't any on the driveway. Did you teleport here?"

"I parked at the bottom of the driveway in case we had to get out. But it's looking almost useless now."

I stare at him. He looks relaxed on the couch. This was supposed to be my time to *relax*. Not Mason's time.

"I'll be back," I state matter-of-factly. I sprint to my temporary room for the weekend. My phone screen lights up with notifications from Vivi.

Violet

Are you okay?

Did you make it yet?

If you don't answer, Dustin and I are going to come out there to make sure you're alive.

Olive

I'm here and safe. But S.O.S. Angry face emoji.

What happened, do you need me to drive out there?

No. I was having a relaxing bath when Mason showed up.

Laughing emoji.

This isn't funny!

He's probably worried about you. It's supposed to snow two feet. Plus, I texted him to make sure you were okay…

Oh. So you're the traitor.

I didn't even think of checking the weather. I'd rather go with the flow. Anyway, everyone is so dramatic over a little bit of snow. This is nothing. We live in northern Pennsylvania for crying out loud.

I can't believe she texted him.

Violet

> TTYL. The goats are kidding right now. It's going to be a long night. Have fun with Mason. Wink face emoji.

Now that Vivi is happily married and living on the farm with Dustin, she has less time to talk and hang out. I get it. She's so busy with her shop, The Not So Secret Garden (NSSG), during the day. And helping on the farm after work. I've been spending a lot more time hanging out with Mason lately.

I throw on some sweats and brush out my hair while it's still wet before it dries. I enter the living room and sit on the couch draping my legs over Mason's.

This couch is small. He was right.

His voice breaks the silence. "Are you still mad?"

"Nope." *Not at all.* Even my mind is sarcastic.

"I'm sorry. When I saw the forecast, I wasn't going to let you get stuck here alone. Also, Vivi texted me. She was worried about you getting stuck out here." He grabs my hand across the couch. "The only heat in this cabin is the woodstove, and I figured you wouldn't want to be feeding it all night to keep warm. Going outside and back through the snow. You won't even know I'm here. I'll feed the fire and keep my mouth sewn shut."

I give him the side eye. "We both know you aren't exactly the silent type. But I appreciate the gesture."

Mason's always been protective of his sisters. And it spread to protecting Oakley and I as well. I can't stay mad at him for more than five minutes, especially when he apologizes. It's sweet how much he worries about me. How much he cares for everyone in his life.

"What is Dough-Lene doing here?" Mason's eyes track to the kitchen counter.

"She was lonely."

"Do you really need to take your sourdough starter everywhere you go?"

"Yes." I cross my arms. "I was planning on making a loaf for breakfast. The bread is proofing on the counter. I just finished the stretch and folds, and now it has to rise overnight."

His lips form a lopsided grin. "I'm not going to argue over that. Warm bread and butter sounds like heaven."

"It will be heaven. That's one thing I can promise you." I guess I might as well include him in the plans I made for my relaxing evening. "How about watching a movie?"

"I would love to, but I don't want to be a burden on your vacation," he says, looking genuinely concerned.

"You're never a burden, Knight."

Now I feel bad for making him think he's being a burden on my mini vacation. I wanted some time alone, but now that he's here, I'm having a lot of fun. We bicker back and forth like an old married couple. I mean, come on, would it have been more fun by myself staring at the television and feeding the fire all night? No. The best part of him showing up is the dog cuddles. And it's also nice to have someone to laugh with. When I'm with Mason I don't have to think about how I talk or act. I'm free to be my chaotic self with him.

"Well, since you're no longer using my full name, I must be back to nickname status, and that means you're not mad anymore." He chuckles as he gets up from the couch. "I'll go get some firewood. It'll only take a few minutes. Don't eat all the popcorn before I get back, or else I'm picking the movie."

I put my hands up in surrender. "I wouldn't dare. I'm picking the movie. And I brought a jumbo container of kernels anyway. We have an unlimited supply."

I air-pop some popcorn kernels in the microwave and cover them with butter. Once I plop onto the couch, Mason comes inside.

"Think fast!" I say as Mason opens his mouth, and I throw a popcorn kernel. It lands directly in its intended target.

"What are we watching? Wait, let me guess." He catches another piece of popcorn. "*White Chicks?*"

I shrug. "You know me."

The corner of his mouth lifts. "I do. You're so predictable."

I press my palm against my forehead. "That's only because you know everything about me."

"That's true."

"You secretly love watching this movie over and over again with me. You laugh hysterically every time. It's funny, admit it, or else you're not getting any popcorn." I pull the giant bowl to my chest.

He peels his coat and boots off and settles next to me on the couch. "I enjoy watching every movie you like just to hear your laugh, Firefly." He pokes my nose and steals a handful of popcorn.

We lounge on the couch for an hour. Mason, Moose, and I. It's a tight fit but comfortable. A fuzzy throw blanket covers us. He leaves a few times to grab firewood and feed the woodstove adjacent to the TV. A bit of smoke fills the cabin with a woodsy scent when he feeds the fire. The lights are dim; it's peaceful. I'm glad he's here with me. If not for him—for Moose—my cuddle buddy. His fur is soft against my lap. I don't care that he's way too big to be sitting on me. Moments like this make me want to get a dog of my own, but I'm not home half the time. My betta fish is the perfect amount of commitment.

"It's my favorite part!" I shake Mason's arm. "A Thousand Miles" by Vanessa Carlton plays. We sing along and laugh so hard there are tears in our eyes.

Chapter 9

MASON

The credits roll on the movie. Olive yawns softly as the fire crackles and pops, filling the dark room with an orange glow. Her head rests on my shoulder. Her body presses against my side. Moose snores loudly from his spot in front of the wood stove.

I knew coming here would piss her off. She insisted on being left alone this weekend. There's no way I was listening. The mountains are brutal when the snowstorms come. Two feet or more of snow is expected, and I wasn't about to leave her stranded alone.

There were so many what ifs circling. What if the power went out? What if she was stranded there longer than the weekend? What if she ran into a bobcat outside while grabbing wood? I know Olive can protect herself; she's the toughest person I know. But I knew I wouldn't be content until I showed up. Vivi's text was the sign I was looking for. Her concern sent me into action. I

72

A MERRY PAIR

packed up a few warm clothes, closed the bar, hopped in my truck, and picked up Moose on the way. I barely made it up the road in four-wheel drive. I had to park at the bottom of the driveway; it was already looking worse for wear.

Olive yawns again.

"You look exhausted. Which bedroom did you take?" I ask. "I'll take the other."

"There's only one." She shifts closer to my side for warmth. "The cabin I won from the spring competitions was one of the smallest ones. I cashed in the prize this weekend. It's a one bedroom."

"Oh, I've never been to this one before." I'm not sure I heard that correctly. "Wait—what?"

She yawns. "Yeah, only one bed too."

"You're kidding."

"Do I look like I'm kidding?" She raises a brow.

"No," I put my knuckles against my chin, "I'll sleep on the couch."

"Don't be absurd. This couch is tiny. Where are you going to put all six feet of you?"

"Well—" When she puts it that way.

"Exactly. We can share the bed." She shrugs, as if it's no big deal.

Two best friends. Sharing one bed. Good idea, right?

I don't know. *No.* Not when you're secretly in love with said best friend.

73

"I don't want to overstep. I can go," I mutter.

"Too late for overstepping. You're here now. Besides, look outside."

Dammit.

There's already over a foot of snow. My truck made it up here, but I don't know about getting out. The plow trucks don't touch the roads on the weekends. It would be a squirrelly drive.

We make our way to the bedroom, where the log walls are decorated with paintings of peaceful landscapes. The carpet is patterned with bears, fish, and canoes, adding a rustic charm. A wooden door on the right leads to the bathroom, while another on the left opens into the bedroom itself. The room is small. Barely enough room for the full-size bed. Olive slides under the covers, and Moose lays on her feet. I turn out the light and head to the bathroom. I grab a quick shower. Scrubbing off the scent of firewood and lingering beer from a long shift today. The hot water eases my mind and the tension in my spine. I toss a pair of sweatpants and a T-shirt on. I carefully climb into bed, hoping not to wake her. I stare at the ceiling as the patterned quilt slowly drapes down over me. Olive smells nice... like Glittery Snow. The body wash bottle sitting on the side of the bathtub clued me into the exact name.

I had no idea snow had a scent. Nevertheless, it's a wonderful one.

The heat radiates off our close proximity. Minutes tick by in silence until the low howl of coyotes shatters the quiet. Snowflakes flicker along the window, reflecting shapes on the log walls. My mind is foggy, similar to the condensation covered windows.

"Are you awake?" Olive whispers in question.

"Yes," I breathe in response.

"I can't sleep."

"Me neither."

After a few beats of silence, she asks, "Do you think we could go sledding tomorrow for old times' sake?"

My voice comes out quiet. "Sure, Firefly. Why not?" *I would do anything she wanted. All she has to do is ask.*

"I know you might be thinking we're too old for sledding, but I don't care."

"I know you don't care what anyone thinks of you." I chuckle. "There's no age limit on sledding. A little joy never hurt anyone, and it sounds like a good time," I say into the darkness. "I always beat you every time anyway."

She laughs softly. "That's because you weigh more, Knight. The law of physics—it can't be attributed to skill or merit."

"You'll have to prove your point tomorrow."

She sighs. "There's only one sled. I found it in the closet."

"That's okay. We'll ride together."

I hear the blanket ruffle as she turns over to look at me. "I'm glad you came—and I know I never said it before, but thank you."

I roll over to face her. "For what?" I whisper. Her green eyes slowly close, lazily blinking shut. I could barely make out the color in the dark room if it weren't for the faint glow of moonlight.

Just before she falls asleep, her lips curl into a smile. "For always being there for me. For being such a good friend."

I stare at her, memorizing every dim freckle as my mind races, repeating those six words.

For being such a good friend.

If only she'd notice the way I look at her. And see that I want so much more than friendship.

Chapter 10

OLIVE

I'm so comfortable. I can feel the rise and fall of the stiff surface underneath me. My leg is wrapped around something solid and elevated. It's a perfect combination. My feet are uncharacteristically warm underneath something heavy. Whatever I'm on is radiating heat like a furnace, and I can't get enough. I snuggle my head deeper, grasping for every inch of warmth I can steal.

Where am I?

"Olive." I hear a faint voice pull me out of my dream state. "Olive." There it is again. "Wake up." It's deep and far away. "Olive." Something pokes my arm.

What the heck?

I peel my eyes open and scream in surprise.

This is awkward.

"I'm sorry to wake you. I didn't want to. But you were gripped on me so tight, I couldn't get free. I need to feed the fire before it goes out and we're freezing. The cabin's already chilly," Mason says.

My mind is still fuzzy, but I remember where I am now. I'm in a cabin in the woods.

Not that cabin! This one isn't haunted. The only ghosts around here are Mason and Moose, and they're not ghosts. Nothing bad has happened here. *That I know of.*

I'm in a totally *not* haunted cabin with my best friend, fake boyfriend—Mason. It's still weird to think of him as my boyfriend in any capacity.

"I'm sorry." I peel my head from his chest. I remove my foot from under Moose at the end of the bed and unwrap my thigh from the grip it had over Mason's legs. I have no control over my limbs when I sleep.

My body suddenly feels cold from the sudden departure. It felt nice to be held by someone else. I shake the thoughts from my mind.

No way. He's your best friend.

"Don't apologize. It was—"

"Nice," I whisper.

"Yeah, it was." He slides out of bed smoothly and pads into the hall.

My phone chimes with an email. As I read it, I pet Moose in the early morning light.

Time: Saturday, December 7th
From: thornwoodvalleytowneventscommittee@email.com
To: olivewatson@email.com
Subject: The Cookie Chronicles Commence

Dear Eager Couples,

I hope this email finds you well.

I'm so glad you've shown interest in our town's first annual Cookie Chronicles. The competition will commence on Saturday, December 20th. Please make sure to be prepared. There will be a judge's panel composed of five town members, myself included. We will be scoring based on appearance, texture, and taste.

Assigned cooking locations will be sent in a separate email. Everyone will meet at Annie's Diner on Saturday, December 20th at noon to judge. Please make three dozen cookies so everyone can share.

A list of participating couples will be sent in a follow-up email.

See you soon,
Constance

"Come on, Moose, let's go." He hops from the bed and follows me into the hall, tail wagging in excitement. As I walk into the living room, I call, "Mason."

"Yeah?" He looks up from the woodstove.

"It's official. We got our first Constance email."

He rolls his eyes. "Can't wait to read it."

I trudge my way up the mountain behind the cabin. Each step is labored in the powdery snow. My feet crunch against the cold compressed layer. Enormous pine trees layered with puffs of white surrounded by thicket. It's a hiking trail regularly used in the warmer months. I come here every so often to connect with nature. Nothing but trees, forest animals, and the crunch of sticks and leaves under my feet.

A few red cardinals glide against the slight breeze in the air, dotting bright vermillion. A stark contrast against the whitened glare. Mason trails beside me. Moose stayed in the cabin; it's too cold for him to be out for extended periods. He gave me that "please don't leave me here" look with wide puppy eyes. I felt so bad.

We walk in comfortable silence. A wooden toboggan hangs on Mason's shoulders. I'm sure it's heavy, but he insisted on carrying it. The path to the top is steep, and the open slope is in view.

My thoughts drift to how things are going to change once we get back to town tomorrow morning. Our new fake relationship will be in full swing. We'll have to act like a couple in front of everyone.

I like my normal, no faking, drama free life. Mason and I already spend our free time together, but being in public in front of townies is a different story. I will have to put in a ton of effort to make it look as though we're together. Instead of being carefree and oblivious to what anyone else thinks.

"Are you ready?" He questions, releasing me from my musing.

"Huh?"

"We're at the top. Are you ready to go down the mountain?"

I didn't realize we already made it. From the highest point of the ridge, the cabin looks like a spec among the vastness—a bird's eye view. My breath catches at the tremendous splendor. I've never hiked this trail in winter; it's transformed into a snowy wonderland. I smile, letting the magnificence seep into my bones. Snow falls gently from the sky. One perfect snowflake lands on Mason's crimson nose. That's when I notice the hat he's wearing; it's the one I crocheted for him last Christmas. I can't believe he kept it and still wears it. The notion tugs at my heartstrings.

"Yes, I'm ready." I gulp. A lump forms in my throat. Although it's extraordinary, the drop is not for the faint of heart. "The question is, are you?"

"As ready as I can be." He adjusts his glasses. "Good thing I'm not afraid of heights."

I poke his plush arm. "Yes, you are! You're lying." The indent pushes back out. There's no give. "We look like two marshmallows in all our winter gear."

"You look like Randy from *A Christmas Story*." The corners of his eyes crinkle.

"Hey! You do too!" I giggle. "Aren't you afraid of heights, though?"

The silence is deafening until he speaks up. "Uh—no—I'm not." He clears his throat. "Do I look like someone who's afraid of heights?" He scratches the back of his neck.

"Not really. You look tough on the exterior. But I remember everything. You screamed like a little girl when we rode a roller-coaster."

"I was twelve. You begged me to ride the Storm Flight with you. It was fast, dammit." His lips curl into a smile.

"It wasn't *that* fast." I grin.

"It went over seventy miles per hour. I almost peed my pants."

"And you just about broke my fingers off squeezing them so hard."

"Are you going to keep torturing me with flashbacks of my embarrassing gangly teen years? Or are we going down this mountain?" He holds a gloved hand out to me, grasping my fingers. "Front or back?"

"I'm done. I swear. You have filled out since then. You're not so gangly anymore." I give him a once over, raising my eyebrows suggestively. He rolls his eyes with a smile tipping the corners of his lips.

"Pick, or I'll choose for you." He reaches out to lift me.

I blurt quickly, making a split-second decision. "Front so I can see!"

"Now we're getting somewhere." He helps me onto the toboggan. I tuck my feet under the front lip as he settles himself behind me. His strong arms come around my sides; he brushes his fingers against my arm while grabbing the rope from my hands. If I didn't see it, I wouldn't have felt it with the amount of layers I'm wearing. I hang on to the rope directly below his grasp. "Hold on," he says, voice shaky. His tone doesn't give me any confidence whatsoever.

We descend at a rather fast pace. Taking off like a two-liter when you throw a few Mentos in. That thing soars in the air faster than you can say *shit*. Imagine that feeling, multiply it by ten, and that's me right now on the front of this death trap. Soaring downward like the Grinch on his sled. Clumps of snow continue to pelt my face. Snowflakes fly into my eyes, blurring my vision. "Ahh!" I yelp. The cold wind burns my face as we accelerate. We start gaining momentum, and I'm beginning to wonder how in the world we're going to stop this thing. I don't think I could reach this speed in my truck on the back roads through town. We've got to be going at least fifty miles per hour.

I may be exaggerating a little, but I promise we're going fast enough for me to be rethinking my life decisions.

"Who's the one afraid of heights now?" he shouts over the whooshing wind.

"I lied!" I yell back. "I wasn't ready!"

"You were the one who made me ride the rollercoaster! I thought you loved heights!"

We rumble through stretches of deep snow, almost hitting a tree in the process. He had directed the rope to the right, missing that tree by only a few inches. "Oh my gosh!" My hands tremble with nerves hanging onto the rope for dear life. "No! I only made you ride it with me because I was too scared to do it alone! I pretended to be fearless!"

"Why did you pretend?" He questions. It comes out as a grumble, as we dodge *another* pine tree. I've come so close to losing an arm that I'm pretty sure I might pass out from the adrenaline.

I'm never getting on a toboggan again. Never.

"I pretended because I needed you to go with me!" I confess. "You make my fears go away! You give me courage when I can't find it in myself!" His hands cover mine. He glides his thumb against my shaking fingers. I calm instantly against his touch. How can he be so worried about reassuring me when we're on a ride to our imminent end.

Okay, so I am being dramatic.

Suddenly, the ride becomes smoother. The steep part of the mountain transitions into a gradual slope. We both laugh out loud. Now *this* is what I was hoping for. I feel carefree, like a child again. My fingers grip the rope beside his hands. The cold bites my nose pleasantly. The adrenaline is like a perfect amount of dopamine to my brain.

Not like before.

All my worries fly away with the wind. My mind becomes a blank slate, where I can be in the present. I almost forgot how nice it was to let everything go and relish in the little moments life has to offer. To feel like a kid again.

Everything was perfect, until we reached the bottom.

A large hump in the snow appears. "Watch out!" I yell. Our feet scrape the snow in a lousy attempt to slow ourselves down enough to miss it. He pulls the rope to the side, trying to direct us to the right. It's too late. We hit the hump full force. The sled flies into the air at least a few feet off the ground. It's like we hit a bike jump or a skateboard ramp. It gives us extra speed to soar through the air.

Why did I want to go sledding again?

Why?

Mason holds me tight, but I can't hold onto the sled any longer. My hands ache from the steel grip chafing into my gloved palms. If I wasn't wearing gloves, my hands would be torn to shreds. I'll definitely have some calluses after this *joy ride*.

"Don't let go!" he shouts through the chaos.

Easier said than done, Mason!

I try my hardest, but my grip is shaky. I let go of the rope. We careen into the air as one.

"Shit!" he yells.

"Ahh!" I yelp. Mason hits the ground first. I land straight on top of him. He groans, and the wind gets knocked out of me.

I lift my head from his chest and blow a puff of hair out of my face. I place two fingers on his neck, checking for a pulse. You know, to make sure I didn't crush him to death. It's strong, I breathe a sigh of relief. His glasses are skewed on his face, and his cheeks are a deep red hue. The hat is ripped off his head. I reach out and adjust his glasses to sit properly above the bridge of his nose. The corner of his mouth lifts. I grin back. We burst into laughter. His deep chuckle reverberates his chest below me. I giggle and yelp when he starts tickling me.

"No! Stop! Please—stop!" My voice is shaky with laughter. "You know I hate—getting—tickled." I gasp for air between bits of laughter. He stops his relentless torture, and we continue to laugh for minutes until we're both out of breath. "I thought I killed you!

Remember when you said, *a little joy ride never hurt anyone* last night. Not so sure about that anymore, are you?"

"You can't get rid of me that easily, Firefly. We're both still in one piece." He brushes his hand over my forehead. His touch toasty against my arctic skin. "You're freezing." He pulls away with a look of disquiet. "Let's go get warm in front of the woodstove."

"Okay, Knight."

Chapter 11

MASON

S unday was spent on the couch recovering. There were no more sledding accidents. My back was screaming in agony. We tried to leave the cabin that night, but the roads were still too snow-covered, so we decided to wait until morning. After Olive and I got back, I spent the day preparing to open the bar tonight. And that's how I ended up in this predicament. Convincing Olive to make our *relationship* look believable.

"Do something." I grit through closed teeth.

Olive huffs in vexation. She wraps her arms around my frame and squeezes me in a vice-like grip. *Ow.* She's incredibly strong. Olive may look innocent; she's anything but.

"We have to make this look believable," I plead.

"I know, but this whole *fake dating* thing is so much work," she whispers against my ear. It tingles my senses into overdrive, and I feel her tremble against me.

"It'll be over before you know it." I release her, and my smile falls. "You're freezing." I look away from her gaze to notice what she's wearing. A thin, white, long-sleeve shirt underneath a green suspender dress, and the sheerest pair of pants I've ever seen. She looks stunning, but it's not practical for ten-degree weather. "Where's your coat?" I grumble.

"It was only a two-minute walk. I didn't think it would be this bad."

I shake my head. "Wait here," I say, as Olive climbs onto a bar stool in front of the live edge wood counter. She swings her purse on her lap and shivers. I walk to the end of the bar and open the door to my office. I grab a sherpa lined coat from the hook on the wall adjacent to my desk. I hustle back out, and the bar is filled with boisterous chatter and live music from the Thornwood Valley Heartbreakers.

"Here, put this on." I drape the coat over her shoulders.

"Thank you." She burrows into the large coat. It looks enormous on her. "So chivalrous." She sighs in relief. I can't deny the way my heart is pounding in my chest at the sight of her wearing my coat.

Damn, I'm such a fool.

Just because we're fake dating now doesn't mean our normal routine needs to change. She swings by every night to hang out and have a drink or help behind the bar. Ever since I hired a few employees, she hasn't had to help anymore. She insists on it regardless.

"Mason!" my sister shouts from the other end of the bar.

"Be right there, Char!" I yell over the clamor, and then turn back to Olive. "What can I get you to drink tonight? Martini, beer, whiskey, or mulled wine?"

"Mmm. Mulled wine." She swivels on the bar stool and wraps the coat tighter around her arms.

"It'll warm you up." I grab a thermos full of the hot liquid and pour it into a glass mug. I top it with an orange slice and cinnamon stick. "Careful, it's hot." I slide her drink across the bar.

She blows on it and takes a small sip. "Perfection as always. You know how to make a drink."

"That's my job. I'd hope so." I grin and look to the end of the bar. My sister taps on the bar while waiting, singing along to "I Love This Bar" by Toby Keith. "See you later, *girlfriend*." I emphasize the word and wink. Olive shakes her head and waves. As I leave, Vivi slides onto the bar stool next to her. I pass by Amelia on my way to talk to Char. "Hey, would you have a second to make me a Shirley Temple?"

"On it, boss." She grabs a clean glass and starts adding soda.

"You're the best." I continue walking and put my elbows on the bar once I reach my younger sister.

Char grins wide. "You got it *so* bad, bro."

"What do you mean?" I look back at the bar to where Olive's sitting. She throws her head back and laughs at something Vivi says. Her red curls bounce with the movement. The moment her gaze meets mine, her jade eyes sparkle in the dim lighting. She sticks her tongue out, and I laugh quietly to myself. I wink in reply, and her face instantly reddens.

I could stare into her eyes forever and get lost in the reflections. I wouldn't mind being there, as long as she's the one I'm lost over. She alone has me fascinated with every infectious smile. Every freckle. Every laugh.

"You got it bad for Olive. See, you can't even look away from her for five seconds," Char says. I break eye contact with Olive to look at my sister.

"I—we're dating. Of course I do." I stare at the wood grain on the counter and trace each line, trying and failing miserably at blending the truth.

I almost forgot this was a ruse because it feels so natural. I'm not forcing any feelings that weren't already there. That moment we shared wasn't something I was doing out of the sake of pretending.

I'm sure it's harder for Olive.

"Don't pull that crap with me, Mace. I know you're fake dating her for that cookie battle, whatever it's called. And to get Mom and the rest of our sisters off your back. They're relentless." She places her elbow against the bar.

I didn't think it was that obvious.

"I know what you're thinking. No one else knows. But we're the closest, you and me," she says with a warm smile and pats my arm. "You can't pull a fast one on me. Did you really think you could?"

"You've got me all figured out."

"Yeah, I do. Now where's my drink? I'm parched."

"A mocktail for one obnoxiously and overly observant sister." I hand her a Shirley Temple that Amelia passes over to me.

"Thanks, Amelia!" Char mixes her drink with a black straw. "Only two more months and this baby will be brought into the world. And I can *finally* have a drink again."

"It'll go by fast."

"Says the one who isn't carrying a twenty-pound stomach. And doesn't have to squeeze their feet into a pair of shoes because they're swollen. And can sleep comfortably at night on their back," she huffs.

"I'm sorry. What I meant to say was it'll go by slowly." My smile tips the corners of my mouth.

She gives me a disapproving look. "You're testing my patience, Mace. I don't have much of it lately."

"Sorry, sis."

"Back to business. When are you going to tell her?" She takes a sip of her drink.

"Tell who, what?"

"Tell Olive, silly. That you're a goner for her. That you have been for a while."

I sigh, avoiding eye-contact. "I don't want to mess things up. I don't want to lose our friendship. What we have is great. It would make things *hard*."

"You only live once. Make it count. Sometimes you need to do things regardless of the consequences. Do it scared. Do it worried. You can't hide from the hard. You can't avoid it forever."

"I wish I were like you, Char, but I'm not. You take spontaneous trips around the world. I've never left the state. You met Mateo while skydiving, for pity's sake. You're cracked."

"You," she points a red nail at me, "are the only one holding yourself back—you grew up in the same nut house as me."

I chuckle. "That's why we're all a little squirrely."

"So true."

"There's my beautiful wife." Her eyes gleam with adoration as Mateo pulls her into his arms and kisses her.

"Yuck." Olive groans from beside me.

I turn to my side, and Olive looks up at me with her arms crossed over her chest. My coat is now missing. "What are you doing back here?" I ask.

She looks around frantically. "I needed a refill, and I didn't want to bother anyone."

"All you had to do was ask. What are you not telling me?"

She rolls her eyes. "Constance just walked in. I didn't want to talk to her. I don't need the interrogations."

"Oh, so we're being evasive." I poke her nose. Her eyelashes flutter, and her cheeks flush.

"Duck now." Olive pulls me under the counter into a crouch. She places a finger to my lips; her eyes go round.

I try to tease her by opening my mouth to say something. "Under here, Const—" Her palm slaps to cover my mouth.

"Shhh," she whispers. "*Please*, I don't need her asking a million questions. Do you promise you'll be quiet?"

I nod my head as her hand slowly retreats. I smirk and whisper, "Are you sure you're not using this as an excuse to be close to me?"

Her brows draw together. "I'm absolutely not."

"You are," I breathe into her ear. I could have sworn she shivered. But it may have been a fragment of my imagination. Or maybe it's because she's cold without the coat.

Mateo leans over the bar with a smirk. "The coast is clear. You two can stop hiding now. She's over by the stage with Chuck."

I look at him skeptically. "Do you know?"

"About what?" he asks.

I point to Olive and I.

"Yes, I know that you're not *really* dating. Char told me the instant she heard of you two being together. But I won't say a word."

"Phew," Olive exhales. "I thought we blew it on the first day. It would be like us, to ruin it already."

"It would be," I say in reply.

Chapter 12

OLIVE

I take a long gulp of my third—no fourth mug of mulled wine. Who am I kidding? I have no clue what number I'm on, but I'm having a great time, and that's all that matters. I lean my elbows against the wooden table littered with empty beer bottles, cups, and abandoned half-finished plates of food. I watch everyone on the dance floor swaying and spinning to the high tempo country tunes. Vivi laughs as Dustin twirls her in the air. It's as if no one else is in the room, they are captivated by each other, and it pulls at my heart strings. I long to be on the dance floor, enamored with the tempo and lost in the rhythm of the guitar and twang. I take another slow sip of my drink; the sweet and rich spices help me feel relaxed. I take off Mason's coat as I get overheated again. I don't want to take it off. I like wearing his coat... It smells like him: vetiver, patchouli, and comfort.

My gaze is drawn to the bar where Mason serves Laura from the post office. She grabs the beer and slides a bill across the counter. He smiles, but it doesn't quite reach his eyes. He needs a break; I can tell by his half-hearted expression. As she turns to join a group of her friends, his eyes somehow manage to lock with mine once more.

Earlier, we had a similar moment, and I stuck my tongue out at him playfully. Mason never fails to make me laugh. He's my rock, and I'm always drawn to him. I want to seek him out and steal him away to dance with me. Maybe that's what we both need. Some carefree dancing, if only for a few songs. It wouldn't hurt to help with our fake relationship either. But that's only an afterthought. I want to have some fun, and who better to help me do it than my best friend (who looks as lonely as I feel at this moment)?

I continue to hold his eyes as I saunter to the bar. He smiles when I reach him, and this time his eyes crinkle as well.

"Hey, Knight. Will you dance with me? Please, just for a song?" I widen my eyes for dramatic effect.

Say yes.

He wipes off the counter in front of me and nods. "I'd love to. One song wouldn't hurt. Just let me ask Amelia to cover me for a few minutes."

"Okay." Good, he looks like he could use a little bit of fun. He leaves to find Amelia in the back, and I wait, slowly swaying with my arms crossed as the band starts another song. The bar is electric as I watch everyone I know dance the night away. Oakley and Jamal, Vivi and Dustin, and Char and Mateo are all here tonight. Everyone looks so happy. Snowflakes race past the front doors and windows. It's cozy and refreshing to take it all in.

Mason appears next to me after a few minutes, holding his hand out to me. "Are you ready, Firefly?"

"I was born ready." I giggle and take his hand in mine as we race to the dance floor. He twirls me around and pulls me into his arms. The band plays a new cover song, a rendition of "Last Christmas" by Wham! I sing the lyrics, as does everyone else in the room. I tilt my shoulders, and he pulls me in and out with our hands locked. I pretend to pull a rope, and he chuckles deeply holding his stomach. I continue to do silly moves to make him laugh. I twirl in a circle, waving my hands in the air. I hold my nose and pretend to swim. I bounce on my feet and shimmy my arms. My hair flows around my shoulders and covers my face. His full toothed smile is so wide, and we laugh so loud together.

I never said I was any good at dancing.

Mason looks at me unabashedly. I love that he isn't ashamed or embarrassed by anything I do. He embraces me for *me.* He's not fazed by the quirky and feisty moments I throw his way. He doesn't shy away from joining in on any crazy idea I have planned. He's the best friend a girl could ask for. I spin a few more times and stumble, feeling a bit dizzy, but Mason is there to steady my shoulders. He's always there.

A slower song starts, and Mason takes my hand. Suddenly, the excitement dies down, and the mood shifts. He wraps one palm around my waist, and his other hand covers mine. I place my free hand on his shoulder and smile up at him. His gaze is heated as he meets mine through the frames of his glasses. His brown eyes are slightly golden in the lighting, and his charming disposition is electric. The tension between us is palpable.

My mind is at war within itself. I'm stuck between thinking this is an act to make our relationship believable and wondering if these feelings are real. When he pulls me flush against his chest little zaps tingle my skin. And I almost let out a little sigh of contentment.

Dancing with Mason is comforting. It's almost like a lazy Sunday where you sit in front of a warm fire with a mug of coffee that's the perfect temperature. The crackle of the fire paired with some fuzzy socks on your feet... there's nothing else that compares.

Neither Mason nor I have spoken since we reached the dance floor, but I like it that way. We don't have to say a word to enjoy the little bit of peace in each other's company.

Mason finger combs a red curl that fell in front of my eyes and tucks it around my ear. His breath tingles as he whispers, "This is nice."

Goosebumps form on my spine, and I hum in agreement. I press my head against his chest and listen to his heartbeat as we sway. After another minute or so, the song slowly comes to an end. If I must admit, it ended too early for my liking. We continue dancing, even though the song is over, as the band shuffles around for a quick break. I think we've both come to the silent conclusion that we don't want whatever this is to end.

I'm so glad I whisked him away to enjoy the night. And I'm positive I'm going to convince him to leave his bartending responsibilities a few more times through the evening.

Chapter 13

MASON

I brace my hands on the bar after helping another customer. The night's been flying by, and the crowd's thinned out. The band has five more songs on their set list until they pack up to go home. Olive whisked me away from my bartender duties a few more times to dance with her. Constance hasn't said a word to either of us all night other than to order a drink, which is rare.

"What can I get you?" I ask Dustin when he walks towards the bar.

"A draft and a root beer," he orders.

I grab a chilled glass from the cooler. I hold it at an angle and let the beer slide down from the tap. I straighten it and fill it to the brim. A small coating of foam sits on top. I fill up another glass with root beer and slide them both across the counter.

"Thanks, man."

"No problem."

"Did you get a hold of my grandpa?"

"George said I could buy the wood lathe." I try my best to mimic his grandpa's raspy tone. *"It's been collecting dust for years—"*

His shoulders shake with laughter. "That was accurate. I could've sworn you were him for a minute."

"—that Grandson of mine won't touch it."

Dustin scoffs. "What does he mean, I won't touch it? Why would I? There's no time between the goats, cows, fixing fences, and mucking the barns. I barely have time to sleep, let alone get a few moments with Vivi."

I hold up my hands. "His words, not mine."

"Believe me, I know. When are you stopping by?" He takes a sip of his beer.

"Sometime in the afternoon this week."

"I'll be around. Let me know. I'll help you load it."

"Thanks."

"You do enough to help us with hay season. It's the least I could do." He walks backward. "I better get back to the wife. She's waiting for her drink."

I nod and my phone buzzes with a text. It's the group chat my sisters put me in. Right now, it's named "Our Brother is STEALTHY" with a few shushing emojis. My sisters change the group's name weekly, sometimes daily. Last week it was named "Oldies but Goodies" and had a few grandma and grandpa emojis.

Jackie was complaining about turning thirty in three years, so Hannah changed the name. I don't see how being twenty-seven is old. I'm thirty. What does that make me in her eyes? I laugh to myself.

The texts roll in with non-stop dings.

Jackie

> Mason! When were you going to tell us you and Olive are DATING?

Hannah

> What the hell! Since when? Astonished face emoji.

Char

> Let the man be happy.

Hannah

> You knew!?!

Char

> I saw it in the town's gossip article. Don't you two read it?

Jackie

> NO. Constance and the gossip mill won't let me have access since I live out of town now. Total BS.

Char

LOL

Jackie

Not funny.

Hannah

How did you find out?

Jackie

Mom. She's over the moon. She's already picking out colors. She video called me and shared her Pinterest board. You're having an ocean themed wedding.

Mason

WTH.

Char

Who taught her Pinterest?

Hannah

Me. Face with peeking eye emoji.

Jackie

Meme of a cat screaming *traitor*.

Hannah

BTW, happy for you, Mason. I knew Olive and you were meant to be.

Jackie

I second that.

Char

I third that. Heart Emoji.

Mason

Thanks.

Char is really playing thick into the narrative. But I'm grateful. I don't need it to come out that this has been fake all along. My sisters make me chuckle. They can be relentless and dramatic. I'm used to it by now.

My gaze gravitates to Olive. I haven't been able to keep myself from finding her the entire night. She's leaning back in a chair, smiling wide while watching the band. Vivi and Dustin sit beside her conversing away.

When I reach their table, I say, "You're cut off. Let's get you home."

"Boo. You're such a party pooper. I was just starting to have a good time." Olive giggles and covers her mouth with her hand.

"We're heading out anyway." Dustin finishes his drink.

"I'm ready for a nap." Vivi stretches her arms. "See you both tomorrow."

Dustin yawns. "I probably won't, but I'll see you at the Christmas party on Sunday?"

"We'll be there," I answer.

"Party? Competition. Cookies. I could go for one of those," Olive mumbles, slurring her words.

"Not the cookie competition, that's not for another week. The Christmas party," I tell Olive.

"Speaking of the Cookie Chronicles, I can't wait to *demolish* you guys," Violet teases.

Dustin shrugs. "Sorry, man. Happy wife, happy life. It's on."

"It's all good," I reply.

Violet whispers in my ear on the way out, "Constance has been *cooking* up something for you two. Just thought you'd want a heads up. I know nothing more."

I want to ask her what she means, but they're out the door before I have the chance. I should be concerned, but I'm not. It's Constance. There's nothing I can do to stop her when she gets an idea.

"Come on, let's go." I usher Olive towards the door.

"Okay, Knight. I'm coming. Slow down—the ground is spinning." She staggers and rests against me as we enter the empty street. "Who's going to close up?"

"Amelia can close tonight. Don't worry about it."

"I'm not worried." A flush creeps up her face. "I'm so hot. I'm taking this coat off."

"Don't you dare. It's snowing." She shrugs it off and hands it to me. "Put it back on." I drape my coat over her arms and pull the zipper taut.

"I want it off." She shakes her arms.

"If you take it off one more time, I'm going to carry you."

She puts her hands on her hips in resistance and wobbles slightly. "You wouldn't—dare."

"You know I don't back down from a dare."

"Wait—no! I take it back!"

Too late. I pick her up, putting one hand under her legs and the other around her back. I carry her the rest of the way to her shop. She hits her fists on my chest and giggles.

"Hey, I'm home," she states with mirth when I stand in front of The Olive Bean.

"Where are your keys?"

"In my purse." She opens it in front of me. Digging around looking for them. She pulls out a toothbrush, sunglasses, a five-dollar bill, and a bottle of hot sauce. None of which would be useful for getting out of the cold. "They're in here somewhere—I know it."

"I'm going to be holding you here all night if you don't find them. What's with the hot sauce? That's new."

"It's always been there—everything's in here. You never know when you're going to need something."

I'm not sure if she's ever going to need any of those things. But I love that Olive is unapologetically herself. I think it's what I admire most about her.

"If we're ever stranded somewhere, as long as you have your purse, we'll survive for months."

"Ha! You'll be grateful for the bag of chips and hot sauce." She pulls out a bag of potato chips and shakes it in front of my face.

I chuckle. "I'm not hungry now. Where are your keys?"

"That's right. Aha! Here they are." She dangles the set with a big pom-pom. You would think she would've found them easily with that on the keychain.

"Okay, Mary Poppins, let's get you inside." I open the door, and I lock it on the way in. I carry her up the stairs to her apartment.

"Now you're home," I state.

"Hi, Jaws." She waves to her betta fish. He swims around the tank in zigzags.

I carry her through the living room. It's full of crocheted blankets and tapestries covering the walls. The faint glow of moonlight highlights bursts of color filling the familiar living space. Her place oozes her personality—bubbly, extraordinary, remarkable. A few words don't even begin to describe the depth of who Olive is. Or her decorating style.

I put her down on the queen-sized bed. It's covered in a blanket with intricate patterns.

"My feet hurt *so* bad." She wiggles her boots. I unzip each shoe and place them in her closet. "So much better. She yawns. "Thank you."

I grab an oversized T-shirt from the closet. It's one of her favorites to lounge in. There are small holes dotting the bottom and sides. She won't get a new one. She says *it's sentimental*. Whatever that means. I'm not going to question it. Besides, I think her quirks are adorable.

"Here, put this on."

"Okay." She hiccups.

I leave the room and hang up our coats. I grab some fish food and dump a scoop into the tank. There used to be two of them. But Jaws, previously named Jack, was renamed according to his shark-like behavior.

"Mason!" Olive calls from her bedroom.

I poke my head in. "Yeah, Olive?"

"Please stay?" she says, as more of a question than a statement. I'm glad she asked because I'd rather be here in case she has to throw up. Or to help her if she needs it.

"I gotta put the chickens in and get Moose. But I can come back if you want?"

"Yes. I don't want to be alone tonight. Lie with me for a few minutes." I lie on top of the comforter facing her. She turns on her side. "You're so good to me, Mason—did anyone ever tell you that you're handsome?" She brushes her fingers along my cheek. Over my nose. They leave a trail of goosebumps.

"Not anyone that I wanted to mean it—until now," I whisper.

Her eyes blink slowly as she drifts to sleep.

My mind is spinning with questions. But two of them linger through my inner thoughts:

Is that how she feels?

Did she mean to say those words aloud?

I slowly get out of bed and wrap her arms around a pillow, careful not to wake her. I prop another behind her back so she stays on her side while I'm gone. I find a comforter on the blanket ladder and cover her with it, lifting it over her shoulder. I tiptoe out of her apartment and lock the door behind me. I rush to close the chickens in and pick up Moose.

Another question plagues my mind.

What am I going to do?

Chapter 14

OLIVE

Thornwood Valley Christmas parties are very *festive*. Or maybe *merry* would be a better word to describe the event. You'll see what I mean soon enough.

A knock sounds on my door. It must be Mason. It's exactly five fifteen. He's forty-five minutes early, uncharacteristically so. He must be nervous, or he knows how I loathe being late. Either way, I'm mentally sighing.

Ugh.

I shake my head as I remember the night Mason brought me home from the bar. I think I confessed to something. Or said something I shouldn't have. I have no clue what was said.

I remember nothing after dancing with Mason the first time, or maybe it was the second time. I don't know. It could be attributed to one too many glasses of mulled wine and maybe a shot of tequila? It's a hazy blip in my memory.

Things have been awkward between us all week. Well, it's not apparent, but I've known him for so long that I can pick up on the hidden cues. The way he avoids prolonged eye-contact and gives me half-hearted smiles. I was out of sorts. All I know is that I woke up with a raging hangover and a note. *Orange juice is in the fridge and take this,* scrawled in his chicken scratch handwriting.

I know one thing for sure. There wasn't any orange juice in my fridge. So he must have brought some over. There was also an arrow pointing to a pain reliever on the note. My heart pitter-pattered in my chest. I could smell the faint vetiver lingering from his cologne. The bed was still warm from where I could see the faint impression of his form. A pillow was wedged under my back and on the front of me. He was so thoughtful; he must have stayed.

I open my apartment to find him standing stiff in the doorway. He looks nothing like the Mason I know. My mouth drops open to the floor. I swear it's on the ground.

Calm down.

"Knight," I greet and wave my arms, motioning for him to come in. "Are you a vampire? Do you need me to invite you in?" I joke.

"I feel weird in these clothes," he admits.

"Why did you wear them? And where are your glasses?"

"I swapped them for contacts for the occasion."

"Wow, really going all out for the Christmas party."

He smiles. "Something like that." He sits on my couch, squeezing between skeins of yarn. "Is that what you're wearing?" He motions to my hole littered T-shirt that sits midway on my thighs.

"Do you have a problem with what I'm wearing?" I question, crossing my arms.

"No. I'm entirely confident in the fact you look beautiful in anything you wear."

"That was a really sweet thing to say. But I'm totally kidding. You look handsome in your dress shirt. Like you could break some hearts with one crooked smile. I've never seen you wearing anything but a T-shirt."

He gulps. "Don't get used to it." He's clearly unhappy with his fashion decision.

"Go home and change. You have time. I'm obviously falling behind today." I twirl a lock of hair around my finger.

He scratches his jaw. "I'm committed at this point. Do you need any help?"

"Follow me." I skip to my room, jumping to avoid a few straggler yarn skeins. "Ignore the mess."

"I've been ignoring it for almost thirty years of my life. I'm used to it."

"Those couple months you had without me must have been the most relaxed of your life."

He rumbles in protest. "No, they were the most boring months of my life."

"You were only a baby. How do you remember?" I scrunch up my face.

He shrugs. "I just have a feeling."

I wave my hands. "He has a feeling, ladies and gentlemen."

I know there is no way he remembers those months when he was a baby. I can't remember what I did last week, let alone something I did in my first few moments. Mason is just being charming. It's the way he always is, and I love it.

He chuckles and sits on the edge of my bed between clothes.

"I have *nothing* to wear." I open my closet and look at the many options. Nothing's screaming, *Christmas party*. I scavenge through the clothes on my bed throwing hangers with clothes in the air behind me like a raccoon scrounging through a dumpster, looking for their next food scrap.

"You have hundreds of clothing options." His eyes widen as I continue to throw them behind me.

I pull out a light green sweater with miniature Christmas trees, a red sparkly sweater dress, and a dark green elk patterned sweater dress. I hold them in front of me by the hangers and ask, "Which two do you like most?"

He scratches his head. "The green ones."

"Pick one." I throw the red behind me.

The seconds tick by as he ponders. He taps his chin and says, "The light green sweater."

"Okay, I'll wear the dark green elk dress then." I'm doing the opposite from what he says because, yeah, I knew I wanted to wear that one. "I need to donate some of these clothes."

"Maybe you should." He chuckles. "I'll wait in the living room." He shuts the door on his way out. I pull the dress over my frame and a pair of thick white leggings in case we're outside for long periods of time. I pair the look with my knee-high brown winter boots. I snatch a candy cane-shaped purse that Vivi gifted me last year. She always gets me a unique purse. I dump the contents from my last one into it, as well as a few other Christmas related accessories.

I swing it over my shoulder and check my reflection quickly in the attached bathroom. I add some sparkly green liquid eyeliner to match the dress. And I part my lips to apply a few swipes of light pink lipstick.

"Ready?" I ask as I enter the living room.

"Ready as I can be." His eyes widen as he notices me. "Firefly, you are a vision in green." His voice cracks when he uses my nickname.

"Will you escort me to the party?" I ask teasingly as I hold out my hand. His face is stunned. "What are you gaping at?"

"It's not every day I get to escort a beautiful woman to a party," Mason stammers. He takes my hand and grins. "Give me a moment to soak it in."

"You're always a gentleman." I smile as we leave my apartment and shop.

We walk along the fresh snow to Annie's Diner. The street is filled with decorations. Every lamp post is wrapped with garland. A monstrous tree is set up across the road in front of the pavilion. Bright white lights and paper houses that the children made in school hang on every branch. Every inch of each business is wrapped in lights. Each one is a different color: blue, white, green, purple, etc.

It's a dream. I'm really feeling the spirit this year.

"White Christmas" by Michael Bublé and Shania Twain plays through a speaker in front of The Hoarder Emporium. Laughter and light filters from the diner. The windows glow in the waning light.

"Can I tell you a secret?" Mason whispers in my ear.

"I would love to hear it," I whisper back.

His warm breath grazes my ear. It tingles against the chill of cool air. "I lied."

My eyes widen. "You wouldn't dare lie to your *girlfriend*." I put a palm to my chest in mock horror.

"Too late. I said you should wear the sweater, but I knew you'd choose the opposite of whatever I told you. I liked the dress better."

That makes me laugh out loud. "You know me so well."

He shrugs. "A benefit of the title."

"Wait a minute." I stop to open my purse. "I almost forgot." I pull out a light up Christmas necklace, and I turn it on so the bulbs glow. "This will transform your outfit from sophisticated to Christmas-chic."

Mason chuckles as he takes the necklace from me and puts it on. "Thanks."

"What in the world?" I gasp.

Mason's brow furrows. "What's wrong?"

"What are the chickens wearing?"

He swears under his breath. "What the hell happened to my chickens?"

Hennifer and Helga strut past, and a few more chickens follow. Each one has tiny arms strapped to them. They look like tyrannosaurus rexes. Some with their thumbs up and muscly arms. They're so tiny. It's the most ridiculously hilarious thing I've ever witnessed. And to make the look even better, each has a tiny Santa hat with a bell. Every step they take the bell jingles. Did I mention each chicken has a different Christmas sweater? No? Well, they do. It's the best thing I've ever seen.

Vivi steps out of the diner wearing a sweatshirt with a chicken on it. *Of course.* It says: "This is my Merry Cluckin' Sweater," and has chickens wearing Santa hats and sweaters.

This town might as well be called Chicken Valley. I think we need to rename it.

"Did you do this?" Mason questions Vivi.

She looks around acting oblivious. "Who, me?" She points to herself.

"You did this," I say with one-hundred percent certainty.

She clutches her stomach. "I—had—to." She laughs between every word. "They needed cute Christmas outfits too. I didn't want them to feel left out."

"They certainly won't," Mason says.

Not now. They fit right in with the holiday.

"Come in and get some food. Everyone brought something," Vivi insists.

Mason and I greet the townies and our families as we enter. Beside the front counter there's a dessert table, a chocolate fountain, fruits, eggnog, cheese platters, and more. Mason and I grab plates and fill them with a little bit of everything. We find a table with Vivi, Dustin, Char, and Mateo.

"The town looks beautiful this year," I say between bites of a piece of fruit cake. My nose turns up as the dense and crumbly texture hits my tongue. It's slightly sweet; it's not *bad* per se.

Who likes fruit cake?

Every year I try it, hoping my taste buds will decide it's good. That never happens. Ada, from Cat's & Novels, makes it. She's the sweetest, and it makes her so happy when people grab some. So I try to put a smile on her face by eating it. No one else took a slice yet.

She waves from the next table, I put on my best "I love it" smile and give her a thumbs up.

"It was a lot of work. Constance had Mason, Mateo, Dan, and I on every roof in town stringing lights. Someone's wife volunteered me," Dustin says, while tilting his head towards Vivi.

"Hey! *Your wife.*" Vivi speaks up. "And we owed Constance a favor after she got us together. We're even now."

Dustin grumbles, "We didn't owe her a thing, but it wasn't all bad. Mason stapled his coat to the roof."

I can't help but feel like someone is watching me. I look around, and my gaze meets Chad's at the table across from us. He looks away quickly when I notice his staring.

Good. Ugh, why does he have to be here.

"You weren't supposed to tell anyone, man," Mason says.

I shake Chad from my thoughts and laugh while looking into Mason's gaze. "How'd you manage that?"

"Oh look! Constance is waving us over. We better go." Mason avoids the topic.

What does she want now? She points to Mason and I and motions for us to come talk to her. He wasn't bluffing. Mason grabs my hand, and as we leave the table, I say, "Pray for me."

"Oh, I will indeed." Vivi grins, and I stick my tongue out at her.

Mason and I meet Constance in the far end of the diner. "Hi, lovelies," she says while tucking a strand of gray hair behind her ear. "I'm so glad you could make it."

"Us too," I mumble, answering for the both of us.

She grins. "Oh my! Look above you! How did that get there?"

As my eyes trail upward, I'm internally screaming.

I should've known.

Why do I fall for her antics constantly? You'd think I'd know better by now. Mason looks pale. Yeah, Mason, I feel your pain. There's no way we can get out of this. We're dating. At least everyone in town thinks so.

I have to kiss him. There's a damn *mistletoe*. It's strung from a line between the cracks of ceiling tiles. There's no getting around it. Couples kiss. If they didn't, things would be a little suspicious. No, very suspicious. I look at the table where Vivi sits; I raise my eyebrows in her direction, hoping she will come up with a distraction. She gives me a thumbs up.

Thank you, Vivi!

I lean into Mason, watching a single bead of sweat trail from his forehead. He doesn't know I had a silent conversation with her.

"Just one kiss," Constance says. I swear the whole diner quiets to a whisper. What in the world is up with this place? This isn't a soap opera for everyone to watch. *Eat your food and look away!*

I take Mason's hand and squeeze it as I lean in closer. I should have come up with a secret code or something to give him a signal.

I stand on my tiptoes to try and peek at what Vivi's up to.

Hurry!

I bite my bottom lip, we're inches apart, and my faith in Vivi is fading.

Mason and I lock eyes as the room slowly fades. He smiles shakily, and I return a nervous glance. His eyes are warm. I suddenly feel like there's a chance I could get lost in them if I let myself. What if I do kiss him?

I trace my gaze over his nose and his bearded jaw, and I stare at his lips. It wouldn't take but a second to close the gap. It'd be so easy. He cups his hands around my face, and I swoon a little inside as he lightly caresses my cheek with his thumb.

Kiss me. My subconscious whispers. Maybe I should let him.

Slam! Vivi throws a glass full force at the floor and shatters into pieces littering the ground. Gasps filter around the diner.

"I'm so sorry!" she cries and winks at me. I can hear Chad's gasp over the sound of everyone else's commotion. He looks at me, and his nose curls. Maybe I should've kissed Mason to prove to him that there's nothing there. And never will be. It's been years anyway. I roll my eyes in his direction.

Constance is momentarily distracted by the scene. I take Mason's hand and run, pulling him along with me through the kitchen and out the back entrance to Annie's Diner. The air is cool and a balm against my skin. Mason sighs deeply, breathing in fresh air and clutching his sides.

"Thank God for Vivi." A fog cloud lingers every time he laughs.

"Let's get out of here before they find us. I'm not staying a minute longer."

That was a close call.

Chapter 15

OLIVE

I open my eyes while stretching my arms above my head. I smile when I remember today's my thirtieth birthday. I yawn and check my phone. It's four in the morning, yet there's already a text from Mason.

Mason

> Good morning, Firefly. Happy Birthday! Now we're almost the same age.

Olive

> Good morning. Thank you!

Mason

> You're taking the day off.

He has the audacity to state instead of asking. Nothing like making demands at four in the morning. *Why is he awake?*

I don't know. Sleep? Nothing? Crochet something? Everything sounds promising. I look to my bedroom floor and at the pile of clean clothes. They're stacked in a large mound, and I haven't touched them all week. I think the clothes made the decision for me.

> Let's pack up some of my nicer clothes, cro-
> chet some blankets, and go on a trip to the
> donation bin and animal shelter. Paw Prints
> emoji.

Your wish is my command. See you soon,
birthday girl.

I smile at my phone. Mason has always done something with
me on my birthday to celebrate. He pretty much goes with the
flow. Whatever I choose, we do together. Whether it be making
blankets for the animal rescues, watching movies all day, or trying
new things like hitting the slopes—snowboarding is not a hobby
I excel at by the way. He's compassionate, putting others above
himself. Or maybe it's putting *me* above himself. I don't know why
he does it, but I sure as heck know he's the best friend any girl could
ask for.

"There's the birthday girl! Happy Birthday!" Mason announces
as he walks through the threshold, hands full of grocery bags. "I
brought reinforcements: orange juice, trash bags, and breakfast
sandwiches."

"I could kiss you!" I squeal.

He stands still, rooted to the spot. "That's not funny. Two days ago that almost happened. I'm still recovering." His gaze trails to the floor, and he rocks on his feet.

Okay, so that was definitely a lie. Maybe he did want to kiss me too.

"Almost, but it didn't—Vivi saved us."

Thanks to my other best friend, I didn't end up making a fool out of myself in front of the whole town. Kissing Mason wouldn't be a mistake. He's easy on the eyes and a total catch in every other way. He pulls out all the stops with grand gestures, and he's sweet and caring. But... I'm content being an honorary member of the singles club. Our relationship is perfect where it stands. Who am I to ruin a good thing when I have it? "Yeah." He looks at the wall behind me. "How about we eat breakfast and get started going through clothes."

"I'm in."

We eat breakfast and share stories from when we were younger. Reminiscing on our days spent without a care. Trading jokes and arguing over who had the worst dating past. I won. He's only ever had flings, nothing serious. So he doesn't count any of them. I go through my entire closet. Sliding hangers and creating three piles: keep, donate, and old T-shirts. I never realized how many I've collected until I saw them all laid out.

"These were outfits from high school." I shove half the clothes to the right. "They can go. I don't know why I kept them all these years. For a while, it was for sentimental reasons, maybe because a lot of them were ones my mom made." I fold up a few dress shirts and place them in a bag. Mason listens to me intently, folding dresses in a pile I handed him. "Now they're just taking up space; they don't fit me right anymore. I'd love for someone who needs clothes to have them, and they're still in good condition. There was a time where we didn't have much growing up, and I want someone else to feel a little bit of joy. It's not much, but it's something I can give."

"I think it's a really nice thing to do, especially spending your birthday thinking about ways to help others," Mason agrees.

We finish bagging the rest of the clothes and carry them to the truck. Once the truck is packed, I start cutting up strips of T-shirts for blankets.

"Can you make them into about one-inch strips, cut slits in the end, and weave them together?" I ask. He's helped me make them before. I normally use cotton fabric scraps my mom has from making clothes as a seamstress. There's always been a plethora of pieces that are too small to be used.

"I can handle that," he says and starts to get them ready for me.

I grab a crochet hook and get to work using a double crochet stitch to weave blankets as tightly as I can. We spend the next four hours making them. By the time we're finished, we have four made. It's only a few, but I already had twenty more ready to drop off at the shelter. We load up the truck, and Mason takes off towards the nearest highway.

"It's a three hour round trip. Hope you aren't hungry," Mason says over the hum of tires on gravel.

"I have a few snacks in my purse." I rifle through the candy cane-shaped purse. I haven't had a chance to switch back to my normal one since the party. I hold up a pack of fruit snacks, some peanut butter crackers, and a protein bar.

His eyes flicker to me and back to the road. "I take it back. We have enough for a few days."

"I have hot sauce too." I wave the half-full bottle.

"That damn hot sauce bottle again, Firefly."

I laugh as I place everything back in my purse and ask, "Why do you call me Firefly? I can't remember how it started."

"You don't remember?"

I shake my head no, making a guess. "Because I liked to catch fireflies when we were kids?"

"Yes and no. You'd cup them in your hands in the summers and run around screaming that your hands were glowing. You'd have the biggest smile on your face. You'd let them crawl on your fingers, and your mouth would be wide open in awe. You were so fascinated with them. That's when I started calling you Firefly."

My mouth was *wide* open? *Embarrassing.*

"Oh..."

"That's not all." He turns the knob for the radio down slightly. "You are like a Firefly in a way. You glow. Your soul is bright and full of unrestrained vigor. You don't hide from any challenge hurdled at you. There's a fire down to your marrow that can't be put out. It's something I admire about you. I always have."

There's depth to Mason. There's meaning behind everything he does. So much thought is put behind every word spoken. He didn't give me a nickname because I caught fireflies. He thought about what they portrayed.

Tears form in the corners of my eyes. "Mason. You're going to make me cry. Why do you have to go and say things like that?"

"I'm only being honest," he admits. "Speaking of nicknames, why do you call me Knight? I mean, other than the obvious."

"Umm..." I cross my leg over my knee and tap my foot in thought. "I'm trying to come up with something as good as what you just said about me," I joke.

"Just be honest, don't think too much into it."

"I will. Would you expect any less?" I bounce my foot. "You are my Knight. That's why. You would drop everything to help me if you had to. But you're not only that way with me. You're fiercely protective of everyone you care deeply for. Your sisters, your parents, my family, me, Vivi, Dustin. Actually... every person in our small town. Every person that's a part of your life. Nothing will get in the way of the ones you love. And that's what *I* admire most about you, Knight."

He glances at me quickly, his smile soft and heated. "I'm glad you think so, because I would do anything for you."

"And I for you."

My heart is warm and tingly, thinking about how much he cares for me. I drum my fingers on the door panel. The trees pass in a blur on the highway. It's weird to be surrounded by buildings and hear so many sounds all at once. I'm used to the quiet life. On a normal day in town, there are many sounds that come from the businesses, but nothing compares to this. Honking of horns, brakes screeching, rumbling of vehicles, cars accelerating, trains passing by. I can't think clearly. My mind is alphabet soup. Each letter is spinning, but nothing comes together to make a coherent word.

Mason shifts the truck into park in front of a clothing donation bin. We put them all safely inside and then stop in front of the Paw Ridge animal shelter. When Mason and I bring the blankets in, the receptionist's face is warm with appreciation.

"Thank you. You don't know how much these blankets make an impact on the cats and dogs," the same volunteer that greeted us says while adjusting her bright purple glasses. It warms my heart to hear how much they appreciate them.

I choose a new shelter every time. Once a month, I call ahead and see if any will take handmade upcycled blankets. I also make them for Ada at Cat's & Novels since she takes in stray cats constantly.

Once Mason and I head towards town, I lean back in my seat, stretching my legs under the dashboard. I pull my phone from my pocket and check the messages from today. I haven't had a moment to look. My parents, Vivi, Mason's sisters, my siblings, and almost every townie texted me Happy Birthday wishes. There is even one from Constance. I fire off thank you replies. A new message comes up, and it's from Chad.

Ugh. Again?

Chad

> Happy thirtieth birthday. I miss you. Have you thought about taking me back? I could make you so much happier than Mason. Think about it.

I'm not thinking about it for a moment. I put away my phone, wanting to enjoy every moment today offers. I don't want Chad putting a damper on the wonderful day I'm having. I'm *not* letting him get to me. It's what he wants. I should block his number. No, I am going to block him. That's exactly what I'm going to do when I get home.

"Open the glovebox," Mason insists.

"Why?" I question.

"Just open it. There's something in there for you."

"You didn't have to get me anything."

"I wanted to. Would you just look already and quit being so stubborn for one second?" His lip curls into a smile.

"I'm not... Okay, I am being stubborn."

131

When I open the glovebox, a small black box sits on top of his registration and insurance papers. I pick up the box carefully and tilt my head. "Is this a surprise engagement?" I tease.

"No!" Mason's answer is clipped as he smiles shakily.

I open the box, peeking inside. A silver firefly charm sparkles from the glare of sunlight draping in the windows.

"Mason. This is beautiful." I pluck it from the felt and hold it in my hands. "Does it glow?"

"Yes. If you charge it under light, the end will glow. So no matter where you go, there will always be a little bit of light with you, a reminder of how much you light up my life and everyone else's by being a part of it. The charm can be clipped onto your purse. That way you'll always have it with you."

"Thank you," I say wholeheartedly. He's so thoughtful my heart feels like it's going to explode. "I'm at a loss for words, and that's rare."

"You don't have to say anything. Your smile says more than enough." He taps the steering wheel. "It wasn't anything extravagant."

"Oh, Mason, but it is. It's the most thoughtful thing I've ever received. I'm going to cherish it forever. I can promise you that much."

I clip it onto my purse, repeating his words in my head. *So no matter where you go, there will always be a little bit of light with you, a reminder of how much you light up my life.*

Chapter 16

OLIVE

I t's finally the day of the Cookie Chronicles. I'm brimming with anticipation. I've been antsy all week for it. Today has been dragging slower than a cheesecake takes to set in the fridge once you've baked it. Slow and painfully tempting with the prospect of what's to come. Delicious, sweet, and nowhere near my stomach. Or close enough to touch but far enough to cravingly stare at.

I want to bottle up the giddiness I get when I'm racing against a clock to put together ingredients and store it in my purse for safe keeping. When I get the timing just right and make something people will enjoy, I love it.

I skip along the sidewalk and see Mason sitting on a park bench in front of Annie's Diner. He looks disinterested, leaning back, arms stretched on his sides grasping the bench. He stares at a chicken pecking snow—Hennifer of course. She's always around wherever we go. I swear she has some kind of Olive and Mason chicken radar.

Mason tips his head up, and his gaze meets mine. His face brightens the instant he recognizes me. "Firefly." His voice comes out gravelly.

"Knight." I skip the last stretch to meet him in front of the diner.

"Do you know what kind of cookie we're making?"

"No—"

He cuts me off. "Please tell me you're joking."

"I have three options."

"Okay. This is going to go well." He scratches his head and looks to the sky. "Do you remember my cookie skillset? We're doomed."

"You made soup instead of cookies. Pretty impressive if you ask me. Don't worry. I'll tell you what to do."

"Thank God."

"So, thumbprint, lady locks, or pinwheel cookies with icing?"

"The third sounds good to me."

"That was easy."

"I'm not a very complicated person. I went with what my stomach was telling me, and that was the pinwheel."

I smirk. "We better get in there before we miss an announcement."

"I can't wait." He rolls his eyes.

I shrug. *I'm excited.* But not for Constance's spiel or rule word vomit. Sometimes, I wonder why there needs to be rules. We're grown adults. I think we can handle acting like civilized human beings. Even if it's only for one day.

I take his hand in mine and swing it back and forth. "It's cookie time. And time to pretend we're in newly relationship bliss."

The door to Annie's Diner swings open. The instant warmth is soothing against the chill outside. People are conversing. I wave to Vivi, Dustin, my parents, and Mason's parents.

Constance taps on a microphone in a rapid staccato with a manicured nail. Short, loud, and pestering. "Good morning, lovebirds. Welcome to the Thornwood Valley's first ever Cookie Chronicles! All is fair in love and war. But please try and follow the rules. Rule number one: There will be no sabotaging anyone else's cookies or pushing and shoving people to get to ingredients first. Rule number two: No one else can help you from other teams. Rule number three: You are not permitted to use any outside ingredients. Treat this like the show *Chopped*. You can use whatever ingredients you like, as long as they are stocked in the kitchen. Rule number four: Please stick to edible ingredients only. The whole town will be eating these, so don't try to be funny. Rule number five: When the timer goes off, you're done. As soon as the clock strikes noon, you are to put everything down. Don't touch another thing." She adjusts her reading glasses. "Per my last email, groups of two will be separated at each of the designated cookie stations: The String

Cheese, here at Annie's Diner, Rooster's, and The Olive Bean. If you missed my email, please come forward now so I can tell you where to go. There are limited ovens in each shop." She pauses, waiting for someone to come forward. A few couples meet her to ask about their designated locations.

I came prepared. Our baking station is The String Cheese. It would've been nice to be in a familiar kitchen, but they didn't want to give us any advantages over anyone else. Joke's on them. I've helped Joe a few times when he needed help making pepperoni rolls on a busy tourist day. The small business owners in town like to help each other out whenever they can. And this time it paid off for me.

The microphone crackles again with Constance's voice. "Okay, your time starts at nine. Good luck! At least one of the five judges will be in each area, so don't worry if you need anything or have questions. We'll be right there to help."

"So many rules," Mason grumbles as he grabs my hand. We stroll along the sidewalk to The String Cheese.

"There are always rules when it comes to Constance."

"You've got that right."

I wrap an apron around my waist and tie it in the front. Mason puts his on as well.

His apron is printed with the words "She's my sweet potato" and an arrow points to mine, which says "I yam."

"You're my sweet potato." He waggles his eyebrows as he ties the string behind his back. It looks so tiny on him, whereas mine fits perfectly.

"I yam." I grin. "I can't believe they got us different funny aprons with sayings on them."

"It's a nice touch. You look cute."

"I mean, I yam," I joke. "These *are* cute. I'll give it to Constance. She knows how to plan an event."

"There are two minutes until nine. Everyone, get ready to grab your ingredients. Remember, you have three hours after I say go," Harvey says from the front of the kitchen.

I poke Mason on the arm and whisper, "Can you believe I was matched with him on a dating app?" I chuckle. "I hope he finds someone. It must be lonely after losing his wife so many years ago."

His face pales. "You're on a dating app?" he whispers.

That's the only thing he paid attention to?

"*Was—is the* key word. I can't be anymore if we're *dating*. Besides, there weren't any options that were feasible. I was matched with Chad and Jackson too. Yuck!"

I can't read the expression that crosses his face. Before I have a chance to ask, Harvey's voice bursts through the room yet again. "Your time starts in three, two, one, go!"

"Grab the sprinkles and food dyes. We need red and green. Also, about four sticks of butter. I'll get the rest," I shout to Mason. All three teams push and shove each other to grab items. I didn't think they'd be this aggressive about it. *We're grown adults. I think we can handle acting like civilized human beings.* Yeah, that thought was purely naive. Oakley body checks me on the way to get a bag of flour.

"Hey!" I shout.

My normally innocent—*wouldn't hurt a fly*—sister just totally shoved me like I meant nothing to her. Like the twenty years as roommates was a blip in her memory.

Oh, it's on.

I snatch the flour from her arms and dash around her as if I'm an Olympic athlete who can see the finish line just in reach. Oakley tugs on the edge of my apron, swinging me back towards her. I unwrap her fingers from the fabric and dive. Sliding across the floor with the utmost swiftness. With as much grace as a newly thirty-year-old could exemplify as they skid across a slightly dirt-littered tile floor.

"Get back here!" she yells.

I glide with the flour bag tucked under my arm like a bird protecting its baby under its wing. The floor resembles ice, and I'm Mario in a penguin suit in *Super Mario Bros.*

Yes. Penguins are cool!

Hmm...why am I always comparing myself to penguins? I guess they're cute, so it's okay.

I don't hear Oakley anymore. She must have decided it was easier to grab a different bag of flour than fight over this one. There's no way she could pry it out of my hands.

I slide to a stop in front of a pair of dark boots. I trail my eyes upward, seeing a familiar sweet potato apron. Mason's eyes crinkle. "Careful, Firefly. Pretty soon we'll be disqualified if you keep breaking the rules."

I raise my brow. "As long as you don't tell on me, I'll keep breaking them. Rule number one is the first of many."

"Never," he promises. "We're partners in crime."

"Harvey didn't see me?" I ask, as he grabs my hand and helps me up.

"No. As soon as he said go, he left." He shakes his head. "Constance would be pissed if she'd known."

"Good, the less she knows the better." I brush my apron off.

I grab the rest of the dry and wet ingredients. He sets the items that he grabbed on our section of the counter with mine.

"Okay, so we're going for red, green, and white swirled sugar cookies with vanilla buttercream and sprinkles," I say as we make our way to the sinks and wash our hands.

"Sounds like a walk in the park." He pats his hands dry using a paper towel. His expression is filled with skepticism.

"It will be. As long as you follow my directions. It shouldn't be too hard."

"What goes first?" he asks, grabbing the butter.

"You can handle the wet ingredients, and I can work on the dry."

He smiles self-consciously. "I think I can handle it."

"You can't mess this up."

His eyebrows pinch together at the bridge of his nose. "Are you sure about that?"

"Yes." *Sixty percent.* I'm not going to tell him, though.

"What do I need to add?"

I recite the ingredients from memory. "Four sticks of butter and two cups of sugar. Beat those until combined on the first setting. Turn the mixer off. Add two eggs and a hefty dash of vanilla. Once it's all in the mixer, turn it on the first setting again, and mix it with the beater until it's smooth and fully combined."

Mason nods shakily. "Got it."

While he mixes the wet ingredients, I mix the dry ones in a large bowl, making sure to combine them thoroughly so no one gets bits of salt or clumps of flour. That would be a disaster. Oakley, Jamal,

Joe, and Hannah's voices are muffled in the background as they make their dough and bake cookies.

"What's with Joe being here?" I ask Mason.

He scoffs. "He has Constance wrapped around his finger."

I turn to Mason and give him a skeptical look. "I thought we weren't allowed to cook in our own kitchens so there weren't any unfair advantages."

"Me too. But Joe is a charmer. He probably begged Constance for a spot here. I wouldn't doubt it." He shakes his head.

I giggle. "You're right. I could see that." I finish mixing the dry ingredients and say, "Turn the mixer on slowly, and I'll add in the ingredients a little at a time." I scoop a cup of the flour into the mixer. He pushes the lever surpassing the slowest settings to full speed.

"Shit!" he grumbles. He scrambles to shut it off. With a few clicks, the beater stops moving. The air fills with a cloud of flour. It coats us both in a white dusting. I stare at the bowl and then at Mason. He looks horrified.

Does he think I'd be mad?

The corner of my mouth tilts. The laughter I tried so hard to restrain bursts out loudly and wildly. There's no containing the merriment I feel in this moment.

"Your hair is white," I say out of breath. I tousle his hair with my hand, another cloud of white poofs out with the motion.

He pats my shoulder emitting another cloud of flour. "Yours is too. And it's all over your apron."

"Holy crap, you two are a mess!" Hannah yells over the radio playing through the kitchen.

"Thanks for stating the obvious," Mason says.

Joe jokes, "The flour's supposed to go in the bowl. Not all over you, guys."

"We'll take your unwanted advice under consideration. I thought you weren't supposed to be allowed to cook in your own kitchen." I chuckle.

"Touché." Joe smiles slyly. "I can't give away my secrets. All I can say is that it must be a *coincidence*."

Mhmm. Coincidence.

We scrub our hands yet again, and when we return, I add the remaining flour. Mason figured out the settings this time, opting for a slight push on the lever. We separate the dough into three bowls.

"Okay, add the red food coloring to one, green to another, and leave the last one plain."

"Aye. Aye. Captain." He begins to add the dye and starts mixing. "Oh no."

"What's wrong?"

"I added the green and red to the same bowl by accident. It's turning brown." He wipes sweat off his brow with the back of his hand.

"This relationship is really going south," I tease him. "You would think with how good you are at making mixed drinks, you'd be just as good at baking."

He sighs. "It is. Maybe I should leave the baking to you. I can be your moral support." He looks to ponder something and says, "Drinks are different. I've made so many that I know them by heart. Plus, you're distracting me."

"With what?"

"With that apron you're wearing." He chuckles.

I purse my lips. "Oh, so sorry that my apron is distracting you. Don't worry. We can make them purple and green. I'll just add a few drops of purple and blue, hopefully they don't turn brown, but if they do it's okay. It doesn't matter what they look like as long as they taste good. I don't really care if we win or lose."

His eyes widen in shock. "You don't?"

"No," I confess. "I just wanted to participate."

"Oh—" I can tell he's waiting for me to elaborate.

I want to be honest with him. I know I can be. He's never once judged me for anything I've said. I'm comfortable around him.

"I'm sick of missing out on things because I'm single. Like the cookie competitions I can't enter because they're for couples only. Double dates. Where it's not actually a double date, I'm the third wheel—not that Violet or Dustin have ever made me feel anything but welcome. I see the way their worlds begin and end with each other. As if they can't comprehend how they've found something so remarkable. Part of me is envious. While the other larger part of my heart is beaming with glee. Vivi's found her soulmate. She deserves the world after losing so much in life. It makes me feel selfish. To want what they have. While I avoid having a relationship because I don't want the complications." Mason takes my hand and soothes his large thumb across my knuckles in reassurance.

I bite my cheek. "Then there are the Christmas dinners where I show up single year after year while everyone else is in love. It's—discomforting, I guess." I look at everything but his eyes, from the ceiling to the scratches on the table's surface to the cookie dough. My confidence wavers with the confession I'm about to make. "I wanted to fake a relationship between us for that reason too."

"Olive." His voice cracks. "I understand it more than you think. It's alienating. You are not selfish one bit. You want something like they have—a love that is all consuming, effortless, not forced, and one that is stumbled upon without looking for it. Can I confess something too?" he asks. I nod for him to continue. "I've never wanted to bring anyone home for the holidays before. I've never wanted to pursue something more than casual. I've always felt a surface connection but never desired continuing a long-term relationship. I've wanted something remarkable too."

My skin prickles. "That's something we have in common. One day we'll find it. I'm sure of it. I feel it in my bones."

Mason's right. We don't normally talk about these kinds of feelings together, but it's nice to relate to him, knowing I'm not the only one struggling. I'm not alone. We're not alone.

I want to feel a spark. I want to be so sure that when I find the person that is the one, I couldn't bear the idea of losing them. I don't want to search for it; I just want it to come out of nowhere. Isn't it human nature to desire something grand that almost seems unattainable?

I felt a fragment of a spark the night Mason and I danced at the bar. When he spun me in his arms and held me close, I could feel the heartbeat in his chest. I want to experience something like that again but stronger.

Lingering questions from last week resurface in my thoughts. "What happened between us the night you brought me home from the bar?"

His eyes widen as he blurts, "Nothing happened!"

I place my palm against his arm reassuringly. "Not that. I trust you unconditionally. Did I say something? You've been acting weird since that day. More distant. And more quiet, I guess."

"You mumbled some incoherent sentences, asked me to stay, and passed out. That's all." He fidgets with the spatula, stirring the cookie dough.

"Okay." My eyes narrow.

"I'll put these in the fridge so they can chill."

"Thanks," I say.

There's still something he's holding back from me. I know it. It's written in the way he deflects and squirms. I'm not going to push him for it. I'm just worried that I said something to make things weird between us. But if he doesn't want to talk about it, I get it. I'm not going to bring it up again after today.

Chapter 17

MASON

After an hour passed, our cookies were ready to bake; we rolled the dough together and sliced them. The cookies baked beautifully, coming out with purple, green, and white swirls. They almost resemble Mardi Gras. *Oops.* At least they taste delicious; I can attest to that. I've eaten a few already. I had to make sure they weren't poisonous. Everyone else finished making their cookies early and left to hang out at the diner until the judging commences.

Olive finishes icing the last cookie and blows out a relieved breath.

I lean against the counter. "This wasn't as horrible as I thought it would be. It seems as though if you follow directions properly, baking isn't so bad."

"See, I told you," Olive retorts.

"I know." I smile reminiscing. "These cookies taste like the ones our moms would always make on Christmas Day. I think that might be why I chose this one out of the options."

Olive's eyes glow. "That's why I love baking. If you do it properly, you can successfully transport people to a memory, a place, or a flash of nostalgia. Just like the cookies did for us both. Stirring a memory related to a loved one or a trip associated with the taste. Cooking is dynamic. There are so many nuances: getting the flavor profiles just right, mixing salty, sweet, and savory, and crafting something that pairs well with each other. It is a perfectly curated science."

I wink at her. "I think you nailed it."

I could listen to Olive talk about baking all day. Her smile lights up her face when she's enamored. She has passion behind every word. Did I understand everything she said? No. But I love the fervor she has. It's enough for me to listen intently and hang on to every word even if I don't fully catch on to the cooking terms she uses.

She shakes her head in protest. "No, *we* nailed it. This was a team effort."

"You're right. I think you have a little something—" I smear my icing-covered finger across her nose. "Here."

"Hey!" She giggles. Her nose turns that signature scarlet, and that's how I know she's miffed at me. "Oh, it's on."

I should've known better. Ever since we were young, Olive would wrestle me to the ground. She's like a ninja with practiced swiftness and control. She comes out of nowhere and can take down any grown man I know. It's admirable. But I'm going to regret it. My back is at least.

She launches and wraps her arm around the back of my knees, pushing all her strength against the front of me. *Oof.* My legs give out. My back hits the cool, hard ground with a plop. She smears a hand full of leftover icing across my nose, lips, and beard. She straddles me—her freckle-covered face hovers above mine with a triumphant grin. The overflow of her ponytail swings over the side of my face with a swoosh.

"You've got a little something here too." She taps my nose, tracing down my beard-covered cheek.

She pops her finger in her mouth and licks the icing. "Delicious."

I wish I were a better man. I wish I had willpower, but all my wild fantasies are coming true. Tension is thick in the air, and her intoxicating perfume is akin to something floral and fruity. It must be her body wash, Glittery Snow—my new favorite scent.

We're friends.

Best friends. I remind myself. *It's never going to be more than that.* It's a painful reminder.

As I stare at Olive with white icing on her button nose and her eyes aglow with felicity, I want to kiss her. I had the chance at the

Christmas party, but it would've made this bone-deep pining so much worse. I knew I couldn't take any more reasons to want what I can't have; Vivi's distraction was a blessing.

My mind was certain it was for the best, but my heart tumbled along the glass as they shattered all the same into broken shards.

My body is at war within itself.

"Hey! Where are you, guys?" Char's voice comes from the doorway.

Olive gets up quickly from my lap, her freckle-dotted cheeks rosy with laughter. She's not embarrassed in the least. Typical Olive to not give a damn what anyone thinks. I wish I had that same nonchalant ease.

"What's going on here?" Char asks, a twinkle in her eye.

"Nothing." I give her the *don't-ask-questions* look. It's part of the secret brother and sister language we've developed over the years. It's more like one eyebrow raised and a slight tilt of the head. "Olive just tackled me like a pro wrestler."

"Oh." Her eyes crinkle. "Sorry to barge in here and ruin the moment, but they're asking for you. Everyone's ready. It's half past twelve. Constance is pacing."

"We wouldn't want that now, would we?" Olive shakes her head.

"No. And you might want to clean up your faces. You look like you bathed in icing." She laughs, bracing on the side of the door.

Once Char leaves and we work on cleaning icing off the floor and our faces, I say, "We broke another rule, Firefly."

Olive grins deviously. "It was so worth it to knock you down like a sack of potatoes and see your icing covered face. I like breaking the rules with you by my side."

"Me too." *I like doing anything and everything by your side.*

Olive and I sit waiting for the results of the competition. My leg bounces up and down. It's not from the anticipation of finding out who won the cookie competition. I think it's the apprehension of my whispered confession. *I've wanted something remarkable too.* My own words spoken hours earlier haunt me. I wanted to tell her that I've already found someone remarkable... her. The sane part of my brain was screeching *don't* with alarm bells.

Constance scribbles across a notepad after taking a bite of a cookie. Bobbie and Annie are nodding, leaning towards each other conspiratorially. Henry and Audrey, the owners of The Laundry Basket and The Valley Harvest, are engrossed in a hushed conversation, lifting cookies, nodding, and shaking their heads at others. Our small town takes competitions seriously. Fiercely. It's all a little bit chaotic. The good kind of chaos most of the time.

Except for when they set up an entire competition for the sole reason of match making. Example A: Olive and I. I knew it from the second Constance stepped in the door with the *news* of a competition Olive couldn't resist. She made it almost impossible for it not to pan out. And Vivi's warning of Constance saying she's been "cooking something up for us" made my suspicions grander. Normally I wouldn't entertain their scheming. Nor would I welcome the idea of putting myself or anyone else in a situation where we had to lie to those we care about. But it got me thinking, why not? They were never going to yield. Olive and I both got something out of it. A reprieve from the vexing questions. I can hear my mother's voice loud and clear in my head, *when are you going to settle down? I would love some grandchildren.* She means well; I know that. However, it's been plaguing my thoughts.

"We have come to a decision," Constance says into a microphone sitting on a fold up table at the front of the diner.

I look across the room. Everyone has their eyes glued to the judge's table. They sit on the edge of their seats, waiting eagerly to find out who won. Some teams made classic-flavored cookies: chocolate chip, gingerbread, and peanut butter. Others made more elaborate ones: cookies and cream, s'more, and root beer float (can't say I've ever heard of something like that last one). I'm eager to try them all.

"Drum roll please," Bobbie says. Everyone pats their hands against their laps. The sound reverberates through the room.

"Oakley and Jamal!" Henry announces with a gleam in his eye. "With a perfect score in every category. Root beer float cookies."

"Woohoo!" Oakley shouts.

"It's rigged!" Hannah yells in protest.

"Even though she has bragging rights for the rest of her life, I'm proud of my little sis." Olive's smile beams. "I don't think she will ever let this one down. She beat me, and I do this for a living." She giggles.

"She won't let it down. It's all we'll hear about at Christmas." I sigh. "Are we allowed to eat these cookies yet? I'm starving."

Olive pokes my stomach. "Let's grab some even though you already tried a dozen of ours. I'm not waiting for someone to announce it."

"And this is why you're the *best* partner in crime."

Chapter 18

OLIVE

"Hi, Olive." Vivi comes bustling in the door and hangs her coat on the hook. Her long brown hair is ruffled from the wind, and her bangs cover her eyes. She blows a breath, and they poof to the sides of her face.

"Hey, sunshine!" I spin around on the bar stool behind the register. This is the slow time of day when I'm just about to close. No one usually comes in, but I stay open for the occasional stragglers. "The usual?"

"Please. I am struggling to keep my eyes open. We spent the whole night taking care of the goats. I'm getting ready to tape my eyes open." Vivi yawns, covering her mouth with her hand. "Plus, everyone's been in all day to buy poinsettias for Christmas. I'm so tired."

"You're closing your shop for the holidays, right?" I ask while pouring a mug full of steaming black coffee.

"Yes. Thank goodness. I'll be closed from Wednesday until the day after New Year's Day. We're spending Christmas Day at Dustin's parents. Then coming back home to do absolutely nothing."

"That sounds like a dream."

"I hope so." She takes a sip of her coffee. "What about you?"

"Christmas Eve and Day will be spent with the fam. You know how the family tradition goes with the Cleary and Watson nut house." I laugh. She smirks while I tug a strand of hair behind my ear. "On Christmas Eve, all the *kids* hike through the woods, pick a tree, cut it down, bring it home, and decorate it while sipping hot chocolate. On Christmas Day, we open presents and eat dinner."

"So, the traditions remain."

My eyes twinkle. "They do!"

"I loved joining you guys. I always had so much fun." Vivi taps her fingers on her mug of coffee. "But it was quite meticulous. Your mom and that schedule of hers. We had to follow it no matter what."

"I know." I sigh. "I'll miss you being there."

"I'll miss it too, but now I can make my own traditions with my new little family: Dustin, Sardine, Fiona, Tuxedo, and I." Her eyes gleam.

"Two love birds and your cats. It's perfect! I'm so happy for you." My grin widens.

"Exactly." Her eyes fill with unshed tears. "We're going to visit my parents and Darcy's graves with Henry."

My heart softens. Vivi lost her parents when she was young and lost her grandmother-like figure, Darcy, last year. It's been hard for her; she's gone through so much loss in her life. It makes me want to cry, but I'm also glad that she and Dustin found each other. "That sounds like a really nice thing to do. I'm so glad Henry will be going with you. Him and Darcy were soulmates. Their wedding was beautiful."

"Yeah." Her eyes soften. "Anyways, I don't want to get all sappy and teary eyed, then you will be too."

A smile tugs at the corner of my lips. "I know. I can't help it."

"Me neither." She swirls her coffee. "I almost forgot! I got you a little something for Christmas." Vivi opens a bag on her arm to pull out a wrapped box and sets it on the counter.

"I got you something too." I grab my purse from my office and pull out a small gift wrapped in newspaper.

I hand it to her, and she tears the paper carefully. "You didn't!" she exclaims. She holds the T-shirt outstretched. "Easily distracted by chickens!" She reads the words out loud. "Ah! It's perfect."

"I knew you'd love it."

"Is this Helga?" She gapes at the shirt and hugs it to her chest.

"Yes, I asked Chloe if she could make it with a picture of Helga for you since she's your favorite chicken."

"This is the best present ever. She's the cutest Buff Orpington that I've ever seen." She smiles wide, looking at it once more. "Open yours."

I rip the Christmas paper and open the box. I'm speechless.

"What do you think?"

My whole face lights up. "Vivi—you didn't."

She giggles. "Well, do you like it?"

"I love it! Thank you. I'm going to switch my purse over to this one now. I can't wait."

"It practically called my name when I saw it in The Hoarder Emporium. Your name might as well be written on it. With the fringe and brown leather. It even has a coffee cup embroidered on it."

"I'm obsessed. It's very boho. It's me to a T. I love it." I dump the contents of my candy cane-shaped purse into the new one and try it on.

A look of awe transforms her face. "It was made for you."

"It was, wasn't it? I can't thank you enough." I spin with the purse on my side and laugh.

"You're welcome." She takes a sip of coffee. "How are you and Mason?"

I take a seat on the stool. "We're good, still fake dating. We will make our debut with family only on Christmas Eve. We haven't had a chance yet without townies around to keep them at bay and on their best behavior." I look to my lap, picking the corner of my nail.

Violet's voice is thick with worry. "Are you doing okay?"

"Yeah. I'm okay." My thoughts have been a bit conflicting lately regarding Mason, but I'm not going to worry her about it.

Vivi shoots me a skeptical glance. "Are you sure? I just don't want to see you get hurt."

I give her a half smile. "I won't. I promise. Mason and I are just friends."

"Okay, I care about you. If you both start catching feelings for each other, that's okay. You know that, right? There's nothing wrong with it."

"We won't. We've been friends for so long. I've never thought about him that way," I say, trying to convince her and myself as I look to my lap again.

She pats my hand on the counter. "I know. I'm not trying to push anything on you. I'm talking about hypotheticals. Just know that I'm here. You can call me or text me whenever. Anytime you need me. It doesn't matter the time of day—it could be on Christmas. Don't ever worry about bothering me."

"Thank you. And you can do the same if you ever need me." I glance up from my lap to smile softly in her direction.

"I know. You've always been there for me. I want to be there for you too. After Darcy passed away, I was in a bad place, but you and

Dustin wouldn't leave my side for weeks. I don't know what I'd do without you both or my therapist." Her voice cracks and a single tear falls from her left eye. I walk around the counter, pulling her into a hug. We both cry together for a couple of minutes until our tears subside. After a few beats of silence, she says, "You also give me the best advice. I don't think Dustin and I would've ended up together if you didn't force me to keep going and quit sulking. You never gave up on me. You were banging on my door for days, no matter how many times I didn't answer."

Tears threaten to pool in my eyes again, but they shimmer instead. "We're just like sisters. I will never give up on you. That's a promise."

"I promise exactly the same thing."

My phone dings with a text.

"Do you mind?" I ask Vivi.

"No, answer it. I'm okay." Vivi's voice is soft as she nods her head.

I look down and see Mason's name on the screen.

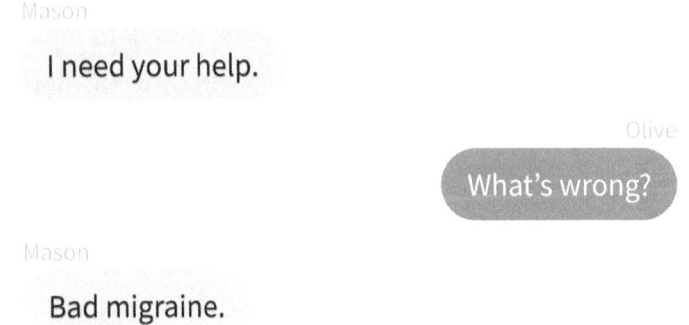

Mason

I need your help.

Olive

What's wrong?

Mason

Bad migraine.

> I'll be over in a half hour, hang in there.

"Is everything okay?" Vivi asks.

"I don't know. Mason has a migraine. You know how he gets them every so often. I'm going to head over to his place." I look up from my phone.

"Let me close up for you," she insists.

My brows pull together. "No, I couldn't do that. You've barely had any sleep. You need to close your own shop."

"That's what we do for each other. We're like sisters, remember? Mason needs you. Go. I'll call Dustin. He'll help me. We help each other." She motions with her hand for me to leave.

"Thank you. I owe you." I squeeze her in a tight hug.

She sighs. "You don't owe me anything. Now go."

I run outside and start my truck in the parking lot across the street; it fires up after a few cranks. While my truck is warming up, I run up the stairs to my apartment. I fill my new purse with pain meds, an ice pack from the freezer, and a few more odds and ends. I shrug on the first coat that I see and book it back to my truck. I drive carefully through the snow ridden streets to the outskirts of town. I grab my phone, dial Amelia, and put it on speaker. She answers on the fourth ring.

"Hey, Amelia, could you do me a favor?" I ask.

"Hey, Olive! Absolutely, hit me with it!"

"Mason's not feeling well. He can't open the bar tonight. Would you be able to handle things?"

"That's what I'm here for. I got it covered."

"I can stop by in a few hours."

"No, no. I have things handled here. You worry about Mason. I'll text a few of the seasonal employees and see if someone wants a shift tonight. I'm sure one of them will stop in for a few hours."

"You're the best. Would you also be able to get someone to shut the chicken coop door before dark?"

"I was already planning on it. Don't worry about anything."

I sigh in relief. "Thank you, Amelia."

"No problem! I better go and get ready to open. I'll let you know if anything comes up. I doubt anything will," she says and ends the call.

Once I reach the long winding road, I see Mason's single wide in the distance. All the lights are glowing in the windows against the dimming sky.

That's not good. He needs it to be dark.

I park in front of his house and unlock the door using the spare key he handed me a few years ago when he bought the place. I always let out Moose when he stays extra late at the bar. Which is few and far between, but nevertheless, I need it in moments like these. He won't tell any of his sisters or his parents about his migraines. He doesn't want to worry them. I worry, though. A lot. They were triggered by a few too many concussions when he was younger.

They flare up occasionally but haven't been occurring as often. It seems he gets them when he doesn't get enough sleep. There are a multitude of things that could trigger a flare up, though.

I open the door to his house slowly, trying to avoid making loud noises. Moose comes up to greet me. He puts his wet nose against my hand. I whisper, "Where's your dad?" I pet him on the head quickly. I hang up my coat and purse gently to avoid making loud noises. Moose leads me to Mason. I follow him through the living room, kitchen, and into Mason's bedroom on the left side of the narrow hall.

His room is lit by the bright light of the ceiling fan. I tug the longer cord to turn it off then draw the blinds down to the window trim. Twisting the wand, I angle the slats until most of the daylight disappears. Finally, I pull the dark curtains closed, plunging the room into complete darkness. Mason groans from the bed.

"Mason," I whisper.

"Olive." His voice is muffled from underneath the covers on the bed. "Thanks for coming."

"You're welcome. You don't have to say anything if it hurts your head to talk. Let me get you some water. I'll be right back," I whisper.

I fill a glass under the tap and bring it to his room. He sits up slowly, and I hand him two aspirins. He takes them and gulps the water. It kills me to see him like this, so weak—so full of pain. The agony it takes to do simple tasks. His migraines are crippling, and there isn't much that helps other than sleep.

He lays back down, and I cover him with blankets. I sink into the bed and press the ice pack wrapped in a towel to the side of his head. He sighs in appreciation. We've got a rhythm down. I know what helps to make it go away. Or at least things that will make some of his pain subside.

After a few minutes, I remove the pack from his head and ask, "Would it help if I rubbed your shoulders?"

"You don't have to."

"I want to," I whisper and sit against the headboard. "Come here." I motion, and he inches in between my legs. I massage his shoulders and neck carefully, hoping to ease some of the tension.

"The bar. The chickens. Your shop?" He sighs.

"I already took care of it. I called Amelia on the way here. She's having one of your seasonal employees come in and someone will take care of the chickens. Vivi is closing my shop."

"I don't know what I'd do without you. Without everyone in this town." His voice chokes up.

"You don't have to think about it because I'm not going anywhere. I'll never go anywhere. I'll always be here for you," I say softly.

"Do you mean that?" His tone is vulnerable as he questions me.

"Yes." *I do.*

He pauses and asks, "Even after New Year's Day?"

My forehead creases at the idea that he thinks I'm not going to be there for him after our deal. "I'm not here because of a fake relationship. Or helping you for the sake of keeping up fronts. Right now, we're just Olive and Mason, two best friends who'd do anything for each other. I'll always be there for you. This is what someone does for a person they care about. You'd do the same for me. I don't need you to tell me because I know you would. You took care of me when I was drunk. You always do."

Mason closes his eyes. "That means a lot to me."

"Good, because we're partners in crime. Who would I break silly rules with? Who would I force to hang up a million and one Christmas decorations with me? There's no one else that would willingly sign up for it." My eyes crinkle.

I can't see him, but I hear a soft laugh escape. "It's not so bad."

"Good." I lie down next to him, and he's silent for a while. I stare at the dark wall. His breath softens, and he falls asleep. I slowly sneak out of the room and leave the door cracked.

I'm staying the rest of the day and night in case he needs me. I open my purse and grab my phone and a book to read. I lie down on the couch and text Vivi.

Olive

> Mason's doing alright. He's sleeping now. Thank you again.

She answers within a few minutes.

Violet

Good to hear. Np. Your shop is closed and locked. I have the key.

Olive

Great, I'll stop by tomorrow morning to get it.

I'm so lucky to have people that care so much in my life. I grab a glass of water and one for Mason and set it on his nightstand, replacing the empty one in case he wakes up. I'm most likely to fall asleep reading on the couch if I don't make it to his guest room. I let Moose outside and fill up his bowl with kibble. I tidy up a few things and wash and dry the dishes. I turn out all the lights, and by the time it's getting dark outside, I check on Mason one more time. I lie on the couch and open the book to resume reading. After a few minutes, I fall asleep to the sound of Moose's snoring.

Chapter 19

MASON

The room is dark. I don't know what time it is. My pounding head has died down to a manageable headache. A relief that wouldn't have been possible without Olive's help. I grab the water glass from my nightstand and guzzle it down. I check my phone. It's five o'clock in the morning. *One more day,* I tell myself. I only need to get through today, and then I'm closed for Christmas Eve and Day. It's a balm against my current state. I can make it through without another migraine.

Bailing on the bar last night added to the pressure on the side of my head. I hate leaving everything to Amelia. The late-night crowd can get rowdy; they tend to do stupid shit. Like throwing punches or slamming beer bottles on each other's heads. It's nothing that I'm not used to. Luckily, it's been far and few between. Amelia can handle her own; I have no doubt about it. But I'd rather be there to oversee everything.

"Are you awake?" Olive whispers from the gap in the door.

"Yes." My voice comes out hoarse.

"How are you feeling?" She stands on the other side of the bed.

"Better. Thanks to you."

Olive's always been the one I reach out to when I'm at my lowest. She doesn't freak out or make me feel guilty for not telling anyone about my migraines. She's there by my side, no questions or judgments. I've been getting them for the past few years. Paula says it's from one too many concussions from my high school football days. Not enough water, exercise, or sleep are all factors that fuse to bring them on as well as stress.

"No need to thank me." She lies on her stomach beside me and props a palm under her chin as her sock-covered feet kick the air. She yawns. "What time is it? I didn't have a chance to check my phone before I came in to see if you were okay."

"Five."

"Crap!" She flies off the bed. Her hair bounces full of perfectly shaped curls. I don't understand how she manages it. Her beauty is confounding. An indented line marks her cheek from where the pillow on the couch must have pressed. Her face is still soft from sleep. Because I know damn well, she didn't make it to my guest room; she never does.

I don't know how she doesn't notice the way I look at her—the smolder in my gaze, the longing glances, and how I can't seem to keep my eyes from hers when we're in a room together. There could be hundreds of people, but I would search for her. There's no other woman that could ever compare. Olive's personality is like a rainbow after a storm. Breathtaking. Extraordinary. Luminous.

I need to get myself together. She only sees me as a friend.

"I'm going to be late!" The look of horror that crosses her face is almost comical. Olive has never been content with being late for anything.

"They can wait a few minutes."

Her eyes widen. "They can't wait! They'll stand outside with pitchforks. Have you ever seen a person who is caffeine deprived?" Her nose turns red the more frustrated she gets.

Why does she look so cute when she's mad?

I raise my arms in defeat. "Okay, okay. You better hurry then."

She throws a pillow at me. "Thanks for stating the obvious."

"No problem, Firefly. Or should we start calling each other *babe* to practice for Christmas Eve dinner with our families?"

Olive's nose scrunches. "Ew, no. Please, anything but that." She runs out of my bedroom yelling, "Bye, dearest. Bye, Moose."

"Dearest. I like the sound of that." I chuckle. "Bye, Sweetie Pie!"

"That one's perfect!" I hear her throw a boot on the floor and grunt a few times. She's probably trying to squeeze her feet in them without untying the laces. I hear her yell, "Yes!" I can assume this is the product of her getting them on. The front door slams, and her engine cranks over. And cranks over some more. And then again.

I drag myself out of bed and pull my shirt off and throw it in the dirty clothes bin. I rifle through my dresser drawers, looking for a clean one. I know Olive will be back any second. I've already deduced I will be driving her back to town. The battery in her truck must be dead.

"Um, dearest? My battery's dead." She comes rushing through the door. "I left the light on and—oh!" Her face blushes, her freckles pronounced against her heated face. "I'm sorry for barging in." Her eyes dart away but then come back and fall to my chest. She gapes at the tattoo on my arm.

"Like what you see?"

Olive stammers, smoothing a hand against her forehead. "What? No—I mean. Yes. Well, no—"

"It's okay." I chuckle, cutting her off. I tug a black sweatshirt over my arms and down my frame quickly, hoping that she doesn't notice the hidden art woven into my tattoo. "You don't have to be embarrassed. I know you do." I wink.

She rolls her eyes. "Can you give me a jump? I have some jumper cables behind my seat."

"I know. I put them there. I'll just drop you off. It'll be quicker."

She scratches her head. "What about my truck?"

"Old Blue will be fine. I'll take good care of her."

169

"Okay." She nods hesitantly. "Thanks."

Once I finish getting dressed, Olive and I head along the road into town. My place is not a far drive away, about thirty minutes. It's mostly sharp bends and winding back roads.

"I loathe being late for anything." She taps her fingers against her lap.

My gaze softens. "We'll make it on time. I promise."

Olive's eyes dart out the window as she murmurs, "I hope so."

"We will." I place my hand on top of hers, giving her fingers a reassuring squeeze.

"How is Char doing?" she asks, changing the subject. "I haven't had time to talk to her lately, just the two of us."

"She's doing good. I can tell she's really excited about having a baby. She's had a hard time sleeping lately, and her feet hurt. But other than that, her checkup this week went well. Paula says he or she is healthy. Only two more weeks and I'll have another nephew or niece to spoil."

"That makes me happy to hear. I can't wait for more little ones to run around."

We sit in comfortable silence for a few minutes until she speaks up again, "Do you still want five kids? When you were little, you were adamant about having a big family."

I smile. "If having kids is in the cards for me, yes, I would love to have a big family. Just like mine. And like yours. What about you?"

She hums in agreement. "I would like the same thing. I would love to have a huge family to take on bike rides, hiking trips, and to fill a house with laughter and little ones."

"And a tire swing in your backyard like your parents have?"

"You read my mind. What else?" She smiles.

I stare out the windshield following the curves of the road. "I'd want my kids to hang out with their cousins. I'd want them to have what I did. A huge family to be born into. Jump on trampolines. Ride dirt bikes. Build tree houses. Enjoy life as it's meant to be."

Olive's voice is light when she agrees. "That would be the dream."

I place my palm on her hand and run my thumb across her fingers. "It would be. Our childhood was a wonderful madhouse. We were all friends. We did everything together. I want that for my kids."

It's something that I'm not sure is possible if I don't settle down. How long can I wait for Olive to realize what's between us? It seems like I might be waiting forever, and I'll never have a chance at a family if I don't do something about it.

"What was that noise?" she asks.

My hand leaves hers, and I grip the steering wheel. "What noise? I didn't hear anything."

"That hissing noise. You don't hear it?" Olive's eyes bulge in horror.

A slow whooshing sound comes from the rear wheel tire. It continues to get louder. *Shit. She's going to kill me.* I slow my truck down and a scraping noise starts. It's loud, and thumping.

I stop the truck on the side of the road, putting it in park. I keep my hands at ten and two and stare out the windshield at the snowy hillsides, praying that it's not a flat. It's impossible, though; I know it's a flat tire.

"Mason." Olive covers her eyes. "Please tell me we didn't just get a flat tire." Agitation oozes from her.

"I won't tell you then." *Ignore the problem, and maybe it will go away.*

She rubs her palms against her forehead. "We're totally going to be late now."

"It will only take me a few minutes to change out the tire for a spare. It'll be okay."

She looks at me skeptically. "Why do I feel like it's not going to be that easy? Nothing about today is."

I step out of my truck and crouch down to look at the undercarriage. *Damn.* I left the spare in my shed. I'm cursing my past self.

I'll put this back on another day. I'm too tired to do it today.

Yeah, that thought is kicking me in the ass right now.

"Don't say it." Olive slams the door and stomps around the side of the truck.

"I won't."

And those, ladies and gentlemen, are my final words.

Chapter 20

OLIVE

"This day couldn't get any worse!" I shout with frustration.

"It really could. You never know. We could trip and fall on ice. Or a meteor could fall from the sky and take out the whole town. Or a bear could show up and attack us. The list is never ending—so, yes it could get worse. However, I'll try my best to protect you." Mason points out with a chuckle

"Now's not the time, Mason." I cross my arms and continue walking across the ice-covered gravel road.

Sometimes I wish cell service worked out here. I would have called Dan's Auto and had him tow us back into town. Or called anyone at this point to pick us up. I'm freezing, *hangry*, and as caffeine deprived as the townsfolk probably lining up in front of my shop.

We'll make it on time. I promise. I keep replaying Mason's voice in my head. He lied. We're late. I know he can't control all the things that went wrong.

To make matters worse, I'm consumed with pent-up tension. When I walked into his bedroom and he was shirtless, my jaw dropped to the floor. He must be lifting weights or something. Because *damn.* The owl tattoo on his upper arm contrasting against his complexion was enough to make beads of sweat roll down my back. I haven't been able to think straight since. We've always been friends. I've never thought about him that way before. It was weird.

Can't a girl admire an attractive man from afar? The answer is always yes.

But now I'll be walking into a coffee shop full of angry people who need their fix of caffeine. And it's *all* Mason's fault.

I'm holding in my rage as good as a cracked foundation supports a house. My patience is thinning to a strand of yarn seconds away from tearing. I could come up with hundreds of metaphors to describe how I'm feeling at the moment.

I'm fine. Everything is fine. It's fine. I repeat the mantra in my thoughts. *Think of the positives.*

"This is all your fault!" I blurt into the silence. There are no positives at the moment.

He rakes a hand over his face. "And how is this my fault?"

I put my hands on my hips. "If you would've just given me a jump, trusty Old Blue would've rolled right over that nail. There's no way she'd let a little something like that stop us. Plus, she has a tire repair kit with plugs. We would be on our way, probably exactly on time."

"Your truck is a tank. I get it. Considering your tires are bald, I'm not sure that would be the case."

"Hello! Anyone out there? I'm accepting best friend and fake boyfriend applications!" I shout to the white covered fields surrounding us.

"Do you hear that? No? There's no one out there. I guess you're stuck with me," he deadpans.

"Yay me!" I blow a frustrated huff. "By the way, my tires are not bald."

They aren't, are they? To be honest, I haven't ever checked to see if they were.

"Yes. They are. Pretty soon you'll be hydroplaning all over the road. I've been trying to tell you for weeks to get new ones."

Hmm... I probably wasn't listening because I can't remember any of those conversations.

"Men," I mutter under my breath.

He shoots me a questioning brow. "What was that?"

"Nothing."

"Hmm. Okay."

I walk beside him in silence, dragging my feet through the gravel and snow. Frustrated huffs slip out every now and then as my thoughts spiral deeper into irritation. We've been walking for what seems like forever. He doesn't say a word. I don't either.

It's silly to fight over something that's a small blip in the bigger scheme of problems. But there's something about being late that makes me go a little crazy. A little off kilter. I can't help it. It makes my skin crawl with the idea of letting someone down.

"Are you still mad at me?" Mason asks after some time.

I take in a shaky breath. "No." *A little.*

He bobs his head. "Okay—so that means yes."

"I didn't say that." But I didn't have to say anything. I think Mason knows me well enough to pick up on the signs when I lie through my teeth. Normally, it's endearing; however, right now it's not helping matters.

I scrunch my shoulders and shiver.

"Are you cold?"

It's just like Mason to care about me regardless of whether we're disagreeing or not. It's sweet. How can I still be mad at him? It makes me feel selfish for being agitated.

"Yeah, getting there. It's chilly this morning, and the wind isn't helping matters. I wasn't prepared for a hike." My feet crunch with each labored step.

"Take my coat," he insists, sliding the sleeves off his arms and putting it around my shoulders.

I stop and cross my arms. "I'm not taking your coat. It's freezing. You'll get frostbite. It's too cold." I shake my head no as he continues to pull the coat over my arms.

"I'll be fine. It's not much further of a walk. I'm warm from moving. Plus, I have a sweatshirt on." His eyes plead with me.

I stand rooted to the spot as he lifts the zipper and finger combs a few curls of my hair from under the jacket. "I'm not happy about you not having a coat." Yet I still burrow into his large one.

Why is he always so sweet to me?

"Just accept it. Got any snacks in that purse of yours?" His eyebrows raise.

I smile proudly. "Funny you should ask, I was getting hungry." I open my purse and dig through the contents. "I have a granola bar and some hot sauce."

He rolls his eyes and continues walking alongside me, taking small steps so that I can keep up with him. "That damn hot sauce again. There's so much stuff in there."

"I bet you're glad to have all that stuff now."

"I am. I'd like to share the granola bar, minus the hot sauce."

"Coming right up." I hand him half. "One granola bar. Hold the hot sauce."

"The key to my heart." He smiles and takes a bite. He tries and fails to not look cold, but I can tell he is. His nose is red, and he rubs the side of his arm with his free hand absentmindedly.

"Who knew it'd be that easy?" I reply. Both of our pieces of granola bar are gone within a few seconds.

We have a long walk until we reach town, so I start to unzip his coat and plan an argument on why he needs to take it back in my head. But suddenly, I hear a low rumble.

"Do you have any water in there—"

"Shh!" I say. "Do you hear that?"

"Hear what?" he asks.

"It sounds like a car's coming." I jump up and down and wave my arms. An old pickup truck comes into view, slowly meandering down the snowy road. It's bright red, stark against the white and that's when I know for sure. "It's Harvey's truck!"

What a relief.

"You can stop jumping. He sees you. You're a walking neon sign. How could you even for a second think he wouldn't see us with your bright getup?" Mason teases.

"It pays off in times like these." I giggle looking at my bright pink jeans. "I'm still not entirely over being mad at you. Just so you know, even if I laugh. But you made up for it a little when you gave me your coat." He made up for it a lot, and I'm not mad anymore. It's more fun to tease him back.

"Okay, Firefly." A smile tugs at his lips as he glances my way.

I hold back a smile. "Whatever, Knight."

Harvey's truck comes to a snow crunching stop next to us. He rolls down his window. "What happened? You guys need a ride?"

Harvey asks, one arm draping out the window. A cloud of fog leaves his mouth with each word.

"Yes." I sigh. "Please, I beg of you. I'll throw in a free coffee and donut if you can speed up a little too."

"We're not speeding over some coffee and donuts. I'm not letting anyone risk their life to get there a few minutes earlier." Mason's deep voice ruins my plans.

Harvey shrugs. "I'd do anything for a donut and a coffee. But Mason's being the logical one right now. I'd have to agree. Hop in. You'll get sick without a coat on. I'll crank up the heat in here for you." He rolls his window back up.

I blow out a breath of frustration and scrunch my nose. "Fine. But I'm sitting in the front with Harvey."

"Whatever you want." Mason pokes my arm, and his smile grows wider.

I whisper into his ear, "Maybe I shouldn't have swiped left on him. He's looking like the knight in shining armor today."

Messing with Mason is so much fun.

"Too bad you already swiped right on fake dating me, your knight in dull armor." He grins a devilish smile. "It's not too late to back out."

"You're being absurd. I'm not backing out of anything. I won't cower at a challenge," I say with a steady assurance.

Mason's brow crinkles. "I don't know. You might."

"Might *not*. I'm seeing this through."

I won't give up on anything I start. Maybe that makes me stubborn, but once I commit myself to something, I want to see it through. And honestly, I'm having a great time being Mason's girlfriend. I don't know if it's because we haven't changed much about our relationship or if it's the fact that it's nice being with him. We're in this together for the long haul until New Year's Day.

Mason runs his fingers over his beard and says, "Good, because I'm quite enjoying it."

Harvey butts in suddenly. "Do you want me to leave you love birds here, or are you coming?" His voice is laced with mirth through his half rolled up window.

"We're coming," Mason says. "I'm starting to get cold standing here." He walks around to the passenger door and opens it for me, gesturing with an outstretched arm for me to get in. My breath catches, and I smile softly. I was only joking with him about calling shotgun, but I feel warm inside—not from the heat of the car, maybe a little bit from that, but from the small gesture.

The back door softly clicks as Mason gets in, and Harvey puts his truck into gear as he drives into town.

After a brief pause, Harvey's voice is full of melancholy as he shifts in his seat and says, "You know, Iris and I were just like you two back in the day."

"Really?" I ask over the muffled radio static. "She always seemed so mellow."

Harvey chuckles and pads his wrinkled hands on the steering wheel. "No, she may have mellowed a little over the years, but you didn't know twenty-year-old Iris. She was a spitfire just like you, Olive." Mason guffaws from the back seat as Harvey continues. "I see a lot of her in you. When I was in the Olive Bean and you threw coffee all over that jerk, Chad, it made me laugh. Iris would've done the same thing as you. We got into an argument when I was young and dumb. She threw all my clothes in a pile in the front yard, and when I got home from work, I was shocked to say the least. I deserved it; I was spending more time at the bar hanging out with my buddies and getting drunk than at home with my wife. I had to wise up after that."

"You must miss her very much," Mason says, sounding somber.

"Every day. But it's part of life, losing people you love. You've got to keep going, knowing they'll always be a part of your heart and soul. My Iris will always be a part of me."

Him talking about her this way makes my eyes water. Thinking about how he had to face each day after losing his other half... It takes a lot of strength to keep going, but Harvey always has such a positive outlook on everything.

"She wanted me to find love again. She didn't want me to be alone. She made me promise. I couldn't break it, and she knew it. Marigold put me on some kind of dating app. I don't know what apps are, but my daughter was adamant about it. You know how

Marigold is. I don't even have a phone; she makes me keep this flip phone in my truck." He holds up a cell from the center console.

"Do you have any dates lined up?" I ask.

"No, nothing yet. I can't complain. I'm not so sure it's a good idea." He pulls the truck into the stretch of town, slowing to park in between Cat's & Novels and The Valley Harvest. "Here you kiddos go. Remember, enjoy every little moment you have together. Promise me."

"We promise," Mason and I both say at the same time.

Chapter 21

MASON

"Hey, Dan. How's it going?" I say as I walk into Dan's Auto. His shop is diagonal from Rooster's. Every tool along the wall is neatly organized. You wouldn't know this is a shop worked in every day by how neat and clean he keeps the place. Crescent wrenches line the wall in order as well as ratchets, screw drivers, clamps, and wire brushes.

"Mason. Good to see you. What brings you by?" Dan asks as he wheels out from under an SUV on a creeper. He sits up and puts a wrench on the floor. His lips turn up slightly. Every tool has a home and the only one missing on the wall is the one he has. "Can you grab a rag for me right there?" He points to the workbench below the tools and a box filled with shop rags.

"I need a tow... or actually, two tows. Olive's got a dead battery, and I got a flat tire with no spare." Letting out a heavy sigh, I grab a rag and hand it to him. "Hit a nail on the way and left the spare at home."

Dan grimaces. "Sounds like someone had a rough morning."

"That's an understatement. Olive was pissed, but Harvey picked us up on Maple Ridge Road about at the halfway mark." I shake my head, remembering how red her nose was. I fight back a smile as I think about how mad she was. Making Olive late is never a good idea. I should know from many years of experience. "Did you get a chance to order those tires for me?"

"They came in yesterday. They're right over there." He points to a stack of new tires and wipes the grease from his hands with the rag.

Okay, so I might've ordered Olive some new tires weeks ago without telling her. I knew she would forget, and I didn't want her driving around on bald tires or getting stuck anywhere. The idea of her getting in an accident because of them was my biggest concern, especially with the condition of the roads right now.

"Do you have any time today to put them on? If not, it's okay. I know you're always busy." I shift, trailing my gaze to where Dan strides to the far end of the garage. He throws the now-dirty rag in the trash can.

He nods. "Yes, this one's an oil change. It'll be done in no time, and I'm free for the rest of the day."

"Great. Thanks, man," I say in a grateful tone.

"You got it." He scratches his head. "I'll pick you up in front of Rooster's in one hour with the tow truck. Sounds good?"

"Absolutely. Gives me some time to get the bar ready. Amelia has the night off." I glance out the garage door windows, watching a few people walk past the front door. I better get started on prepping now while I have a chance.

"See you then," Dan says and waves as he sits on the creeper and scoots back under the vehicle. He never was one for a lot of words; he's straight to the point and a hard worker.

"You can drop the truck at my place. I can fix the flat. They're still brand-new tires, so I'm going to plug the hole," I tell Dan from the passenger seat of his tow truck as the snowy fields flicker past the window. It's later in the afternoon and the sun is bright, with an illuminating glare. I squint trying to continue watching the scenery and flip the visor down.

"Okay, works for me," Dan replies, shifting into a higher gear. "Congrats on you and Olive by the way."

A shadow falls across my features at the thought. It would be nice to accept his comment with an eager tone. It'd be nice to celebrate Olive and I with my friends, but there's no us to speak of or congratulate. It's just me and my sad truth. "Thanks, but we're not actually together." My voice cracks with the honest confession. Might as well tell him. No use in keeping it a secret; he's not the type to care about the town's gossip. I don't have to worry about him shouting the truth to a soul.

"That's a shame." His head tilts towards me, and he gives me a sad smile.

"What's a shame?" I raise an eyebrow. It's definitely a shame for me, but I'm not going to bore him with the specifics.

"You're good together," he states with certainty. After a few beats, he continues. "You balance each other out."

He's right... We do. I stare out the windshield watching the trees pass by and think about his words. Olive is the vibrancy and light that I'm missing. Where she fights and goes after what she wants, I'm more of an observant, silent protector. When we're together, we complement each other.

Dan pulls into my driveway. He detaches my truck and then backs up to the rear of Olive's truck with ease. He hooks it up and heads along the road back into town in no time.

"How'd you catch on to that?" I question him.

He replies instantly, "I get coffee every morning. You're always there."

"I'm not always there." I drag a hand along my face. *Hmm. Maybe I am there a lot.* "I can't help that she makes good coffee and pastries."

Dan looks at me and shakes his head in disbelief.

"Or maybe I go to see her—fine, I'm there to see her," I confess.

He's right yet again. I don't go there for anything other than Olive's company. Who am I kidding? The pastries and coffee are a nice benefit... but she's why I'm there—to hear her laugh, to brighten my day, to tease and joke around with her. I can't help that she's captivating. I never know what's in store when I show up each day. One minute, she's puffing flyaway strands of hair out of her eyes while biting her lip and pulling croissants from the oven; the next, she's dancing behind the counter, whipping up some kind of coffee concoction. One day, she's humming and crocheting a blanket in her office, and the next, she's spinning on that stool behind the counter waiting for customers to enter. And maybe that's why I always find myself there, just to get a small piece of time with her.

"Now the truth is coming out," Dan says while turning the wheel around a sharp bend.

"How's Marigold? You spend an awful lot of time getting *parts*."

He shifts in his seat. "I run an automotive shop. I need parts," Dan says this with a heavy sigh, and his lips form into a line.

I must have hit a sore spot with that one. Maybe I should change the subject before he decides to push me out the window. "Right—anything planned for the holiday?"

"Going to my parents' place for Christmas Day." He backs into the shop. "You?"

"Same as every other year, you know how it is." I chuckle. *One action-packed, huge-family get-together.*

"One gigantic, joint Christmas," Dan says. He took the words right from my mind.

"Indeed." I nod. "I'll stop by before I open. Is that good with you? I'll write you a check to cover everything."

"Perfect, I should have it ready by then. Stop by the front desk. Char will have a receipt for you." He pulls to a stop and shuts off the engine.

"Thanks, man," I say as I open the door.

"You got it."

Chapter 22

OLIVE

I scrub the last coffee pot and place it on the drying rack. Everything is clean and ready for when I reopen on the twenty-sixth. Everyone is finally gone for the day. I flip the sign to *Closed* and breathe a sigh of relief. I'm so tired. All the morning mayhem was enough to burn my energy. My phone dings with a text message.

Mason

Your truck is outside.

Sorry about this morning.

Olive

Don't apologize. I was overreacting. Will you ever forgive me, dearest?

Mason

Nothing to forgive, Sweetie Pie.

I giggle. Taking off my apron and hanging it on the wall. I slide the zipper up my coat and walk across the street to check my truck. *Wow.*

I can't believe it. I crouch down and place my hand on one of the tires. New tread. *He got me new tires.* I open the door and start the engine; it comes to life in an instant. I look around the inside and everything is sparkling clean. It smells like cinnamon. The seats are spotless. I swipe my finger against the dash, it's dust free.

I pull my phone out of my pocket and dial Mason's number.

"I love you," I say into the phone after the call connects.

"Do you like it?" He laughs.

"Do I like it? Of course I do! I love it. I can't believe you went to all the trouble just for me. I'm literally speechless. Old Blue has never looked better." My heart feels all warm and fuzzy. No one has ever done anything like this for me.

"It wasn't any trouble. Dan did all the work. I just went with him to get it."

Classic Mason to brush off something he went to great lengths for. I know it wasn't easy. He probably hitched a ride on the tow truck to his broken-down one, brought it back to his house to fix it. Because I know he insisted on repairing the flat himself. Then they towed my truck to Dan's for repairs. At least, I assume. He must've walked over to the garage once it was ready and scrubbed it at the self-service car wash station, Suds in the Bucket, before the bar opened for the night. All to drive it back here for *me*. That doesn't sound like an easy day.

"Still. Thank you. You're the best. What do I owe you?" I smile, looking over my truck once more.

"You're welcome. Nothing—are you kidding?"

"Are you sure, what time can I stop by to bring you home?"

"Yes, I'm sure, and no, I'll hitch a ride from someone at the bar."

"You will not," I protest.

"I will."

"Nope. I will be there at midnight. Try and stop me." I put extra emphasis in my tone, daring him to disagree with me.

His deep voice reverberates a chuckle through the speaker. "Fine, Firefly. I will see you then."

"Okay, Knight, see you tonight." I end the call. I shut the door on my truck and walk across the asphalt to the front of the shops. A few chickens peck the fresh snow on the sidewalk. I recognize Hennifer, a Plymouth Rock, and Bernadette, a Wyandotte. I pet each of them and ask in a sweet voice, "How are my girls doing?"

They strut off in reply. While the cold-hardy chickens scavenge the streets and woods during the day, others prefer solace in the heated coop.

I open the door to The Hoarders Emporium. It's a one-stop shop for used eclectic items. I'm looking for something perfect to give to Mason for Christmas. We've always swapped them for as long as I can remember. When I was in third grade, I gave him a pinecone. Don't judge me! It's all I could get my hands on at that time. He gave me a rock, so don't go thinking his gift was much better. At that age we thought the world of those little things. I kept the rock after all these years. I cherish everything someone gets me. Last year, I got him a leather wallet with a Rooster stamped on the front, and he got me a metal keychain with a whisk engraved on it. The gifts are always small, meaningful, and useful. I love the tradition.

It's my last chance to find something before everything closes. I almost forgot about it. I already picked up a few things for Octavia, Logan, and Emma: jump ropes, a mini trampoline, and Skip Its. I always spoil them with my favorite things from when I was younger—because I can. I picked out some diapers and essentials for Char's baby on the way. For the adults, we do a Secret Santa because there are way too many people to buy presents for with a fifty-dollar limit. This year I got Owen; he was easy to buy for. A case of beer and a gift card for groceries is what he asked for. He's a simple man.

Every time I come into this shop, my mouth drops to the floor. Jane, the owner, is an acquirer of things. Or in other words, a hoarder, but the good kind—if there is such. Stacks of boxes cover the room, floor to ceiling. She finds everything while traveling the continental U.S.: unique lampshades, jewelry, signs, knick-knacks, vintage toys, and more. It's a picker's dream. I don't know where to begin. The amount of boxes is imposing; they tower over me.

I rifle through a few items off the first stack. A pen engraved with the words "Best Dad." That might be a little too soon since he doesn't have any kids yet. A bedazzled watch with a glitter band. *Maybe a little over the top.* I drop it back in the pile. I pull out a unicorn stuffed animal and a framed picture of someone's grandma. The former would be received with a good laugh; the latter would earn me a raised eyebrow. I wouldn't blame him. It would be really weird to hang a picture of someone else's grandma in his house.

Something meaningful would be nice.

I pick up a perfume bottle that looks like it's from the Middle Ages. It still has some liquid left in it. I spritz it on my wrist. *Why not?*

Bad idea.

I begin to cough into my arm. Gagging on the wretched odor. It smells like something died in there—ash, fish, rotten flowers, and a hint of orange spice. It's so potent that it makes me itch all over in disgust. It's putrid; an instant pain flares at the bridge of my nose. Sweat drips from my forehead. I want to throw up everything in my stomach.

Let's spray a questionable perfume directly onto your wrist. Nothing could go wrong.

My thoughts deceived me. *Why would I do this to myself?* In a split second, I made a decision that was arguably *very* stupid. I'm too curious for my own good. And the only thing I got in return is regret.

"Is someone in here?" Jane's voice emits over the coughing fit I've found myself in.

I shout in the direction of her voice. "It's me, Olive. I'll be back to see you in a minute. I'm going to use the ladies' room."

Like right away!

"Take your time, honey." *I will indeed.* I run into the bathroom and scrub my arm with a purpose. My skin is raw and red by the time I'm done cleaning every last ounce of fragrance that lingers on my body.

Phew. I'm glad that's over. But I can still smell a hint of the nasty perfume in the air when I exit the bathroom. I need to get out of here soon.

Sorry, Jane!

I walk through each aisle. Jane left three feet gaps between each one. So, at least you can get through it like a maze. I finally find her in the last row with a clipboard tucked close to her chest. She smiles wide. Her hair is poofy and unkempt. She's covered in jewelry. The silver and gold bands pair with multicolor beads. They jingle with every movement she makes. Her clothes are flowy and colorful.

"I'm so glad you stopped in. I haven't seen you in a while. After I got back from my trip to Florida, I've been hiding out in this place.

I'm not too fond of this snowy weather." Her bracelets jingle when she checks something off her clipboard.

It must be an inventory checklist. How in the world does she keep her sanity?

"I know. I thought you'd stay in Florida until the weather cleared up."

"That was the plan until my grandson called asking me to spend the holidays with him. I had to drive back." She looks up from her clipboard. "What are you looking for?"

"A gift for Mason for Christmas. Something special with meaning."

After the firefly keychain, I know that I need to find something unique this year. Which is nearly impossible, but one can try. With Jane's help I'm certain I'll find something great.

"I have just the thing." She taps her pen across the clipboard and looks down at the scribbles. Her smile widens more when she hovers over one line and nods. "Wait here. Let me grab it for you."

Jane always seems to have this penchant to pick out exactly what you're looking for, without ever asking what you need. It's like some kind of magic; no one in town understands it. We just go with it. There's no use in denying what is clear as day. She just knows.

After some time, she emerges into the aisle. "Here you go." She hands me a figurine. It's a knight in armor with a sword and shield.

I gasp, covering my mouth with my palm. It's perfect. I couldn't have found something more fitting if I searched through the aisles myself.

"Thank you. It's exactly what I needed."

There's a twinkle in her eye, and I know she's proud of her find. It may be a little concerning that she doesn't know that I call him Knight. Maybe she overheard it? Or maybe she just knows—I'm not going to question her magical powers.

Mason's going to love it.

Chapter 23

OLIVE

"Y ou're early," Mason says while stacking chairs on each table.

"Is that even a question?" I grab a wooden chair next to him and flip it onto the table. My purse swings on my side and hits my leg with the motion.

"No." Mason chuckles. "I shouldn't be surprised. The world will stop spinning if you show up late somewhere."

"Don't be ridiculous. I'm only half an hour early. I was late this morning." I look around the room. "Looks like the world is still spinning."

"Says the one who was ready to tackle me on the walk to your shop."

"I was not." I giggle, covering my face.

I was definitely thinking about tackling him when he walked around the truck and said there wasn't a spare, but I could see the guilt written all over his features. Everything that went wrong was out of our control, anyway.

"See, I knew it." He shakes his head in humor.

"That was a nice thing you did for me. Getting my truck new tires. And having it cleaned... I don't really know what to say." I glance around.

"You've said enough already. I want you to be safe. I figured I'd do it for you."

I lift another chair. "I would've gotten around to it eventually."

"I know." He sighs. "But I was worried. Since Dan already had to tow my truck home, I figured I might as well get it done. It was nothing."

"Well, thanks. It means a lot to me." I gaze at him, touched.

Why does he feel the need to do so many sweet things for me? I have no clue. But I know that I can't take Mason for granted.

"No problem. I just have to sweep and mop, and then we can head out."

"I'll help." I insist as I flip the last chair.

"You don't have to. Why don't you hang out in my office until I'm done? Take a nap on the couch."

"No way!" I defend. There's no way I'd take a nap while he's out here cleaning by himself. He should know this.

"You look exhausted. Please?" he begs.

Ugh. When he looks at me that way and begs, I almost want to say, *Sure, I'll go sit in your office.* But I can't fall into his deep brown gaze this time. It's not happening.

I put my hand on my hip. "No, I want to help. I'm not taking a nap while you're out here scrubbing the floor. You need to sleep too. When you don't get enough sleep, you get migraines. I'm not trying to harp on you, but the faster we both get the floor done, the sooner we can go home and sleep."

This is why Mason gets migraines more often than not. He takes care of everyone else but himself. So, I need to be the one that takes care of him in any way that I can. If I have to argue with him until he relents, then I will.

"Fine." He rolls his eyes. "I'll grab the broom."

I stick my tongue out. "Good. I'm glad you're done being so infuriating. I'll fill up the mop bucket."

A smile tugs at his lips. "Fine."

"Fine." I cross my arms and grin.

Sorry, Mason, we're in this together.

I fill up the mop bucket using the utility sink and pour some degreaser solution. I wheel it out to the tables while Mason's busy sweeping the floor. He does it swiftly and turns to look at me with an apologetic glance. I shake my head. Nope. He's not going to feel guilty about my helping. He didn't make me help. I wanted to. He shifts his gaze away quickly.

Good.

After a few minutes of mopping, I groan, thinking about Christmas Eve. "Tomorrow's gonna be a long day."

He stares at me uneasily for a moment. "Yeah, we'll be tired."

"I'll make some coffee when you pick me up."

He pushes the broom along the floor. "That would be the perfect medicine."

I swallow. "Do you think they'll believe that we're together?"

"I hope so. It would be so nice to enjoy those two days without them trying to set us up with someone. I have a hard time saying no, especially when they invited a girl to dinner for me last year." Mason suppresses a groan.

"Oh my God. I forgot about that. What was her name again? It was something starting with a B or maybe an E. I can't remember." I tap my chin trying to think of it.

"Brooklyn," he states.

"Yeah! That's her name. Whatever happened between you two? You went on a few dates, and then she disappeared."

"I only did it because she was so nice. I didn't want to tell her no. My mom promised her that I'd be interested. I wasn't at the time." There's a brief pause until he says, "There was someone else."

I raise my eyebrows. "Ooh! Who? Do I know her?" I try to think of any person in town that Mason was interested in. None come to mind other than Marigold and Daisy. But he doesn't talk to them much.

"No one you know. It was a long time ago," he says bluntly.

Ouch, touchy subject. I shouldn't push him any further after that one. I get it. Some things are better left in the past.

"Sheesh. No need to be so grouchy. What's gotten into you? You're normally the positive one," I tease.

"I'm just tired." He finishes sweeping the rest of the crumbs into a dustpan.

"You're right. I'm sorry. I shouldn't be heckling you right now. I can't help that I'm a ball of energy all the time."

His rough expression softens. "You never heckle me. You are the most kind and outgoing person I know. Maybe a little rough around the edges when you tackle me as if I weigh nothing and pound on the ground like you're a WWE wrestler. That can be overlooked." His eyes dance with mirth.

I laugh out loud. "That's good to know because I am your fake girlfriend. You're supposed to like me no matter how much it stings your pride that I'm stronger than you." I flex my left arm jokingly as I finish mopping the final stretch of floor with my right. "And I'm one hell of a multitasker."

Mason shakes his head. "Let's get out of here before you mop the floor with me next."

Chapter 24

MASON

"I need to prepare myself for the chaos that is our families." I grip the steering wheel tightly.

"Do you want to try some breathing exercises? Breath in, one, two, three—breathe out, one, two, three," Olive says.

"I'm thinking about trying it. That's how nervous I am to walk in there. They can smell fear."

"They're not that bad. We already dealt with them at the Christmas party." She brushes the idea off.

I stare, eyebrows raised, blinking at her a few times.

"Okay, your sisters can smell fear. Hannah and Jackie can, not Char. Your mom too... Sophia has a way of telling when you're lying." She pushes her curls off her shoulders to her back.

"Beth isn't so innocent. She's just as bad. Oakley and the guys don't care, and our dads couldn't give a shit." I pad my fingers over the wheel.

She laughs, covering her mouth. "They don't care if we're single for eternity as long as we're happy. Regardless of who we attach ourselves to. Or who we bring to dinner."

"Exactly—at least someone looks like they're ready to go in there with the wolves. Moose is about to jump through the cab window."

"Awe, Moose. You're so cute. You're going to get all the food scraps. I'll sneak you some under the table. Give me a kiss." Her voice reaches a higher pitch as Moose licks the side of her face, and she giggles.

I'm jealous of the way she talks to my dog. *What is wrong with me?*

"So, what's the plan?" she asks.

"There's no plan." I tap my fingers on the steering wheel some more.

"Just act like we're obsessed with each other, right?"

"Pretty much." I swallow hard.

"We can do this. Don't act weird about it. Don't try too hard. But don't try too little where it isn't believable." Olive makes it sound easy.

I don't have to act with anything. I've been in love with Olive for years. Nothing's going to change for me. She smiles at me reassuringly, and I can't help but notice how beautiful Olive looks. Her face is warm with color, and her red hair is in tight curls. She has those red lips and soft green gaze. She shifts to the side, gazing at the front door of the house with a mixture of anticipation and uneasiness. That's when I notice the green ribbon tied into a bow holding her hair out of her eyes. It matches the festive Christmas sweater with bows.

She turns back towards me, and her head tilts in silent question.

I clear my throat. "Got it. I should be able to manage that." *I won't even have to try.*

I walk around the side and let Moose out. Then I open her door. I take her hand in mine, and the small gesture shoots tingles through my arm. My impending doom is approaching. Each step forward is painful as I force myself closer to the front door. The stress of everything is causing an ache to form in the back of my head as my jaw clenches.

Dammit. Now is not the time for a migraine. I rub my head with my free hand. I realize the door isn't getting any closer. We've stopped. My feet are cemented, but my mind is miles away.

Not now.

"We can make it through the day together. If you don't want to go in there, we can make an excuse and leave right now," Olive whispers reassuringly.

Her voice is an anchor, grounding me in sanity, strength, and confidence.

"No. We have to do this. I love both our families. I want to spend the day with them—sometimes it becomes too much stress. It's Christmas Eve, though. I need to be here."

Olive squeezes my hand. "What about your migraines?"

"I won't get one as long as I have you by my side. You keep the stress at bay."

She looks into my eyes, and for a split second, I think I notice them watering in the corners. It's almost as if it were a look of something more than friendship.

The door swings open suddenly. "What are you guys doing out here? It's freezing. Come in. The party's just getting started." Ryder greets us. "Watch out for—oh shit."

Oh shit is right. Greta, Ryder and Jackie's miniature dachshund, comes running full force from the gap in the door. Olive jumps into my arms. It's no exaggeration on her part. Their dog is undisciplined. Greta starts barking uncontrollably. A sound loud enough to make my ears ring. Olive covers her ears. Greta latches onto the corner of my jeans with her teeth and starts tugging. For being such a little dog, the thing is vicious until you pet her and prove to her that you aren't a threat.

Ryder shouts, "Stop, Greta! Quiet! Now!" Greta continues to bark and gnaw on my jeans. "I told Jackie that we should have left her at home and hired a dog sitter like we did on Thanksgiving!"

"It's okay!" I manage to yell over the barking and the snagging of my jeans. Moose struts through the door.

So much for a loyal and protective dog. Abandoning his owner when I'm clearly being *attacked*.

Ryder manages to tear her off my jeans and holds her in his arms. The barking stops as soon as Olive pets her head. He sets her down, and she runs inside. "Sorry about that. She's a hard one to train."

Olive jumps back on the ground, and we follow Ryder inside. She whispers in my ear, "They've been training her for four years. She doesn't seem to take direction very well. You would think by now she's seen us enough times to calm down."

"No, she doesn't listen very well." I chuckle under my breath.

"At least she's cute. It makes up for it."

We greet everyone with quick hellos. I make a few trips to the truck and back, bringing in presents for tomorrow. I set them with the others in the corner of the room. We won't have the tree until later today. Once we bring it in and decorate, we can set them around it.

I lean back on the couch and put my arm around Olive playing into the doting boyfriend role.

"Want anything to drink?" Mom asks.

"Beer," I reply evenly.

"It's not even nine in the morning." She puts her hands on her hips.

"Okay, I'll settle for a black coffee." Olive raises an eyebrow. I know what she's thinking. Something like, *should you really be drinking that right now? You already had one this morning.* "Never mind. I meant water," I say.

She's right. Well, she never overtly said it, but I know what she's thinking. My migraines are triggered by a combination of things, caffeine being one of them. It wouldn't be good to experiment with too much of it today in front of everyone. I don't want my mom or sisters to find out. They'll act like I'm dying.

"A glass of water please," Olive says.

After a few moments, my mom returns. "Here you go." She hands us each a glass of water. She sits on the recliner next to us. "Can I say something?"

Oh no. No, Mom. Please don't say something.

No one in the history of the universe has said, *can I say something,* without it being something negative... or at least with some underlying implication.

"Don't give me that look, Mason. It's not bad. I'm happy for you both. It brings me to tears to think that you were meant for each other."

I'm in trouble. Not now, no. When this ends and she finds out we were lying... I see it as bending the truth a little; I don't think she'll see it that way.

"Thanks, Sophia," Olive says and grasps my hand, squeezing my palm slightly.

"You're welcome. So, I had a few things I was thinking about. I was on Pinterest and saw some lovely photos for an ocean themed wedding. We could put little bowls on each table with seashells and driftwood. The tablecloths could be blue, and we could get some sand delivered to make a mock beach out back. You can have your wedding here if you want; otherwise, you could do it in town. I'm sure Constance would love to organize the whole ordeal," Mom says with a chipper tone.

Olive's hand feels clammy in mine, and I see fire in her eyes. Her face paled the instant my mom said "wedding."

My eyes almost pop from their sockets. "Are you out of your mind? Firstly, there will be no *ocean* themed wedding. We live in Pennsylvania. Do you see an ocean anywhere?" I don't pause long enough for her to answer. "Secondly, there will be no wedding. And if there ever is... you and *Constance* will be the last to plan it. You could be involved with planning, sure. But it's ridiculous to think that you'd be planning something without asking."

"Thirdly, we aren't getting married. We *just* started dating." Olive's eyes are lit ablaze.

"Yes, I second that. I forgot the part about not getting married," I say, giving Olive an apologetic look.

"I'm sorry. Can't a mother have a dream for her son?" She taps her chin in thought. "Hannah taught me how to use Pinterest—it's a wonderful place where you can save things you like. There's a board where I pinned all my ideas if you want to look at it."

"Of course, you can dream all you want. But now's not the time or place to suggest a wedding. And no, yet again, I don't want to look at a board," I say.

My mom sighs in defeat. "Okay, I'll show Beth instead. I'm sure she'll appreciate what I've come up with."

"I'm sure she will." Olive laughs, covering her mouth. Olive's mom is just as bad as mine. We can let them live out their wedding planning dreams on their own time. My patience is thinning.

After finishing our conversation and listening to a few more of my mom's grand *ideas*, we bundle up for the long hike through the fields to find the perfect tree. My parents, Olive's parents, Char, and Mateo stayed to make lunch. Char and Mateo stayed to help since she said her feet hurt too much to make the trek, rightfully so. She's due in a matter of time. Everyone else walks in front of Olive and I. We trudge through the snow-covered field behind the house to the Christmas Tree Farm. Beth and Alex have a hundred acres of farmland and woods. The Christmas trees are planted far from the house, so it's a trip to get there.

"It's a beautiful day for this at least." Olive sighs happily, looking around at the snow-covered pastures.

"It is, isn't it?"

Olive swings my hand back and forth. She skips along the snow and hums a Christmas song. The sun is bright. It glows against her face making the freckles stand out over her wind-bitten nose. Creases paint lines on the edges of her closed lip smile. Her eyes find mine, locking onto my gaze. It's like looking through a forest covered in moss, as if everything is full of life and wonder.

"What?" She smiles wider.

"Nothing." *Everything.* I want to tell her all the thoughts that come to mind. The way she is so inadvertently striking. The natural beauty of what's inside her soul...

But I can't.

"This is the tree I want!" Octavia points to the tallest tree in the field. It sits apart from the others. Grand and imposing.

"Yeah! I want that one too," Logan says.

"Me three." Emma smiles wide and runs with the other two.

Of course they want that one. The tallest and widest tree. I don't think it will fit through the door. Let alone be easy for us to carry the trip back.

"This one it is then," Jackie says, staring up the length of the tree. Her eyes widen as her gaze continues following its height to the top.

"Want to help me cut it down, Mason?" Owen asks. "Joe, Ryder, and Jamal, can you hold up the tree while we cut?" They all answer with head nods and agree to hold it up.

I sigh. "Yeah." I'm exhausted from being up so late yesterday. My early morning coffee is wearing off.

I grab the crosscut handsaw. The diameter of the tree is around a foot. It's huge. *How in the hell are we going to get this inside the house?*

Owen grips the handle on one end; I grab the other. We start pushing it back and forth. It continues to scrape at the surface, slowly cutting into the bark. A small amount of wood shavings starts to form a pile on the snow.

This is going to take forever.

After many minutes of the same motion, my arm begins to feel like Jello. The tree starts to creak as we get closer to the edge. The last bit holding it snaps off; it falls with a big swoosh. And it lands directly on the three guys. They fly with it to the ground. A cloud of snow poofs into the air from the branches.

"Oh my God!" Jackie screams. She sprints over to them, her arms waving. "Help me get it off of them!" She frantically grabs at the branches, trying to move it by herself.

Everyone runs over and tugs at the tree. We pull together to lift it off the three knuckleheads. I could see their shit eating grins through the gaps in the branches. They were holding the tree above them the whole time. They laugh hysterically and roll on the ground, clutching their stomachs. Ryder gets on his knees and slaps the ground in fits of laughter; he wheezes from laughing so hard. Jamal sits up, grinning so wide, happy tears in the corners of his eyes.

There is never a boring holiday when everyone gets together. Last year, Mateo tied a fake snake to Owen's leg on Memorial Day. Safe to say, Owen freaked out. He kept running and looking back and running more. He thought it was following him. He was so scared that he just about pissed himself. It was a good laugh, but he's been planning something big to get back at them. I can't wait for the day but also dread what theatrics are coming.

"Got you!" Joe jokes.

"You're all pathetic." Jackie sighs, and she plops on the snow to sit down. "You could have given me a heart attack. I thought you guys were hurt. I'm so sick of these jokes. They're aging me. You're taking *years* off my life. I already have a few gray hairs."

Ryder tries to hold back his smile. "Oh, Jackie. I'm sorry honey. You know we just like to mess around. No harm done."

I think Ryder might want to shut his mouth before he makes things worse, but I'm not saying a word. She is my sister and all, but how's that saying go? *Never get involved with the affairs of the heart.* I'm not starting today. They continue to bicker and end up making up moments later.

The kids built a snowman through the tree cutting and fallout. Now they run around throwing snowballs at each other.

"Mason, come here," Olive says.

"Everything okay?" I ask.

"No." She grimaces and motions for me to be quiet. "When I walked over to hang out with the girls, I overheard them talking about how we don't seem like we're dating. They think nothing's changed other than us holding hands. They changed the subject as soon as they saw me, but Char wasn't there to back us up. We need to do something to make them buy it," she whispers.

My brows furrow. "Like what?"

"I don't know—kiss me or something?"

Kiss her? *This again.* This woman is going to kill me. I can't just kiss her and not think about it for the rest of my existence.

I gulp. "It's not necessary. We can tell them the truth. We don't have to go through with this anymore."

"No. It's only a kiss. I don't miss the pressure of them trying to hook us up with people. I also don't miss them making us feel guilty for not dating other people. Please? What harm could it do? You've kissed plenty of girls before."

You're not just any girl.

I adjust my glasses and reply hesitantly, "As long as you're okay with it. Are you really sure?"

"Just kiss me already." She bites her bottom lip.

I stare at her dumbfounded for what feels like seconds, minutes, or maybe hours. How can she be nonchalant about it?

"Well?" Olive tilts her head and gazes at me in question.

"Okay." I continue to stare at her flushed face. Tendrils of red curls dance through the wind out the back of her hat. I could admire her beauty forever and never get tired of it.

"Mason?" She brushes her hand on my arm.

I take in a shaky breath. "Yeah?"

"Kiss me," she pleads.

This is really happening.

I lean in and hover my lips over hers. Her cool breath blows fog in the air.

Dammit.

I've wanted this moment to happen for so long; it stings that it'll be fake, with irreversible consequences for me. What will be another meaningless kiss for her will be my *undoing.* Two people sharing a kiss can be a transaction of sorts, but I can already anticipate the agony and fallout that will linger in the confines of my subconscious. I know if I don't take the chance, it may never present itself again. I could play it safe and end things now before it's too late or go for it. The former would be the best choice; the latter is what I want.

I decide on the latter.

What have I gotten myself into? I'm already regretting it, without even kissing her yet. I won't regret the kiss itself—only the torment I'll feel every day that passes after this.

I tilt the bottom of her chin. I brush my thumb along her rosy cheek; she shivers under my touch. Our lips meet in soft brushes. Tentative at first. Slow and calculated. She smiles against me, kissing me as though she has nothing to lose.

But I have so much to lose. My sanity. My self-control. The will to pretend that I only want to be her friend from now on. The remnants of my thin restraint filter away.

I've only had a small taste. I'm lost in what could be or what might be. A future where nothing will change what is between us—where our friendship will never be tainted by foolish mistakes. I won't be able to look at her again after this without remembering every single detail: the softness of her lips, the tingles in my core, the smell of her perfume, and her button nose brushing against mine.

She presses herself against me; I can feel the shared cadence of thudding, our heartbeats rapidly in sync. I dread the inevitable, the moment she deems this enough to prove what we are. For the sake of carrying on our fake relationship.

We're just friends. This is all an act.

My thoughts are painful reminders. But I shove them away. I'm going to let myself enjoy this moment for as long as it lasts.

Chapter 25

Olive

Mason's lips are smooth, warm, and captivating. I feel light, like I could just float away. I wrap my fingers against the back of his head, grasping against his hat. He curls his large hand around my waist, slightly grazing bare skin as the hem of my jacket lifts. The icy breeze makes goosebumps form along my hip, but I couldn't care less. His fingers burn; the touch spreads heat to my core.

Everything leaves my mind. My worries, agitation, and our surroundings are all gone. His lips brush mine with desire. It's akin to something resembling longing. I didn't know a kiss could feel this good. It's like we're the only ones in the middle of nowhere, not surrounded by both of our huge families. For a brief but fleeting moment, I forget that he's my best friend. I forget that he's the boy I grew up pestering. The one I called when each boyfriend broke up with me. The one person that could comfort me and let me cry on their shoulder through it all. I forget that this is *fake*.

My insides melt into a puddle when he brushes his other hand through my hair. My skin prickles. He tastes like peppermint and confusion.

What is going on with me?

Owen whistles. The sound breaks me out of the daze I found myself in. I'm realizing that I don't want to stop kissing him. I pull back from him slowly. Blinking a few times, his brown-eyed gaze is heated. I stare at him blankly. I don't know how to think or behave. The sun overhead reflects a glow across his eyes, boring into mine. I never noticed how deep brown and rich they are; they aren't cold—they're intense. Nothing about Mason has ever been cold. His personality is warm and protective. But now, it's as if I see him a bit differently than a few minutes ago. I've never felt a kiss that stuck with me afterward. That left me reeling in withdrawal. Conflicted.

No. It can't be. This is all part of the act we're playing. He must be really good at making it seem as if I'm the only one he wants.

I turn away. I can't find the words to describe what happened. I can't think about my best friend this way.

Friends don't kiss like that, nor do they get butterflies in their stomach or tingly sensations from a simple touch. I've been waiting so long to experience all those feelings, the ones people say they get when they've kissed—the one. I may have just barely scraped the surface before. None of my exes ever put a dent in what that was. I will never be the same because now I'm treading deep below the surface.

What is happening to me? I can't think rationally.

I know that wasn't fake. I'm almost positive he is thinking the same thing. I can't believe it. Could Mason and I be more? Why have I never entertained the thought—of *us*? I'll admit I'm scared of how things are going to be different now. I don't want them to be. I like my relationship-free life. I promised myself I wouldn't be entertained by the idea of one unless I knew it was serious. This was a one-time feeling, something put on as a show to prove we were in a relationship. I think we've sold it. I'm in shock right now, but it will dull with time.

Oh crap, I'm not so sure about that.

I trudge through the snow, retreating. My face instantly reddens. It's not from the cold. It's from what I know will never be the same again.

Hot chocolate warms my insides. The fire crackles and pops in front of my slipper-covered toes. Moose and Greta are curled up together in a dog bed. The kids are decorating the tree with home-made ornaments. Some of them are from years ago, dating back to my parents' childhood, and others are new ones that the kids made moments ago using paint and clear globes. There's more paint on their fingers and clothes than the ornaments. I smile thinking about how Mason and I used to be the same way. Christmas music plays soothing tunes. I'm happy, deliriously full of merriment.

Mason laughs and tips his head back at something Char says and takes a sip of beer. I never noticed how his nose crinkles when he laughs or how he calms when in the presence of family (when they aren't trying to fix him up with a girlfriend or wife). I think the kiss removed all the doubts our families felt; they've accepted what is the truth. At least, what we want them to think is the truth. It pains me to lie to the ones I love, but when the pressure becomes over the top, sometimes people need to blur the lines a little. If only for their sanity. My sanity. Mason's sanity.

He looks at me from his place in the kitchen. It's like there's an invisible pull drawing us together when we're separated. I stick my mug of cocoa out in cheers. He chuckles, winks, and tips his beer in reply.

I feel the couch dip next to me. "Olive," Jackie says my name.

"Yeah?" I answer, not breaking eye contact with Mason. His face is all hard lines and soft edges; I feel like I'm a snow-woman melting into a puddle in front of the fire. I drum my fingers against my leg. His smile is devastatingly handsome. Why did I never notice it before?

"Earth to Olive." Her voice fills my eardrums once again as she touches my shoulder. I shake my head and turn towards her, trying to shake loose the thoughts from my mind.

"Sorry."

"It's okay. You're in love. It's the honeymoon phase of your relationship. It's okay to be a little lost in each other. Or a lot."

Love? Who said anything about love? I love Mason platonically as a best friend. But true love, I don't know that I've ever felt it. It would be something I feel in my bones; I wouldn't second guess it. "I'm glad you think so," I reply with as much sweetness as I can muster.

That was convincing, right?

"I wanted to say that I'm happy for you both. I've known he has been in love with you for a long time. I could always see it with the way he looks at you. I'm sorry if we've been pressuring or pushing you both. It was only out of love. I've wanted you to have a future together. You both looked so lonely during the holidays."

She thinks *he's been in love with me?* They whispered about something similar in high school. I brushed it off. Both of our families are full of jokesters. I didn't believe anything that came from their mouths, especially not at that age. I still don't. To hear it now makes me reconsider if what they were saying didn't have a whisper of truth to it.

It can't be.

I place my hand on top of hers. "Thank you. I know you mean well. Even in your over-the-top way." Extremely over-the-top if I must say to myself.

A smile spreads along her face. "I am over-the-top in the *best* way." *Right...*

"Sometimes. Not all the time."

What can I say? I usually say what I'm thinking.

"Hey!" She shoves my arm playfully. "I'm never surprised when you're brutally honest. I'm glad, though. I don't need you walking on eggshells around me."

"I would never." My voice skips an octave.

"Are you lying to me, Olive Watson?" she jokes. "Your voice got all high-pitched."

Uh-Oh.

"Jackie, please stop torturing my girlfriend," Mason says. He must have snuck up on us because I didn't hear him coming.

I breathe an internal sigh of relief. I could hug him for showing up right now. I'm a horrible liar, especially when confronted and put on the spot.

The word girlfriend sounds so foreign coming from Mason. I almost turn to look and see if there's someone else behind or next to me. For another moment, I almost forget about our deal. Recognition comes crashing back a second later. *Girlfriend.* Why do I like the sound of that? When it comes from his lips it sounds promised yet outlandish.

The rational side of my head isn't in sync with my thoughts. One kiss rewired my brain chemistry.

"I'm not torturing her." Jackie defends.

He crosses his arms over the broadness of his chest. "Well, then stop talking about me."

"As if we'd be talking about you." She laughs, clutching her stomach. "You think very highly of yourself."

I'll give it to her. She's a good liar. Could've fooled me. We both know that we were talking about him.

He rolls his eyes at Jackie as he lowers himself onto the couch beside me, pulling me towards him with his fingers hovering slightly over my arm. The edges of his lips tilt upward as he looks down at me. My eyes crinkle in silent reply. He rubs my arm in circle motions, sending shivers through my core. It's comforting and distracting. The way my body is responding to his touch is confusing. One kiss has changed the dynamic between us, and as of right now, I'm not complaining.

"Uncle Mason!" Emma runs up to Mason, holding her palms up in front of him. "My fingers are colorful." She wiggles her painted, sparkly fingers in front of him. Her eyes are wide with amusement.

Mason leans forward on the couch to look at her hands. "Wow, they are beautiful. Show Olive. She wants to see too."

"Olive," she says, but it sounds more like Oyive. "My hands are pretty!" She holds her hands close to my face. I grasp one of them in mine.

"Not as pretty as you are." I poke her nose with my free hand. "Now we're both pretty. My hand matches yours. See?" I show her my hand that's covered with paint and glitter.

Emma bounces on the heels of her feet. "We're twins."

"Yes we are!" My smile reaches my eyes.

"Beautiful twins," Mason states. Emma's face lights up, and she runs off to join the other kids.

"I think I better clean them up before they smear the carpet with paint." Jackie chuckles. "I don't think your parents would be so happy, especially after you two destroyed it when you were younger."

Mason guffaws. "We thought the floor was a canvas. That's what happens when you leave kids unsupervised. I felt like Bob Ross."

"I remember it was all embedded into the carpet. It was stained for a good three years before they could replace it." It's funny now, but I'm sure it was devastating for my parents at the time. I would have been so upset.

"Yeah. So, I better hurry." Jackie laughs and heads in the direction of the tree.

"I think we better get you cleaned up too, Olive," Mason says.

I hold out my glittery hand. "Good idea. Unless you want some paint on you too?"

He lifts his hands in surrender. "No—please. Not on my shirt. It's new."

I giggle while wiggling my fingers, inching closer to his chest. "You don't fool me, dearest. All your shirts are the same. It's black. Suspiciously similar to the same style you wear every day. It looks a lot like the one you wore yesterday. The day before. And ten years ago."

"Guilty—if you can catch me first." He races from the living room.

"Get back here!" I shout as I chase him. I follow him through the living room and into the hall.

I love that Mason and I can still joke around with each other this way. We may be in our thirties, but that doesn't mean we won't act like we're thirteen again. This house holds plenty of memories. I skid past the family portraits on the walls and my childhood bedroom where the pencil scribbles on the doorframe are still visible from each year I grew. I can picture the foam darts stuck to the wall where Mason and I played in the hall. I laugh through heavy breaths and call out, "You can't outrun me, Knight!"

We run around the bend that leads to the bathroom. "Looks like I already am!" He boasts over his shoulder with a dimpled smile.

Mason stops abruptly in the doorway, clutching his stomach to catch his breath. I skid to a stop inches away from colliding with his back. I can instantly tell something is wrong. His face is unreadable. Anger, worry, and frustration all mixed in one expression.

"Char? What's wrong? Why are you crying? Where's Mateo? Did he say something to you?" His voice is soft. But the fire behind his eyes is wild. My smile fades to a line of concern. Char is bracing the sink in the glow of the bright lighting. Tears stream from her eyes as she sobs uncontrollably.

"No—Mateo went outside—to grab some firewood with Owen," she whispers between crying.

Char pauses for a few beats, but Mason doesn't say anything. He stands in silent patience until she speaks up once again. Her voice cracks as she says, "I'm scared."

He walks into the bathroom and hugs her. "What are you scared of?"

"It's nothing. I'm sorry." Char wipes some tears with a shaky hand.

He examines her face with a look of sympathy. "Don't you ever apologize to me. You are carrying a whole human life right now. You're allowed to feel any way you like. You're allowed to cry regardless of the circumstances. It's okay to be scared. What can I do to help?"

My heart fills with awe for this man. His soul is caring. He would do anything for the people he loves. There's no telling the lengths he would go to protect his sister from whatever is scaring her.

"There's nothing you can do. I'm scared about being a mother... I'm not sure I'd be a good one." She looks at the floor.

Mason puts a consoling hand on her arm. "Don't you ever for a second doubt you wouldn't be the best damn mother there is. You'd give the shirt off your back to someone you don't know if they needed it. You are selfless and kind. You babysit Octavia and Emma twice a week. You're great with them. You will make a great mother."

"Is that really what you think?" Her eyes widen.

"Of course it's what I think."

She smiles through tears. "Thank you, Mason. You're my favorite brother."

"I'm your only brother. You have to say that. You're my favorite sister, but please keep it between you and I." A smile tugs at his lips.

She pulls away and smiles at Mason. "I wouldn't tell a soul." She looks at me and motions for me to come in with a wave of her hand. I walk towards them and grasp her shaking hand in mine. I turn away and find a makeup remover wipe from the closet behind the bathroom door. I swipe it under her mascara stained cheeks. Once I'm finished I squeeze her hand tight with my clean one.

"Thank you," Char whispers as she gives me a hug. "The both of you. Thank you." She puts on a brave smile and walks out of the bathroom to rejoin our families.

"Come here," Mason says.

I hesitate at first, and I show him my glitter covered hand. But he doesn't seem to give a damn about me ruining his shirt. He steps closer to me, and I oblige without thinking. I wrap my arms around him. He places his chin on my head and engulfs me with his body heat.

"You would make a really good mother someday too," he whispers.

My voice comes out muffled from against his shirt. "You think so?"

His chin bobs. "Yes. Back there with Emma... you were so good with her. She looks up to you. They all do. And how you cared for Char too. You were patient and silent. You respected her space until she welcomed you in."

Thinking about having a little family of my own makes my eyes feel damp. I can picture a future for myself. A happy one filled with laughter.

Mason pulls back for a moment to kiss my forehead. We're not pretending anymore; there's no one here to see us. This isn't a show put on for the sake of proving we're a couple in front of others. This moment is something I want to pocket and save. It's sacred to both of us.

"I'd like that one day—to be a mother," I whisper.

Chapter 26

MASON

Christmas Day is no less haywire or action-packed. Everyone sits around the tree decorated with hand-painted ornaments, garland, candy canes, and multi-colored lights. The top of the tree touches the popcorn ceiling, and it extends further than any one we've had before. It's so tall that we didn't have enough room for the star. And so wide that it barely squeezed through the front door jamb.

I give my Secret Santa gift to Hannah. She squeezes the poorly wrapped box with silver ribbons and bows to her chest. "I can't wait to see what I got this year. Thank you. You're the best brother."

"Char said the same thing. I'm your only brother. You guys have to say that." I chuckle. "I hope you love it."

"I will love whatever you got me." She smiles in delight.

"I got you this year," Joe says while handing me a large overflowing bag with festive tissue paper. Hannah is the tissue paper queen, so I know she wrapped it. When we were kids, she kept a drawer overflowing with crafting items, tissue paper, and bags for each holiday.

Joe scratches his head. "I didn't get anything on your list, but it's something you've needed for a long time. You just didn't know you needed it."

"I can't wait to see what it is. Thanks, man." I pull out the tissue paper until I get to the box for an automatic chicken door. "You didn't?"

"I did." He grins.

"You were right. This is exactly what I needed."

"Hannah and I saw it in the back of a gardening magazine a few weeks ago. We had to get it for you. We know how you're always trying to get them locked up before dark every night. Now you don't have to worry as much." He smiles proudly.

"Thank you. I appreciate it." I really do. I've been scrambling every day to get someone to close the coop door for me if I can't get to it myself before dark. The chickens aren't safe with foxes, raccoons, and coyotes at night. Now that I have the automatic door, I can set a timer for it to close at a certain time every day.

"It has a solar panel and battery. I also made sure to get the one with a sensor, so it doesn't crush any chickens."

I wince. "Yeah. That wouldn't be good. The townies would be devastated. Thanks again. I'm gonna install it tomorrow."

Olive laughs at something Oakley says, and it draws my attention away from my conversation with Joe. Olive sits next to me with her feet tucked under her thighs, and her hair cascades over her shoulders. I'm pulled toward the sound of her voice like a moth to a flame. She could be talking about the most mundane thing, but I am captivated. I could spend decades listening to her go on and on about baking or crocheting. Or anything. She could be describing the color of the sky, and I'd be enthralled. Maybe that makes me obsessed, but I don't care.

Olive has an effect on me. Her eyes get a glint full of fervor. Her freckles draw me in. But it's the passion behind every word that makes me want to stay and listen for a lifetime.

"I can't believe you did that to him!" Olive exclaims while placing a hand against her face to stifle more laughter.

"It was so funny. Watching him open box after wrapped box until he finally got to the present in the smallest one. I think I wrapped thirty of them. His face was priceless." Oakley grins deviously.

"I need to try that next year on Mason," Olive says to her sister. Even though I'm listening, she's oblivious. I'm going to keep this secret and pretend I didn't hear it. It's something to look forward to in the future. *A future of us still being friends.*

Damn. My inner thoughts are sabotaging my happy mood. Our fake relationship is over in seven days. I've been counting down as a reminder. Not in anticipation for this to be over—no—to drive it into my head that this is only temporary.

The kiss we shared was a fluke. But for me, it was life altering. Her racing heart could only be described as a side effect of being without another's touch for so long. Or maybe it was nerves from having to kiss in front of our families for the sake of keeping them from nagging us. Who am I kidding? Olive doesn't seem to get nervous very often. She always seems confident in every decision she makes.

"Mason," Olive says.

"Yeah?" I mumble in reply.

"Everything okay?" Her brows knit in worry.

"Yes—of course. Why wouldn't I be?" I stumble over my words. *Get it together, Mason.*

She places her hand on my thigh; the touch feels electric. "I know you, Knight. I can tell when something is on your mind. If you need someone to talk to, I'm here. You can tell me anything."

If only I could tell you. But I don't want to lose you.

It's not worth the risk. I can't sabotage a lifetime of friendship just because I'm in love with her. That would be reckless. The words are on the tip of my tongue; it would be so easy to confess. "I know I can. I'm just thinking about some paperwork I have to get done for the bar. It's stressing me out."

It may not be what I was truly worried about, but it is something that's been working on me. Running the bar comes with a lot of responsibilities: expenses, hiring employees, and inventory. There's a shit-ton of paperwork and not enough time in the day to get it all done. I need to figure out if the band can play on New Year's Eve. I also have to check inventory to make sure we have enough drinks in stock for the night. Everyone gathers there to celebrate the countdown to midnight; it's the busiest day of the year. That's all I can think about... other than Olive.

She exhales through pursed lips. "Don't stress right now. I need you to be worry-free. We're going to enjoy the rest of today with our families, open these presents, and then eat a boatload of ham, mashed potatoes, and pumpkin pie. Once that's finished, we'll eat some more. So much that the buttons on our pants are going to shoot off in protest—"

"That sounds—"

"I wasn't finished," she scolds me. I chuckle and wave my hand, motioning her to continue planning. "Then you're driving us to your place to watch *National Lampoon's Christmas Vacation* by the fire with Moose. And sip on a little bit of spiked eggnog." She grins wide. "You'll most likely fall asleep. Then I will too because your couch is so comfortable... Now I'm finished. What do you say?"

"I say that sounds like a perfect night. One ticket please." Olive's right. One worry-free night is just what the doctor ordered.

She beams. "Well, let's start now, and soon enough, we can leave."

Chapter 27

OLIVE

"Who's ready to eat?" my mom asks.

"Everyone's ready to eat, Beth. It's been hours. We're starving." Hannah sighs.

"Okay." My mom waves her arms. "Bring the stuffing and mashed potatoes into the dining room." She points to Dad. "Alex, honey, can you bring the gravy and the green beans?"

"Yes, dear," Dad says as he grabs the food. On his way out of the kitchen he whispers under his breath, *"Bring the gravy,"* in an attempt to mock Mom.

I giggle, covering my face. "You better hurry, or you'll be in trouble."

"I'm going. I'm going." He disappears into the dining room.

"Olive? Can you grab the rolls and butter?" Mom asks.

"On it," I say as I grab them. I set the bowls on the china cabinet, and I take a seat at my *assigned* chair. My mom was always relentless over *order*. So, we don't change where we sit—ever. It's ridiculous if you ask me.

Mason carries the carved turkey into the room, setting it into a water-filled pan above the flickering flame from the Sterno. He pulls out his *assigned* chair next to mine. Owen sits on the other side of me and sets an armful of water bottles and beer on the table.

"Thank you, Owen. I'll take one of those." I eagerly accept a beer.

"Mason?" Owen asks, holding out both options for Mason to choose.

"I'll take one of these." Mason grabs a bottle of water. "Thanks, man."

Ryder sits across from me, and Joe sits on the other side of him. Moose and Greta wait patiently under the table for food to drop.

After a few minutes, everyone takes their seats in the dining room. We collectively decide on lining up at the china cabinet to load our plates with food. Once everyone finishes filling their plates, we start eating.

"Jackie, the stuffing is out of this world," Owen mumbles between open mouthfuls.

"Thanks, Owen. I tried out a new recipe this time. It's got a bunch of butter."

"I can tell. It's delicious," he says before finishing chewing.

I sigh dramatically. "Really, Owen? Again?"

He rolls his eyes. "Focus on your own food, Olive, and you might not notice what I'm doing."

"Yeah, Olive!" Octavia repeats. Paula just shakes her head. My brother is a bad influence, but he's hilarious. So, it makes up for it most of the time.

"It's so nice to have the whole family together," Sophia says. I turn my head to the left, finding her happy expression at the head of the table.

Liam takes Sophia's hand and says, "Sophia's right. I'm so proud of the men and women you've become. When we got married thirty-one years ago, I never thought I would have a family like this. A house full of my kids, their significant others, grandchildren, and another little one on the way." He tips his head to Char and Mateo. "Plus, a whole bonus family: Alex, Beth, their kiddos, and their grandchildren. It's a blessing to be surrounded by all of you."

My mom's eyes look glassy from the other end of the table. She adds onto what Sophia and Liam were saying. "We are so grateful for each other. This year has been one of the best in a while. With Char expecting so soon. Jackie and Ryder moving to Maine... Even though we miss them, we're so happy for Ryder and his career growth. Most of all, we're just tickled pink about Mason and Olive finding each other. We've always known there was something special between them. And now it's proven." She wipes a few stray tears from her eyes.

Are they right? Is there something between Mason and I that I've missed?

"Cheers to that," my dad says at the right side of the table, holding his condensation-covered glass in the air. Everyone lifts their drinks and clinks them together. I clink my bottle with Mason's. His smile is warm, and I look at him thoughtfully.

"What?" he mouths.

"Nothing," I mouth back.

It's not something I can exactly discuss at the table full of our families. And it's definitely not something I'm ready to divulge to Mason either. I'm busy contemplating what's going on between us, but I can't tell him that. Something is different between us. I can't put my finger on it. Or, maybe it was that toe-curling kiss.

"Earth to Olive and Mason!" my mom says loudly.

"Huh?" Mason replies. They're all looking at us with shit-eating grins. Well, everyone except for my mom and Sophia.

Oh no.

"You didn't hear what I said?" my mom asks.

"No? I missed it. Can you repeat it?" I answer.

"I was asking you guys... dark blue or teal tablecloths for your wedding? Sophia showed me her *board.* Is that what it's called? Anyway, I think the ocean theme is a wonderful idea. Bring a little bit of the beach here since we don't have any around." Mom taps her chin lost in thought.

Owen chuckles next to me, and I slap him on the arm. "Ow." He laughs some more, rubbing his arm.

What's up with these people and the ocean themed wedding? And why in the world are they thinking they can plan a wedding in the first place? We've been *dating* for one month. Marriage is out of the question. It'd be different if we've been together a while. Just when I think we can avoid the dramatics and nagging. They find something new to latch onto and run with it. And what about Oakley and Jamal? They got engaged. Why can't she worry about their wedding?

"There will be no *ocean* themed wedding. There will be no wedding at all. How do you know Mason and I want to get married in the first place? Maybe we're going to break up before that ever happens because you two—" I point to Sophia and my mom. "—are going to drive us mad. So much that we'll break up. End up alone. And move back home to live with you again." I squint my eyes and tilt my head. "And drive you nuts. How does that sound?"

"Oh no! I'm sorry, Olive, honey. We're just trying to help. We'll stop bringing it up. You're right," Mom pleads with me.

Thank you!

"That was a lie. There's no way they're going to stop bringing it up," Mason whispers in my ear.

"I know. But maybe they'll let it go for the rest of dinner until we leave. One can dream."

"Let's eat and get out of here."

"Deal."

I start by eating some turkey when Owen decides it's the perfect time to pull a fancy fork out of his pocket.

Who in the world carries a fork in their pocket?

"Do you have a special fork you like to eat your food with?" I question him.

He shrugs. "Nah. I'm gonna mess with Mom. Seemed like the perfect opportunity. She's too busy gossiping with Hannah to notice."

"Notice what?"

"You'll see." His eyes sparkle with whatever he's planning.

Oh no. This must be one of Owen's famous pranks. One of two things could happen. One: He could do something hilarious. Two: He could take the prank too far and ruin dinner. Hopefully the former and not the latter. I'll never forget when he started a campfire in the center of the table on Oakley's fourteenth birthday. He was roasting s'mores. The smoke alarm started going off. The house filled with a cloud of smoke as he ran outside with the makeshift campfire (kindling, leaves, and paper ablaze on a plate) with his tail between his legs after being hollered at. Mom and Dad weren't very happy with him. Neither was Oakley, who just wanted to enjoy her birthday without any hiccups.

Owen extends the end of the fork when Mom isn't looking. It spreads two feet behind his back. He wears a grin full of mischief. He swings it around the top of the table over my plate and then

Mason's, spearing a chunk of turkey from Mom's full plate. He quickly whips it behind him and sets it on a bowl conveniently set up on the china cabinet. I'll give it to him: he doesn't come unprepared. He scrapes the turkey off the fork swiftly using the bowl's edge. Octavia, Emma, and Logan catch on and giggle. Owen motions a finger over his mouth, and they all quietly laugh covering their mouths. He slowly hovers the fork over our plates once again and swipes the gelatinous cranberry sauce right from her plate into the bowl.

Mom is animatedly moving her arms while in a conversation with Hannah, oblivious to what's happening right under her nose. "Jane found me Mateo's Secret Santa gift. I can't believe she knew he needed a new leather wallet. His was all worn and weathered. It's miraculous the predictions she makes. I'd love to have that kind of magic. I didn't even show her the list of items he had come up with. It was the first item he wrote. She's a psychic for sure. She has to be!"

"Crazy! She found the gift I got for Joe too. It was a pizza peel. He needed a new one for The String Cheese." Hannah smiles and takes a bite of green beans. She covers her mouth when she notices Owen's fork whip through the air. He lifts a big clump of stuffing. Mason puts his finger over his mouth when she looks at us with raised eyebrows. She scratches her nose in the secret code we all came up with when we were younger. It means "I'm in." With the amount of pranks they pull on each other, we had to come up with one.

Just when I thought things couldn't get more comical. They do.

Owen pulls a large spoon from his never ending pocket full of surprises. He extends it behind his back. Mostly everyone at the table has now noticed the disappearing food. And they're all trying to suppress laughter. Our mom still hasn't noticed. She continues a conversation with Hannah and my dad. Completely blind to what is happening right under her nose. She doesn't look down at her plate; she just scoops up a bit of mashed potatoes and takes a bite all while keeping up the conversation. If she would've glanced down even for a moment, Owen would've been caught red-handed.

This is getting too entertaining. I'm nervous she'll catch on. I want to see if he can clear her whole plate before she notices.

Next comes an extendable spatula.

Where are these coming from? His pocket is similar to my purse. And that's saying something because one could get lost in there.

He scrapes the potatoes and gravy in one full swooping motion, plopping it in the bowl of food. All that's left is a serving of green beans and a dinner roll.

"I think we should stick to cupcakes for Char's baby shower, right? We need something that is grab and go," Mom says to Hannah, continuing to plan other things she's *volunteered* herself for.

Owen pulls an extendable pair of tongs from the *same* pocket. This is unreal. He grabs the roll, and her entire plate is empty except for a few green beans. It takes everything in me not to cry of laughter. I'm going to fall off my chair if I don't settle down.

I poke a forkful of mashed potatoes, and I almost take a bite when I hear a noise across the table over the chatter. It almost sounded like someone passed gas.

Are you kidding me?

I look around the table when I hear it again. It's faint, almost silent, but I know what I heard. Mateo's talking to Char, looking the least bit guilty. Jamal and Oakley are staring into each other's eyes, still oblivious to everyone else. They're in a love haze. Jackie and Ryder are immersed in a conversation about work. Joe and Hannah are being entertained by my mom's clearly exaggerated storytelling. My dad is eating food, trying and failing to suppress a grin as he looks at Mom's empty plate. The kids all sit together next to Sophia and Liam. None of them look suspicious.

Maybe it was in my head.

The noise starts again. Louder this time. There's no mistaking it. Someone is farting at the damn table. This family is out of control. Liam's voice sounds in my head: *I'm so proud of the men and women you've become.* I laugh to myself. Half of us still act immature. They haven't outgrown their teenage years. Owen was just stealing food from our mother's plate. And now someone's passing *air biscuits* at the table.

I can understand if they aren't feeling good; I get that. Half of the people at this table are lactose intolerant. Heck, I have my moments. I understand it all too well. But at the table? It's taking it too far—go to the bathroom—please!

I hear it again. I put my fork down; my appetite is gone. "Mason? Did you hear that?"

"Hear what?"

"Someone is bottom burping."

He chuckles. "I've never heard it called that before." He gasps for air between laughter. "But no. I didn't hear anything." He shakes his head and shovels another mouthful of turkey.

"That!" I exclaim. His eyes widen in realization. Everyone looks at me. The room quiets to a whisper. And someone cuts one loose again.

"Heard it that time." Mason scrunches his nose.

The guys all look at each other, sharing a few nods. "I knew it!" I shriek. I point to Joe, Ryder, Mateo, Mason, Owen, and Jamal. "This is some kind of cruel prank."

Mason holds his hands up. "I wasn't involved."

Mateo shakes his head. "I wasn't involved either." He takes a big swig of water from the bottle Joe handed him moments earlier. He spits it across the dining room wall. "What in the hell is this? Salt!" He runs to the bathroom to wash his mouth out.

My mom looks down at her plate. "Where in the world is my food?" She stares in horror at her empty, once filled plate. "I barely took a bite." She shakes her head in disbelief.

Sophia slams her hand on the table. "What in the world is going on? Someone needs to speak up *right now!*" Somehow, she managed to miss Owen's extendable utensils. She was too distracted with her conversations with Liam, Oakley, and Jamal.

Octavia and Logan hold up whoopee cushions and break into a fit of laughter.

Owen holds up his fork, spoon, spatula, and tongs. He pulls the handles all at once and extends them.

"You ruined dinner. You should be ashamed of yourselves!" My mom stomps out of the room. Dad shrugs, following her from the room.

"I thought it was funny," I tell Owen.

Paula looks furious. "Where did you get those, Octavia?"

Octavia juts out her bottom lip. "Daddy told us to sit on them and make noise."

Paula points to her husband. "Owen, you're ridiculous. Why would you do that at dinner? The extendable utensils are funny but sweeping our kids into the prank with whoopee cushions? Too far this time."

"That was for the tree. They pranked us first." Owen shrugs, pointing at Jamal, Joe, and Ryder. Paula stomps out of the room. "Wait, Paula, it was just a joke."

"And the salt in the water?" Sophia questions him.

"That wasn't me," Owen calls over his shoulder as he runs from the room.

"It was me," Joe says. "That was for last week when Mateo wrapped my car in plastic wrap. It took me an hour to get to work. He needed a *taste* of his own medicine."

"Dinner is ruined. Christmas is ruined." Sophia sighs and drops her head.

"It's not ruined. Let's calm down. Laugh about it. And try to enjoy the rest of dinner. It will be okay. Nothing could get worse, right?" Mason reassures her.

Our Christmas dinner continued thirty minutes later. Everyone sat back at the table again after they quit arguing. There are some lingering glances laced with a sliver of frustration, but everyone made up after disagreeing (for the most part). I don't think Paula has fully forgiven Owen yet. One thing I know for sure: No one in this family stays mad at each other for long. There isn't a holiday that passes by without a prank playing out. Though, I'll admit, Owen really hit the nail on the head with the best prank ever. I don't think it was too far. It was hilarious. And it got the conversation away from wedding planning, which I'm grateful for.

"That is the first and last time you'll ever steal food from my plate in this dining room." Mom points at Owen.

"Yes, ma'am. Sorry, Mom." Owen looks down at his plate to hide the slight curve of his lips. There's no way he's listening. He's bound to do it again.

"Now that's settled," she says. "Olive? When are you planning on blessing us with some grandchildren?"

A part of me would love to rip the tablecloth right from the table after that question. My intrusive thoughts are at an all-time high. I want to throw my plate across the wall and let it shatter into a thousand pieces. Then I'd storm out the door. "I—"

Mason cuts me off and puts his arm around the back of my chair in a protective manner. "I can't believe you just asked her that." *I can.* He grumbles, "We're leaving." He stands.

"I was only kidding. Trying to loosen up the room," Mom says. *Oh she loosened up my anger alright.*

Mason's eyes shrink to slits. "I'd hope so."

"Anyway, the Sternos worked out great this year. I knew it would be a good idea. No warming up food multiple times. This way, it can stay warm for a few hours," Jackie says, changing the subject. It was her idea. The company Ryder works for uses them at events.

"It was a wonderful idea," Sophia says.

Mason slowly lowers himself into his seat. He looks at me, searching my eyes. I can tell he's trying to make sure I'm okay. I nod at him, giving him a half smile. It doesn't seem to appease him fully, but it's enough for his shoulders to relax slightly. He takes my hand under the table and smooths the pad of his thumb over my knuckles. It eases my racing thoughts and lingering agitation. I sigh softly as he turns his head towards me, quirking a brow. My smile grows wider as he tucks a strand of hair behind my ear, sending butterflies through my stomach. I'm so caught up in the moment that I forget we're surrounded by people. Mason has successfully found a way to make everything else disappear. I only feel the warmth from his hand, his small touch dropping from the side of my face. I watch his eyes blink in rapid succession through the frames of his glasses.

Soon enough I lose his gaze and rejoin the table conversations, but this time with reluctance. I'm counting down the minutes until we go back to his place to watch a movie.

Once we're all finished eating and completely full of the main course Mom asks, "Can someone help me put the Sternos out? I can't get the flame to go out."

"Sure. I'll help you, Beth," Jamal says. He tries and fails to put the lid on multiple times; he struggles to put it out. He grabs the Sterno from its slot and tries to move it out from under the tray of food. It spills slightly. "Ow. That's hot," he says as the Sterno pours out even more. The liquid engulfs the cabinet and counter in flames. They shoot across the surface, spreading fast.

"Oh my gosh!" Mom screams.

Dad comes rushing from the other side of the room, as Mateo and Char leave the dining room.

"What do we do? How can we put it out? I don't know what to do!" Mom's frantic as she paces in front of the flames.

I don't know what to do either, so I stay out of the way watching everything unfold.

Jamal runs to the kitchen saying something about looking for a pitcher of water or some flour. The flames shoot higher across the cabinet. Mason pulls the shirt off his back trying to put it out. He slaps it against the counter; his shirt starts to catch fire in the process.

"Shit," he grumbles.

Greta decides now is the perfect opportunity to get a bite to eat. She jumps on the table using a chair and starts devouring Mateo's plate of turkey and stuffing. She gobbles it down as Ryder screams, "Get off the table, Greta! Now!" She doesn't listen and continues scarfing it as fast as she can. He picks her up, and a piece of turkey dangles from her teeth.

Jamal comes rushing into the room and pours a couple of gallons of water over the fire. It stops a little but continues to burn. The paste is thick across the counter. The room is in complete mayhem.

It keeps getting worse. The telescopic utensils, salt water, and my mom's comment were enough to send me over the edge for the day.

"Does anyone have a fire extinguisher?" Jackie yells over the hectic room.

"We do. I don't know where it is," Mom says.

Liam comes back in and scrapes up the paste. He takes it outside, putting out the rest of the lingering flames.

The counter is scorched black from where it was burning. "I don't think the Sternos were a good idea," Mom says.

"Me neither," Hannah says as she looks around the room with widened eyes.

You could hear a pin drop in the dining room. Everyone is quiet as we sit in what I assume is shock. No one says anything for a few minutes. I stare at the scorched counter and replay the crazy events in my mind.

My mom starts to laugh, cutting the tension and unwavering silence. We all begin laughing. "Life's too short to be mad over something that was an accident. This will be a holiday we'll never forget."

She's right. I will never be able to wipe this memory from my head. That's for sure.

Chapter 28

OLIVE

"When you said we were going to eat until our pants were blowing buttons, I didn't think you would take it seriously," Mason says while taking the last bite of a slice of pumpkin pie. The chill of a breeze blows in from the open window after the fire catastrophe.

"When have I ever bluffed?" I question him.

"Never," he admits through a sigh.

I lean my head back. "You might have to carry me to the car. I ate so much that I can't walk."

"You and I both. You can carry me." He slouches against the back of his chair.

I finish the last bite of my pie, and my eyes snap to his face. "There is no way I can carry you, silly!"

"You fling around sacks of flour like nothing every day. What's the difference?" He laces his fingers and stretches them behind his head.

"They are fifty pounds. Not two hundred. I may be able to drop you to the floor with a wrestling move, but I won't lift you." I double over laughing.

"There's a first time for everything. And I'm probably sitting closer to two hundred-fifty for how much we just ate."

"So, definitely not happening. You can carry me." I shrug playfully.

"Fine. Climb aboard," he teases by outstretching his arms and smiles.

Mason's grin is devastatingly charming. I almost want to jump into his strong arms just to be closer to him.

I flutter my eyelashes. "Why, that's mighty fine of you to offer your *services,* my Knight. But I think I'll walk."

"Suit yourself." He shrugs and lowers his arms.

I'm kicking myself for passing up the opportunity. But we have to say goodbye to our families that are currently watching TV in the living room before we go. Plus, I don't want Mason to hold me for that long.

We say our goodbyes and hop in Mason's truck with Moose on our tail. Moose pouts on the way out of the door, looking at Greta like she's the love of his life. It breaks my heart to separate them. But I have had enough social interactions for the day, especially after Owen's grand stunt at dinner. Not to mention, the counter literally caught on fire. It was a recipe for disaster. At least I can say the night kept me on my toes.

I thought I'd be able to say it was the first holiday where no one prodded or pushed either one of us into a conversation about settling down. Or missing our window of opportunity. Or anything like that. It was a foolish way of thinking. They still continued with other avenues.

One good thing came out of dinner: I realized I sort of like being in a fake relationship with Mason. I could get used to it. He stood up for me when my mom questioned me in front of everyone about "blessing" them with grandchildren. But that's what Mason does. He always stands up for me. This time it felt different, though. Maybe it's because of the unspoken thing lingering between us. Neither of us addressed our kiss yesterday. The kiss was toe-curling, and I still don't know what to think about it.

Now, in the cab, it's silent. We're both a little on edge. It's awkward, and I don't like it. Nor do I want anything to change what we've had for so long. He's my best friend—my partner in crime. The silence is palpable. He drums his fingers on the steering wheel. I look out the fogged-glass of my window to watch the snow-covered trees fly by, lit by nothing other than the soft moonlight. The heat from the vent is blowing a steady stream of hot air. Moose's head is between our seats from the rear of the cab; I pet his fur.

I decide to break the silence and get what's bothering me off my chest. I was never one for bottling things up. Confront it now, and figure the rest out later. Or regret it later. "Let's talk about the elephant in the room."

"There's no elephant in the truck with us." He tilts the right corner of his mouth.

"I know." I place my palm against my forehead. "That kiss yesterday."

His grip on the steering wheel tightens. "What about it?"

"It didn't make things weird between us, did it? You would tell me if it did, right?"

He sighs a soft and shaky breath. "No, Olive, it didn't make anything weird. I would've told you."

I look out the window. "Okay—"

I have a hard time believing his answer. His iron grip on the steering wheel says otherwise. He's never so vague or fidgety. I've come to learn the little things he does when deflecting.

He pulls the truck into his driveway, shutting off the engine. The porch light is the only thing illuminating the way to the front door. He walks around to my side and opens the door for me. Once we're inside, I hang up my coat, hat, and gloves on the hooks next to the door. I open the fridge and pull out a carton of eggnog while Mason grabs some firewood and throws it into the wood stove on top of coals. Moose runs to the front of the wood stove to lay in his favorite spot.

I fill two glasses, adding a shot of bourbon in each. I hand Mason his, and I take a sip of mine. It burns going down my throat.

Mason drags the ottoman to the front of the couch. We both get comfortable, and Moose lies next to us. Mason drapes his arm around me, and I lean back against his side.

"Today was really nice. For the most part. Except for the questioning and counter catching on fire. I lost my favorite shirt." He tries and fails to sound somber.

"It was." I giggle. "You could do without one shirt. You have plenty that look awfully similar." I flick on the television to put on the movie we watch every year.

His eyes flicker from the screen to me. He tucks a strand of hair behind my ear. It zaps my senses. "Wait here. I have something for you."

I completely forgot about his gift. I'm glad I put it in his truck. I set down my drink, throw on my coat, and grab it quickly from outside. He's already waiting for me, sitting on the couch. I shrug my coat, dim the lights, and sit next to him.

The fire crackles as large snowflakes float past the windows. The small tree in the corner is covered with twinkling multicolored bulbs. Christmas music plays from the movie. The faint smell of wood smoke is relaxing, as Mason shifts and looks at me nervously. He grips the present close to his chest.

"Here." He hands me a box wrapped in festive paper. I can tell he wrapped it himself, and it makes my heart so warm.

We don't need to exchange gifts, but we do so regardless. The only gift I need, I already have. It's the best one of all—the gift of Mason in my life.

"I got this for you." I place the small bag in his hand. We both tear into our presents. The fire reflects a glow over his features, and he smirks once he sees what I got him.

"I love it." He turns the knight figurine over in his hands. "It will look nice on the mantle. That way I'll see it every day and think of you."

His words melt my heart. "I thought you would. It's a reminder of who you are. Always the protector of those you love."

I pry open the box to see a wooden bowl with a spiral carved into the side with two holes. The wood is dark, smooth, and polished to a shine. I can almost see my reflection in it. I flip it over, and my name is carved into the bottom.

It's beautiful.

My eyes begin to water, and I glance up at him. "Did you make this?"

"Yes. For your yarn. It's a yarn bowl holder," he says, like it's no big deal. It is a big deal to me. "I got a wood lathe."

Mason doesn't even realize—this is the sweetest thing he's ever done. If he wanted to win my heart, he accomplished it.

"When did you get a wood lathe?" I ask.

He pushes back his hair. "I bought it off Dustin's grandfather. He wasn't using it anymore. He taught me how to turn wooden bowls so I could make this for you."

My eyes continue to fight the urge to cry. "Let me get this straight. You bought a wood lathe. Spent the time learning how to make things on it... just so you could make me a yarn bowl for Christmas?"

He looks at his lap shyly. "Yeah."

"This is so nice." A few tears form in the corners of my eyes. "Thank you." I pull him into a hug. His touch is warm and inviting. So much has shifted for me since we've kissed.

I can't believe he made me this. I love the yarn bowl more than I thought I could love any gift. I don't deserve Mason. He's too good for me. My heart skips in my chest at the realization.

Who does this for someone that's only a friend?

That's who he is though. Mason is caring and thoughtful. He spent his limited free time learning how to use a wood lathe to make it. I'll cherish this gift forever.

I wrap my arms around him tighter.

"Don't cry," he whispers into my hair. Mason holds me tightly against him.

"I'm only crying because I'm so happy."

How did I get this lucky? He is the most wonderful, caring, and observant person I've ever met.

He wipes a tear from under my eye with the pad of his thumb. "I guess it's okay since you're happy. I just don't like to see you cry."

I can't help but cry when he goes and does something so grand. This Christmas is wonderful because of Mason. My favorite part about today is this moment. The sparkling lights. Our annual Christmas movie playing in the background. Moose's soft snoring next to us. What could be better?

I shift to lean my head on his shoulder, and we slouch against the back of the couch, watching the movie.

"I got you something else!" I blurt.

His gaze is soft when I turn to look at him. "You didn't have to."

I wanted to. "It's for both of us. You'll see tomorrow."

His brow crinkles. "Should I be concerned?"

My voice is chipper when I reply, "No. You should be excited!"

"I can't wait then." *Me neither.*

Chapter 29

OLIVE

"Please keep your hands over your eyes," I beg Mason.

"I can hear the chickens. I know where we're headed," he states.

"Why don't you play along then? Humor me. It was supposed to be a surprise."

"I'll start over." He clears his throat, and his voice is higher with an elated tone. "Where are you taking me, Olive? I can't wait to find out where we're going!"

I beam with a smile he can't see. "Now that's the spirit! Perfect excitement level."

I steady Mason to the back of the chicken coop, and I open the door. I'm so excited for him to see what I got. I can't contain it any longer. I want to jump for joy and burst into happy tears.

His tone is wary as he says, "That sounds like a lot of chirping."

"You can uncover your eyes now," I say.

He stands there speechless, mouth agape, staring at the chickens.

"What do you think? Do you like them?" I bounce on the heels of my feet and crouch down to pick up one of the adorable chicks.

"How many did you get?"

"Twenty. Why?" I look up at him, and my smile falls. "What's wrong?"

"Nothing." He shakes his head and scratches his chin.

"You look. Well, I don't know how you look. Your face is blank."

"That's a lot of chickens, Firefly." He gulps.

"Is it too many?" I pet the chick's head, and I smile admiring how adorable they are. "I'm going to name you Fluffy—look at how cute they are." I hold out Fluffy to Mason.

"No." He sighs. "They're adorable. I've never had Bantam chickens before. Look at their feathered feet."

"I know, right?" I look at him with wide eyes. "Is this the best present ever?"

"Yes. We'll have to add some more egg boxes." He nods, taking a moment to marinate in his thoughts. "But the more chickens the merrier."

"Do you mean it?" I question with an elated tone.

He runs his fingers over his mustache. "Yes. But you're going to help me take care of them?"

"I already was and now there are more to run around town. The townies can name the rest, but Fluffy is my favorite one."

He picks up a chick. It looks so small in his large palm, and he smiles brightly.

I stare at his features. He's so handsome. I don't know why I didn't notice it before. If I did, I didn't let myself really look at him. His thick trimmed beard. Those glasses, fitting his face perfectly. The creases at the corners of his lips as he smiles. And his devastatingly cute dimples. The gruffness of his voice. The glint in his eyes.

Ugh! Get a grip on yourself, Olive! You're in a fake relationship.
Fake being the key word.

Chapter 30

MASON

"Good morning," I announce to the chickens when I open the coop door. I grab a drill from the tool belt around my waist and take out the few screws holding the wooden door. I screw on the new automatic one and hook up the solar panel. It's Sunday, so I finally have a chance to do a few things I've been putting off.

The chickens peck the snow in their run and gulp on water from the refillable system. I test out the automatic door; it works smoothly. I leave it open, so the chickens can wander the town through the day. I walk along the path back to the bar, preparing myself for a long day of work. There are only three more days until New Year's Day. So, the preparations start today.

And only four more days until Olive and I are done *dating*.

I open the back door and get hit with the sound of people. There was no one here when I left to install the door. Violet and Dustin are standing on A-frame ladders, stringing fishing lines along the ceiling. Olive is standing behind the bar with a clipboard. She taps a pen on the board while talking to a group of townies. Each one scurries off as she tells them what to do. At least, that's what I'm assuming.

I walk to her once everyone disperses. "What in the world is going on here?"

She jumps in place and looks up from her clipboard. "Oh, good, you're here."

"This *is* my bar," I reply matter-of-factly.

"Thank you for the observation. Do you remember the favor I owed you?"

What favor? Olive doesn't owe me anything.

"No? Should I?" I cross my arms.

"You helped me decorate The Olive Bean for the holidays. It was about time I repaid the favor. I was grabbing all the decorations out of the back room of my shop when Bobbie showed up to question me. Of course she did. As an honorary gossip mill member, she has to. I explained my idea and asked if she wanted to help. The news spread by mouth after I told her... or by a single text to the *source*. The source, also known as Constance, posted on the social page asking if anyone wanted to pitch in. That's when the whole town showed up."

"You did this in the thirty minutes it took me to fix the chicken coop?"

"It was nothing." *Nothing.* This woman just gathered an entire entourage to transform the bar. And she thought it was nothing?

"I could kiss you," I say and cover my mouth. Her eyes light up and her cheeks pinken.

"Save it for later, *boyfriend*. We have decorations to put up, drink deliveries to inventory, and coffee to make for these lovely people."

"You're right. What can I do, *boss*?"

"For starters... you can get behind the bar and show me where the coffee maker is. It'd be easier to make it here than to go back to my shop and start everything up."

"I have one under here." I crouch down to open the cabinet doors underneath the counter, sliding around the napkins and boxes full of straws. "Ah! Here it is." I pull out the one pot maker, coffee pot, ground coffee, and filters. I haven't broken this out in years. I had no reason to when I could acquire the best coffee right down the street.

Even if the coffee wasn't any good, I would still go there to see Olive. Guilty as charged.

"I can work with this," she says. "Although, I'll need to scrub off the layer of dust and see if this baby will fire up some coffee."

"Okay, Firefly. Work your wonders."

"I will, Knight, don't even think about doubting my talents." Her brow raises.

I put my hands up. "I wouldn't dare. What now?"

"Can you grab some mugs? I brought a bag of my homemade strawberry pop tarts, so we'll need some plates too."

"I would do anything for those pop tarts. You should've started with that."

"If I'd started with that, you wouldn't have heard me saying anything else." She knows me too well.

"Thank you for helping. You don't know how much I needed it."

"I do. That's why I'm here now. I don't want you getting any migraines from the stress. Even if you do, tell me, okay?" Olive says this quietly, so that no one hears her.

"I will. I promise."

I head towards the kitchen and grab a stack of saucers.

I could kiss you. Why did I say that? Sometimes the words leave my mouth faster than I have time to think. Seeing her blush gave me a shred of hope. A shred that's going to mess with my mind.

Bobbie passes by with a smile when I leave the kitchen.

I needed help today. Somehow—without me saying any-thing—Olive knew. She has a way with knowing me better than I know myself. The bar will be ready in record time, and I'll have time to breathe once the day's over. My chest swells with gratitude. This town. These folks. They'd do anything to help each other, and it shows.

"I'd like to make a toast." Everyone quiets down around the bar. Vintage style bulbs and streamers hang from the ceiling. Christmas trees left over from around town sit in each corner with little *Happy New Year* decals. Each one is covered with bulbs matching the ceiling. Everything is decorated with Olive's vision in mind. Leaving a timeless look that matches the antique signs fastened along the walls. The bar is glowing, but it's the faces around the room melting my heart. Everyone looks so proud to have lent a hand.

"I couldn't have done this without you all." I look around the room. My family, Olive's family, Constance, Jane, Vivi, and Dustin. Everyone I love and care about is here. "You can thank Olive for organizing today. The bar looks phenomenal. The camaraderie in our little town is remarkable. I never expected to show up today with so many people lending a hand. Thank you all again. A free round of drinks on New Year's Eve for everyone who helped today." They cheer and clap.

Constance walks over to me while people start to file out. "Today was a great success, wouldn't you say?"

"Yes, it was. I couldn't have done it without you." *Even though you drive us all nuts.* "I appreciate your help."

"No need to thank me. I have nothing better to do at this time of year. There isn't much commotion in town. Everything slows down in winter. When the tourists start coming. They give me plenty to write about."

Thirty articles posted in the past few weeks say differently. What do I know?

"Anyhow, I needed to talk to you somewhere quiet. I have a few things I want to say to you alone. Without any prying eyes."

Oh dear God, what is it now?

"I don't have much time," I grumble.

She tucks a strand of gray hair behind her ear. "I only need a minute of your time."

"I'll meet you in my office in a few minutes," I say and adjust my glasses.

I spot Olive behind the bar cleaning up, and I make my way to her. Fuming with each step.

I blurt, "What does Constance want, Firefly? Did you have something to do with this?"

"Woah! Calm down. What do you mean? How would I know what in the world is going on in her head?" Olive asks, looking perplexed.

"I thought maybe you had something to do with it. It came out of nowhere. She wants to talk to me *alone* about something." I suppress a groan.

"*Ha! Alone!* Funny for you to think I would have anything to do with her scheming. I have no part in her dramatics. Go see what she wants. I'm curious now." She stares off in the direction of my office, watching Constance entering the door and shutting it behind her.

"Thank you. I want no parts of it either."

"But you're already involved. It's too late to save you." She chuckles, covering her mouth.

"This isn't funny." I back away towards my office.

"Oh, but it is." She sticks her tongue out. "Good luck in there. Take one for the team!"

I grin. Olive never fails to make me laugh, even though I'm dreading sitting in my office alone with the town's gossip mill executive. I have to filter myself around her. I never know what little thing she'll draw a story from until it's too late. And then *poof,* there's a lengthy 2,000-word article written about your deepest, darkest secrets.

I open the door to my office hesitantly. I grip the handle loosely and twist it, releasing the latch. My cool-and-collected restraint is waning, as I push open the door.

Constance is sitting at *my* desk. In *my* chair. It's becoming very difficult to keep my composure.

Calm. Calm. Stay Calm. She wants to get to you. Don't let her get to you, Mason.

"Mason. Glad you showed up. Have a seat." She motions to the chair across from my desk. The one I normally have other people sit in when they come into *my* office.

This has to be a power tactic. Constance is in charge; she's proving her self-appointed *authority*.

"Is this an interrogation?" I ask. This has to be. I feel like I'm at the therapist or some kind of appointment where I'm the client who paid for the service I'm about to receive. The only thing I'm receiving is a load of cow manure. In my own bar. Let me reiterate that. This better be some kind of prank.

"No. No. Nothing like that, dear." She sets her glasses on her nose. It's getting serious. "It's about Olive."

"What about Olive? Is something wrong?" I take a seat across from her. Might as well play into the charade.

"No. Nothing's wrong. Will you just let me talk? You haven't let me get a word in." I nod. Although in my mind I want to tell her, *Get out of my office.* But I hold it in for the sake of keeping my name out of a messy article. Plus, she did help decorate today. So, I can't go being rude to someone that helped me when I needed it. "I fear you are losing the very small window you have left to tell her how you really feel."

What the heck? What is she talking about?

"We're dating. I don't know what you mean by that." I look everywhere but her eyes. How would she know we aren't?

"Do you really think I fell for the whole *'we're dating?'*" She puts her hands in air quotes. "Olive looked devastated as soon as I mentioned the Cookie Chronicles was for couples only. And you jumped in like the hero you always are for her. It was so predictable. So, if you think I didn't catch on, you're in la-la land."

I press my hand to my chest. "It hurts me that you'd think we're not. I'm highly offended."

"Oh, cut the crap. If you won't admit it, I'll tell you anyway."

Ouch. Someone's impatient.

"Innocent until proven guilty." I shrug.

"The girls, Bobbie and Annie, and I made the Cookie Chronicles up for one sole purpose. Do you know what that purpose was?"

"I don't know." I do know. But it's more fun to make her explain to see if my suspicions are true.

"To force you and Olive into a forced proximity trope—"

"What in the hell are tropes?"

She rolls her eyes. "I guess you don't read books. Let me finish explaining, and maybe it'll come together for you. Just like in all the romance novels we read, there are tropes: friends to lovers, enemies to lovers, and my favorite—forced proximity where two people are forced to work together towards a common goal and fall in love in the process. We knew it would work. And for a little while, we thought it did. Best of all, you kept the ruse going for your families. But I caught on to you. You've got that pining look. The one you only do when Olive isn't noticing. You love her. I know it. You know it. But the most important person that needs to hear it and see it, doesn't. So... this is an *intervention*. Not an interrogation. Do with it what you will. But don't make the wrong choice, or this may be your last opportunity. I'm not coming to your rescue again. This is your *last* chance. Last!" She gets up from her chair and storms out; the door slams shut with a loud thud.

I stare at the wall for what feels like forever. For all the nonsense Constance spews... she's right about something. *For once.* It pains me to acknowledge it.

If I lose my chance to say something, I may never get it again. I'm a fool either way. In a perfect world where we didn't have a lifetime of friendship at stake, I could tell Olive how I feel.

My thoughts swirl in my mind. Seconds and minutes tick by until I hear a knock on the door. It doesn't make me flinch. I sit grounded to the spot in the same chair that Constance left me in. I don't look away from the wood paneled walls as I hear footsteps.

"It's me... Mason, are you still here? Everyone's gone." Olive's voice rings in my ear drums.

"Yeah, come on in." My voice comes out scratchy.

"Why are you sitting there?" Olive rushes to my side. I place my hand on my temple, massaging out the worries in my head. To no avail. "What did Constance say? Do you have a migraine?"

"She just wanted to know some information so she can post an article about what drinks the bar will be serving on New Year's Eve. No migraine. Don't worry about me."

"Oh—okay. Is everything alright?" Her voice is laced with worry.

"Everything's fine," I say and force a tiny smile.

I wish it were. I wish I could say, *it's fine,* and mean it.

Chapter 31

OLIVE

"Come in!" I yell over the music blaring through the speakers in my apartment.

"Hey!" Vivi walks in carrying bags on her arm. Sardine, Tuxedo, and Fiona are on leashes. "I brought the necessities and my cats."

I turn down the music using the remote. "So, that means candy, yarn, and books?"

"Exactly." She unclips their leashes. The cats take long strides to me as they hop on the couch.

"Do you need any help?" I ask while petting Sardine and Tuxedo. Fiona jumps to sit at the foot of the couch. After a few seconds, she starts to fall asleep. The trip here must have been exhausting for her. "You two are adorable." My voice reaches a higher pitch. Sardine and Tuxedo purr loudly in appreciation.

"Nope. I can handle it."

"You didn't bring me any chocolate bunnies this time?"

Sardine jumps from the couch and hops on the stand next to the fish tank. He watches my betta fish swim while Tuxedo falls asleep on my lap.

She rolls her eyes. "No. They obviously aren't in season right now. But even if they were, I wouldn't allow you within inches, let alone five feet of them."

She never got over the time I tackled her over the chocolate bunnies she got before Easter from The Valley Harvest. She took them from me because *it's mean to eat them.* Her words, not mine. So, I tackled her John Cena style. All is fair in chocolate and war. That's the saying, right? No? *Too bad.* I changed it because I like it better that way. Suits me just fine.

"Sorry, not sorry about that," I say.

"Mhmm. I knew you weren't sorry."

"Oh, crap!" Vivi shouts as she stumbles over a ball of yarn and catches herself. "That was a close one."

"Maybe I should clean up so you don't fall." I laugh.

Sardine pounces to the floor and plays with the yarn.

"No way. You don't have to clean up for me. I can't help but be clumsy. Even if there was nothing on the floor, I'd still trip."

I rake my hands over my forehead. "Don't I know it."

"Hey!" Vivi retorts. "I can't help it." She shrugs and grabs a few bowls, filling them with assorted candy: chocolates, gummy worms, and jolly ranchers. It's a sweet addict's wet dream. "Where do you want the yarn?"

"You can put it in the yarn bowl right there." I point to the end table covered with ramekins. Each is filled with crochet hooks, scissors, and needles. They sit on crocheted place mats. "Thanks for picking it up for me. I didn't want to leave my apartment today. I practically slept most of the morning."

"No problem. I was grabbing our books in Cat's & Novels anyway." She drops the yarn ball in the bowl. "Wait? Is this what Mason made you for Christmas?"

"Yes. Do you like it?"

"Oh my God! It's beautiful. The wood is so polished." She picks it up and examines it. "That was really sweet of him."

"I know." I sigh dreamily while petting Tuxedo.

"Do you want to read the romance novel or the thriller?" She brings over the candy bowls and sets them on the coffee table.

"I'm feeling a good romance for a change."

"Ooh! Does that mean what I think it means?" She sits down next to me on my mustard yellow couch and tucks her feet under her legs. She hands me the romance book with a couple on the front.

"Honestly, I don't know what it means."

Sardine takes the end of the yarn with him as he jumps onto the fish tank stand once more. He swats at the glass, following Jaws, yarn hanging from his mouth. Everywhere the fish swims, Sardine tilts his head and tracks Jaws like clockwork.

"Do tell. Don't hold anything back on me."

"You better watch out for Sardine. Jaws might attack. He already took out his roommate."

Vivi laughs. "I think it might be the opposite. But Sardine and Jaws will be fine. The tank's cover makes it impossible for either to get to each other." Vivi reaches into a candy bowl and takes a handful. "Please don't leave me in suspense. Fill me in."

"I don't know—I think I might be starting to form some feelings for Mason. More than friend feelings. After we kissed, my mind was fuzzy. All I can think—all I dream about—is his lips on mine. And how it felt to be held. He treats me so well too. The yarn bowl. He learned a whole new skill to make something for *me*. It was the grandest thing anyone has ever done. Am I being silly? Please tell me I'm being silly."

She shakes her head quickly. "No! You aren't! Hold up. Did you just say you kissed? Since when? You didn't tell me."

"I didn't have a chance to. I forgot. We've both had so much going on. But yeah, on Christmas Eve. All of his sisters and their husbands were there. I overheard his sisters talking about how they didn't buy us as a couple. So I told him to kiss me."

"How was the kiss?" She puts a palm on her chin and crosses her legs on the couch.

I sigh wistfully, and I close my eyes for a moment, replaying the feeling in my head. "It was—out of this world. Toe-curling. Electrifying. Out-of-a-movie good. I don't think I'll recover. He set the bar way too high on first kisses for me."

Vivi taps her chin and lights up. "Maybe you should give it a shot. A *real* relationship."

My voice deflates. "I don't know. I like being single. There are no complications. Chad ruined relationships for me."

She scoffs. "Are you seriously going to let Chad stop you from being happy?"

"No," I say with as much confidence as I can. *At least I'm trying not to.*

Her expression turns into one of relief. "Good, because how many times do I have to tell you that his name is Chad? I think the name speaks for itself."

She has a point.

"Yeah, that's true. It does. I learned a lot of important lessons with him." I chuckle.

She nods in agreement. "The number one lesson: *Never* trust someone named Chad." She flips open her book. "So, back to Mason. Are you going to try it for real?"

"I don't know," I say, looking down at the book in my hands. I'm still so conflicted. I shift my legs on the couch, careful not to disturb the sleeping cat.

Her expression softens. "Just think about it. You don't have to make any decisions. I see the way he looks at you."

A line forms between my brows. "And how does he look at me?"

She smiles. "Like he's in love with you. He has for a while."

"Oh." I've never noticed. Maybe it's because I haven't opened myself up to the possibility.

"Yeah." Vivi's voice is soft.

Sardine runs into my bedroom, yarn in tow, making us laugh out loud. Tuxedo leaves my lap and follows him around with different colors of yarn. Within thirty minutes my floor is a yarn art board. All the while, Fiona is still fast asleep.

Vivi and I read in silence. When I'm a few chapters in—and the heroine's shut out all ideas of love—I feel as if I'm the one in her shoes. There's this unnerving connection forming between us both. Did Vivi pick out this book on purpose knowing I'd choose it? My gaze wanders to her. She's engrossed in her story: nose tipped, pages flipping, and popping candy. She couldn't have. But if she did... it was smart. She knew she couldn't convince me to give him a chance. I'm too stubborn. I needed to see it on my own terms.

Is this what I'm doing? Shutting out Mason?

My mind's reeling with questions. I don't know the answers to many of them.

Chapter 32

MASON

"Hey, man. Thanks for coming." Dustin greets me as I open the barn door.

"No problem. I don't mind helping out." I push my hair back and slide a ball cap over my head.

"Good, because I need plenty of it. The cows need hay; the goats need milking. Vivi's spending the day with Olive. So, I'm on my own. I'm glad, though. She needs a break. She's constantly running between her flower shop and helping on the farm. She's gotta be exhausted."

"Olive needs the break too. She's been non-stop helping me with the bar and running her coffee shop."

I could probably use a break too. I'm sure Dustin could as well.

I'll get one eventually, but helping on the farm is like a day off for me. The fresh air. Some time away from the bar, responsibilities, and the small town gossip. I'm free to think out here without any distractions. It clears my head.

"Thanks again for helping get the bar ready for New Year's Eve. It helped a lot." I've been meaning to thank him but didn't get a chance yesterday.

"What are friends for? We help each other." Dustin grabs the keys to the tractor off the hook. "You're unusually quiet today." He observes.

"Got a lot on my mind." I scratch the back of my head.

"Olive?" His brow lifts.

I chuckle. "How'd you know?"

"Because I've been in your shoes. It feels like déjà vu. Not too long ago you were giving me advice to be patient with Vivi. To let everything work itself out. It did. Just like you said. Now here we are. It's coming full circle." He makes a circle motion with his hand.

"So what's your advice, oh wise one?" I wonder out loud.

He grins and flips me off. He climbs up on the tractor. "Go for it. Tell her you love her. That you want a go at a real relationship. She's oblivious, but it couldn't hurt. Damn the consequences."

"I don't know," I say with uncertainty laced in my words.

"If you don't say something now you never will." He closes the door and starts the engine, pulling from the barn. I hop into the side-by-side and follow him through the pasture. I veer off towards the goat barn.

I scratch my head with my free hand. I don't know if I'm willing to tell her. What if I do... and she doesn't feel the same way? What if it makes things awkward, and then our friendship changes forever?

I don't want to lose what we have. She's always been my friend. After I tell her, what if she doesn't want to be friends anymore? I shake my head, no... Olive wouldn't stop being friends with me because of me loving her. She's not like that. She loves me in her own way—platonically. It'll make things different. That's for sure. But she wouldn't throw me to the curb and never look back.

Damn, all I keep saying is what if?

But what I need to be asking myself is: what if she felt the same way?

I'll never know if I keep quiet.

I drive through the open field. Globs of snow land on the windshield. Everything is covered in white—the trees in the distance and the grass under my tires. I park in front of the goat barn and open the doors.

Dustin's right about something. Constance said the same thing too. If I don't say something now, I never will. Damn the consequences. I'm going to tell Olive I love her.

I'm in love with her. It's time I quit hiding it. I've been in love with her for years.

It could all come crashing down. I could end up losing a lifetime of friendship.

If I don't risk it, I'll never know.

Those will be my final words. I'm sure of it. Eight words to my downfall.

Chapter 33

OLIVE

There's so much snow. It came out of nowhere. The forecast started out at only a few inches. Now there are six and counting. It wouldn't be so bad if it weren't for the fact I have to shovel the sidewalk by hand. Where is a snow blower when you need it? As if the universe decided now is the perfect time for my dreams to come true in a snap. They do. My knight in shining armor appears out of thin air, pushing a snow blower down the sidewalk.

"Sweetie Pie! Why are you shoveling the sidewalk? That's my job!" Mason shouts over the sound of the engine. As he gets closer, he revs it down and takes the shovel from me.

"Hey! I was trying to get this place cleaned up so people could use the sidewalk and not have to trek through snow to get to the bar."

"That's my job. You have me to do it for you."

I put my hands on my hips. "I don't need anyone to do things for me. I have two hands. I'm perfectly capable."

He grabs my hands and swings them back and forth in his. "I know you're fully capable of anything. But let me help you."

I blow out a breath. "Fine." He tickles my armpits, and I giggle. "Stop!" I protest against his continuous tickling. "Please, I can't take any more." I wiggle out of his hold, but he continues to try and torture me.

I push him on top of the mound of snow I piled, and I land on top of him.

I tickle him back and poke his nose. Between breaths he says, "Careful, Firefly, you're making me want to kiss you."

I blush. *Kiss me then,* I want to say but I don't. Instead, I let him go. "Let's call it a truce. I can salt behind you as you plow."

"We have a deal." We shake on it. I can feel the buzz of tingles when our hands meet through our gloves. It's becoming more difficult to fight the attraction that's been growing out of nowhere.

The bar is booming with live music, laughter, and the clinking of glasses. It smells like fried food, grease, and beer. The perfect combination if you ask me. I left my hair down with a piece braided around the side, secured by a million and one bobby pins. I opted for some mascara and silver eyeshadow. I wanted to look special for tonight. New year, new Olive. My black boots are perfectly paired with my faded jeans and leather jacket. I wore a pink shirt under my coat with the words "Happy New Year" written across it. I was going for fierce yet colorful. I think I nailed it.

"We're over here, Olive!" Vivi waves me over from a table with Jackie, Hannah, Char, Paula, and Oakley.

"Where are the guys?" I ask.

"They went to grab us some drinks," Oakley says. Her gaze is focused on her fiancé as he walks to the bar counter.

"I can't believe the year is almost over!" Hannah exclaims.

"Me neither." Jackie lets out a long breath. "It went so fast. And our kids are growing faster than weeds sprout in spring. I guess time flies when you're having a good time."

"I'm eager for this one to be in the world," Char says, rubbing her stomach. "I can't wait to meet him or her in a week or so."

"It will be in no time," Jackie replies. "You're getting extremely close to your due date."

"Yeah. The baby is healthy and happy. Only a matter of time." Paula is steadfast in her reply.

"I'm grateful you're by my side." Char puts her hand on Paula's. "I feel a lot better that a doctor is with me practically everywhere I go." Char laughs and rests her other arm on the wooden table.

"Me too," Mateo says as he comes up from behind Char with the other guys. He rests his head on Char's shoulder and kisses her cheek.

"I want to dance," Hannah says. She whisks Joe off to the dance floor. He's smitten as she runs towards the band. Dress flowing and heels clicking against the tiled floor with each step.

"Olive, would you like to hit the dance floor?" Mason out-stretches his hand. "I have a few minutes."

"Well of course, dearest. I would love to." I shoot him an amused smile. I grab his fingers.

"You look beautiful, Sweetie Pie," Mason whispers into my ear.

His breath makes goosebumps prickle my arms. I blush under his admiring gaze. "Thank you!" I manage to blurt, voice cracking. My heart pounds wildly in my chest.

Once we find our way onto the dance floor next to Hannah and Joe, Mason twirls me around. The Thornwood Valley Heart-breakers play a cover of the song "We Danced" by Brad Paisley. We sway back and forth to the smooth sound of Chuck's voice (the singer of the cover band and Constance's husband). My feet move perfectly in time with Mason's. We settle into a slow rhythm.

He tucks a strand of hair behind my ear. "You look beautiful tonight. I wasn't kidding," he rasps. I blush under the heat of his gaze and the sincerity behind his gruff words.

"Thank you. You clean up nice too." I smile in reply. He's wearing his signature black shirt and jeans. But he looks different tonight. Lighter. Happier. I can't pinpoint it. He looks handsome with the owl tattoo peeking from the edge of his T-shirt. His arms wrap around my waist, pulling me close against him.

His breath is warm against my ear when he says, "I love being your fake boyfriend."

I don't give myself a chance to think. I blurt the first words that come to mind. "I love being your fake girlfriend!"

I do. I meant what I said. I never thought I would enjoy being in a relationship again. But Mason gives me a whisper of hope. Maybe this might not end tonight. It's only the beginning.

The song changes to one with a more upbeat tempo. We hold each other still in place. I sigh when he lets me go. My heart beats wildly against my chest.

"I have to serve some drinks. If you need anything at all, let me know. Meet me at midnight, here, in the same spot," Mason says.

Midnight. A New Year's Eve kiss. I'm almost certain it's what he's implying. It would make sense. We're a couple to everyone else; it's what people do when they're together. When the clock strikes the new year, they share a kiss to embrace a future, solidifying a strong relationship.

He saunters off, and I'm left reeling. What if Vivi's right? What if I could give this a real shot? What if things didn't have to end tonight like we planned? We could make it real.

I run to the bathroom to fix my makeup after my racing mind dies down. I dig through my purse and pull out a makeup palette.

I touch up my silver eyelids with a few swipes of my finger. I dig through my Mary Poppins purse again to find a tube of mascara. I apply it slowly, carefully brushing it through my lashes so I don't smear any against my skin. I watch my reflection in the mirror. My lips are curled upward; it's an out of body experience. I'm unconsciously smiling. My cheeks are rosy, and my face glows. I'm in awe of my ability to exude mirth.

I'm absolutely delirious... but in a good way. I've never felt so giddy. I shove everything back into my purse and pull it over my shoulder. I check myself one more time, smoothing down some unruly curls.

Chapter 34

Olive

When I exit the bathroom, a voice to the side of me stops me dead in my tracks. My smile falls to a thin line and turns into a frown at the recognition. It's the voice of the man I threw a cup of coffee all over. It was an iced coffee—for clarification purposes. But I wouldn't be opposed to using coffee a little warmer or even boiling right about now. I would do it again if I had to because I'm the one boiling.

"Hey Olive," Chad says again, slurring his words.

I heard you the first time. I chose to ignore you.

For crying out loud.

"What do you want?" I hiss through clenched teeth. "You won't stop texting and now this?"

I'm on edge in his presence. He wants nothing but to rile me up.

"We never had a real chance to work things out. Give us one more chance—please. I'll change for you. I'll quit hesitating and ask you to marry me this time. We dreamed of a life together. Mason and you aren't going to last." He sways on his feet a little.

"No. You'll never change. I've moved on. There's no more *us*. The second we broke up to take some time *off* and figure things out, you started dating other people. But that was the best thing you could've done. It made me realize we weren't meant to be. And that's okay."

"Come on, Olive, we had so many good times together. We would hang out at the diner. At the bar. All the late nights planning our future under the stars. You said you loved me."

I swallow and sigh heavily. "What are you not getting Chad? Yes, we had some good times. Yes, I once loved you. I'm grateful for what I learned about myself when we were together. But there was also so much *bad*. So much overshadowed the good. You and I weren't meant to be. You didn't want to do anything I liked," I retort. "You hated hiking. You despised my crocheting. You couldn't stand my *messy* house. It wasn't messy. It just didn't fit your so-called *normal* appearance. You wanted to put me in a box. To hide me from the world. To strip me of my light. My colors faded when we were together. I wasn't myself. I pretended to be someone you needed. Now that I'm finally happy with Mason and embracing who I am, you want to tear it away from me? Do you want to see me as a shell of myself again? Does that please you, Chad?"

Chad grabs my arm. I can tell he's obviously had too much to drink. "Just give me a chance." His eyes plead with me.

But no one touches me without permission. "Get. Your. Grimy. Hands. Off. Me." I grit through my teeth. "Before I rip your arm out of its socket. You know I'm not bluffing."

He grabs on tighter. I twist his arm sideways and he screams. His yell in protest reverberates in my ears.

"Dammit!" he bellows. "That hurts!"

Good. I could do much worse. Test me more, asshole.

Just as I am about to flip him on his ass. Mason grabs Chad by the shirt and pushes him against the wall. He yells in his face, "Don't you ever touch her again! Do you hear me?" Mason pulls back a fist and it lands straight at his jaw. It connects loudly, crunching in the now silent bar. I could hear a pin drop until his punch made contact. A few gasps filtered around the room. "If you ever step foot in my bar again, you'll be a dead man. Now get out! And don't you ever come back," he growls. "There are no police officers out here that are going to make it in time to arrest your ass—you and I both know it. I'm the *law* in this bar."

Chad rubs his (what I assume is sore) jaw and nods up and down.

"Get the hell out! Now!" he yells.

Chad disappears out the door faster than I can blink. "Shows over. Sorry about that everyone," Mason announces. The chatter starts to slowly turn from whispers to full on conversations. In an instant, you would never know a fight just went down. Dustin runs up to Mason's side. They share a few hushed words. Mason says, "Can you make sure he doesn't drive home in his state? He could get someone hurt. Or hurt himself trying to drive in his intoxicated condition."

Even though Mason's fuming, his ability to care about others surpasses his rage. It's crazy to me how much he thinks of everyone else.

"Yeah, I'll take him home," Dustin states.

"Thanks, man. Sorry to ask that of you." Mason claps him on the shoulder.

"It's no problem. It'd be better if someone that's out of the situation took him home. That doesn't mean I'm not angry with how he acted. Plus, you might get into a fist fight in the car if he breathes a word about Olive. Not a good mix with driving," Dustin replies and follows Chad out the door.

"Olive? Are you hurt?" Mason's eyes scan over my arm; they're blazing with fire. He pulls off my coat, and his brows furrow when he sees the black and blue fingerprints forming on my arm.

I shrug. "No, I don't feel a thing. I'm mad though."

"You may not feel it now, but you will later. You're full of adrenaline right now." His expression hardens. "Mad at him? Because I am too. I'm more concerned about you right now, and the nasty bruise will continue to form if we don't get some ice on it."

"No! At you! Well, and more so at Chad. I had him right where I wanted him. I was about to flip him on his behind. It would've been so badass if you hadn't run in and saved the day. I can take care of myself, you know?"

"I wouldn't let anyone lay a hand on you. I know you can take care of yourself. But I would burn this place to the ground before I let something bad happen to you. You're going to have to come to terms with that fact because I mean it."

My heart skips a beat. The way he protects me with no hesitation sends goosebumps over my skin. *I would burn this place to the ground before I let something bad happen to you.* I let his words seep into my bones again.

Mason would let go of every bit of what he spent years improving to make it the beautiful place it is now...*for me?* The thought is confounding.

He clenches his fist at his side. I reach out and fold my fingers over his hand. I rub my thumb over his knuckles.

"Does it hurt when I touch them?" I ask.

"A lot less than it's going to hurt for him when he wakes up sober tomorrow morning." He shakes his head.

"You really didn't have to do anything. I could have handled it. Now you have to work the rest of the night with your hand aching."

"I don't know what you're not understanding? So, let me make it crystal-clear. I would take every bit of pain aimed towards you so that you wouldn't have to feel an ounce of it. I don't care what it is. Let me be the one in agony. As long as you are safe and comfortable, that's all I want." His warm, brown eyes lock with mine.

I can't help but wonder if Mason and I would make a merry pair—a real one, not some ruse we're playing with now.

Chapter 35

MASON

O live hisses when I press an ice pack against her arm. It makes my blood boil remembering how Chad's fingers were curled around her bicep, digging into her flesh. It makes me want to run out of the bar and find him and make him feel pain once again—a flicker of what he put this beautiful woman through. It's sickening that he thought he could grab her. But I had already done more than enough, and he was so drunk hence I'm not even sure he'll remember any of it tomorrow. The only clue will be the ache in his jaw as a painful reminder of him doing something careless. And there were consequences. Well-deserved ones.

Besides, Olive needs me right now. She needs someone to make sure she gets ice on her arm to lessen the bruising. Otherwise, she'd be on the dance floor with her friends acting like nothing happened. And tomorrow her arm would sting with a reminder of what happened tonight. I don't want her thinking about that asshole another minute. I don't want her pondering why she was even with him in the first place. Nor do I want her dimming any of her bright smile, the one she's shooting my way at the moment.

"What are you thinking?" she whispers as she sits on top of my desk, dangling her feet.

"You don't want to know," I mumble.

"Try me?"

"Only about how furious I still am over what Chad did."

"Oh—that." She shakes her head as if clearing her mind of all thoughts pertaining to Chad. *Good. That's what I want.* "What are we going to do about your hand?" She prods.

"Nothing. I'm worried about *you*. Not me."

"You're being insufferable. If you're going to inflict this *torture* on me. We're going to get an ice pack over your knuckles." She motions to get up, and I steady her in place.

I breathe a slow sigh out my nostrils. "Fine. I'll get another ice pack. Don't move a muscle." She places her hand holding the pack to her arm, and her fingers brush mine, sending tingles straight to my heart.

She dangles her feet and smirks. "Does this count as moving a muscle?"

"You're the insufferable one here. I don't know why you think it's me." I chuckle, opening the freezer door of the mini fridge in the corner of my office. I grab the other small ice pack that I keep just in case.

"You'd be bored if I didn't make your life a little insufferable... and exciting... and totally so much better than it could've ever been without me in it. I'm the bestest—best friend and fake girlfriend."

Isn't that the truth?

Olive makes my life exhilarating. Or what I meant to say was, she makes every day exhilarating. When I'm not with her, I feel empty. I seek her out for a semblance of that bubbly personality. It's contagious and ends up rubbing off on me. She transforms every day from mediocre to electrifying. She lights up any room she enters with laughter and encouragement for her friends. I'm so in love with Olive; it's not even funny.

I transition to holding her ice pack again, and I hold my own in my palm. She lowers her arm and says, "Here." She grabs it from my hand. "Let me hold yours at least." She places the pack on top of my knuckles. "If you're worried about my arm bruising, let me worry about your hand swelling. We can take care of each other. It doesn't always have to be all on your shoulders." Her voice is gentle.

I swallow, realizing how close we are to each other. She sits upon my desk, and I stand inches from her. Her perfume wafts into my senses. A hint of vanilla and something fruity—raspberry. Her red curls are stunning against the freckles dotting her face. Her eyelids flutter, and her green eyes sparkle in the bright LED lights of my office. A brightness against the dark walls. It makes my heart pound.

I look into her eyes, and they soften in a matter of seconds. I want to tell her how I feel now. I want to tell her I'm in love with her. But I need to know why she won't let anyone in anymore. It's been two years, and she's only been on dating apps because she was looking for companionship and nothing serious.

"Why don't you want to be in a relationship with anyone?" I ask. It's too late to take it back now.She looks taken aback by my question, but she doesn't avoid it. She answers my question with conviction. "Because—I'm afraid of what might happen."

"What are you afraid of?"

She sighs, tracing her fingers over mine. "I'm afraid of falling in love again." I stay silent, hearing the low murmur of laughter from underneath the small gap of my office door. "Love has always proven to be a weakness for me. I don't want to be weak anymore. I want to be strong." She looks to the wall in thought. "I don't want to be constrained or held down by any ties. When it's just me... I'm free to be confident. I can be my true self. There's nothing holding me back. I can do anything I want. I can leave my house a disaster. I can let yarn drape over the couch. I can pile useless, and some useful, things in my purse until it's completely overflowed. There's no one to gripe about it when it doesn't fit their way of living."

I want to tell her that love isn't a weakness. There's so much I want to explain to her. So much I have to say. There isn't enough time in the day for me to spell out the way Olive makes me feel. The way she's perfect just the way she is. How she shouldn't have to change herself for anyone.

But a screech fills my ears and everything goes silent in the bar. I drop the ice pack to the floor and run. I open the door so fast it would've flung off the wall if there wasn't a stopper.

"Help!" someone shouts from the dance floor. When it clicks that it's Mateo's voice my spine straightens. "It's Char. Her water broke! Where's Paula?"

Everything I thought I was worried about fades away except for Olive. Worrying about her is always in my mind, but my sister needs my help more at the moment. I run around frantically, looking for Paula. And then I see her running from the bathroom towards Char.

Chapter 36

MASON

My mind whirls. Everything was a blur after I heard those words, *Char's water broke.* It was as if the dam let loose on everything at the same time. Chad made his debut performance; he's lucky I let him off so easily. I still see red every time I think about it. The moment Olive twisted his wrist back, I was so god-damn proud of her for standing up for herself. But I'm still full of rage. I didn't think at all. I still want to break his hand for ever laying it on her. And then Char's water breaking was the tip of the iceberg. No one suspected it would happen tonight. I, for one, thought we had a few days still. But I guess due dates are predictions and not set in stone.

I pace the hall back and forth. As I've done for the past few hours. I've memorized the chip in the wall and the number of paintings lining it. There are six if you're wondering. I scratch the back of my head with worry. A pain starts to ache in my hand and my head, but I ignore it. What if something's wrong? Is it too early? Did I cause her stress that triggered her water to break because I punched Chad? So many unknowns. And none of the questions I have can be answered. I need to be patient and calm down.

Easier said than done.

I also never got the chance to talk to Olive and confess what I've been holding back. And I never got a chance to tell her love isn't a weakness. I also missed out on giving her a New Year's Eve kiss like I promised. That's when I was planning on telling her, right after midnight on the way home. Confessing everything I've held in for so long would have been exactly the freeing moment I needed. It's agonizing at this point. I need to tell her. I know there's something special between us. I can feel it in my bones. I can hear it when her body is pressed against mine—the racing of our hearts in tandem. There's a deeper connection, even if she doesn't admit it to herself. It's there. We're so much more than best friends. If only she'd put aside her concerns about weakness and let her heart open to new possibilities. But I need to explain it to her. I need to show her I wouldn't change a thing about her. I'd only support her and brighten her bubbly personality.

Olive sits in the waiting room with both our families. She looks just as nervous as the rest of us. She's focused intently on making a hat for the baby. She already made a blue one, and now she's halfway finished with a pink one. Somehow, she managed to store the supplies in her purse without stopping anywhere to grab them. I shouldn't be surprised; her purse is filled with everything.

Technically it's already Thursday, and the first day of the new year. It's around two in the morning. We're exhausted. I can't begin to imagine how Char feels. Everyone rushed to Paula's clinic as fast as they could. Luckily, it's only across the street, so they didn't have to go far. The roads were too bad to make it to the hospital in time. Plus, the hospital is an hour's drive away. It wasn't worth the risk to get there. Char and Mateo had a plan in place to go to the closest hospital a few days before her due date, leaving this morning. Things didn't turn out how they'd hoped. We're all glad Paula has delivered babies before. And she also planned on delivering in case something like this happened. In a small town you have to prepare for the unexpected.

"I have news." Paula steps into the room beaming with a smile. Everyone sits on the edge of their seats and loosens when they see her smile. I quit pacing and relax the tensions I'm feeling. She wouldn't be smiling if it weren't good news to share. "Char had a baby girl. She'll be ready for you to come in soon. In groups of two or three in an hour or so. She's healthy, seven pounds and two ounces, and has all ten fingers and ten toes."

Everyone breathes a collective sigh of relief. It's a baby girl. I'm so proud, relieved, and happy for my sister and Mateo. And for their growing family.

"Boo, why is it a girl? I wanted a boy," Logan whines and runs to me. He hugs my legs.

"Why did you want it to be a boy? Aren't you happy you're going to have another cousin?" I ask him.

"Because I'm the odd one out. There are already Emma and Octavia. Now there will be three girls." His little voice complains.

"Let me tell you a secret." Logan nods his head as I continue. "When I was your age, I had three sisters, one of those being your mom. It was the best thing that ever happened to me. Do you know why?"

"No." He shakes his head back and forth.

"I got to take care of my sisters in school, protect them, watch out for them, and learn some things too. Girls are just as cool as boys. Your cousins build forts in the woods, and they play with cars too, don't they?" He nods up and down. "So what do you think? It's kinda cool. Isn't it?"

"I'm excited!" He jumps up and down. He gives me a fist bump.

"There you go, buddy." I chuckle. He runs towards Emma and Octavia. Olive looks at me, and the corner of her mouth turns up. There's a sparkle in her eye.

Chapter 37

OLIVE

It's a girl, and she's absolutely beautiful. She looks just like her mother. She was born with a full head of brown hair. Mason is sitting next to Char, having a conversation with her and sporting a wide smile on his face. He holds the baby in his arms delicately and smiles at her. He's going to be such a good uncle. He already is, but he was always the closest to Char. I just know this little girl is going to be spoiled to no end. No one's going to tell him otherwise.

They decided on a name right after she was born—Nova, meaning something new. They thought it would be a perfect fit since she was born on the first day of the new year. Nova Sophia Hernandez, her name alone is as pretty as she is. I made her a little pink crocheted hat with a white pom-pom while sitting in the waiting room. I never leave the house without my hook and yarn. You never know when you might need it. Now was the ultimate testament to that. I also made a blue one but obviously didn't need that one unless she likes blue. She can have it too.

The way Mason looks filled with so much love and joy makes me think a lot about what I want in life. I want a family. I want someone to love me so much they would do anything for me. I would do anything for them in return.

But you already found that. A voice in the back of my head drones on.

Why didn't I see it before?

Mason cares for me as no other has. When something breaks, he's the first person there to fix it. Even if it's at the crack of dawn, he's there in an instant. He showers me with grand gestures: flowers for no reason other than to make me smile, replacing my tires when they aren't safe, hanging up Christmas decorations with me (even though it's the last way he wants to spend his time), learning a new skill to make me a meaningful Christmas present, and breaking silly (Constance) rules with me. No matter what we do, he doesn't mind; he *wants* to spend his time with... me.

It's the little things too: the way he makes me laugh over nothing, how he takes care of me, how he *protects* me, and the way he would risk losing everything he's worked for. For *me*. It's more than a friendship. So much more.

Why have I been so blind to the way he treats me? Am I conditioned to think I don't deserve someone who cares this much? *I think so.* All the things he does for me should be the standard. It's what one does for someone they love.

Love.

It's as if someone screams *eureka.* Someone pushes a button. An electric shock connects the pieces together. A switch flicks. A light bulb goes off—blinking with bright lights. A flashing neon sign inside my brain turns on. This is what *love* is. This is what love should feel like. It's the most wonderful, empowering, and enlightening realization. I thought I knew what love was. I didn't know. I barely had a glimpse of what it was. I'm one hundred percent sure—I *love* Mason. I want to shout it from the rooftops and from the top of a snowy mountain. I'm in love! It's everything I've ever wanted. Everything I've dreamt about. I might burst from happiness. Love isn't a weakness like I thought. It wasn't *true love* before.

Mason gives me a puzzled look with one eyebrow raised. "Olive?"

"Yeah?" I shake my head.

"Do you want to hold her?"

"Oh—yes. I would love to hold her." I sit down next to him, and he passes her to me carefully. I stare into her beautiful blue eyes.

How am I supposed to sit here when my mind is screaming, *I am in love?* I want to tell him everything. I'm climbing a metaphorical mountain, searching for any tether to grasp onto. But at the same time, I want to jump off the cliff into the deepest ravine. One where

I expose my newly found feelings. I need to tell him I love him no matter the consequences.

"I'm going to grab some coffee for us from Paula's office. I'll be right back," Mason says.

"Okay. Thanks." But what I really want to say is, *Stay here. I love you.*

Nova stares at me. I hold her tiny little hands. They're so small and delicate compared to mine. I can't keep from smiling and thinking of a future with Mason. I look up to Char, who is lying in a hospital bed, covered with blankets.

"Are you doing okay?" I speak quietly.

"Yeah. I'm exhausted. But okay."

I whisper, "She looks so much like you."

"I know. Isn't it wonderful?" Her expression is drained, but her lips curl into a huge grin despite it.

"It really is." I smile tenderly.

"Do you love my brother?" she whispers it. No one else is in the room to hear us. But it's so quiet I almost miss her question.

I ponder what I'm going to say for a moment. "I've always loved him as a friend—but I've only just realized I love him much more than that. I haven't told him yet, but yes, I do." Saying it out loud is freeing. Now I need to work up the courage to tell Mason the same thing.

"Good. I'm so glad to hear it. Your fake relationship was killing me. I knew both of you would end up together. Now all you have to do is tell him."

"Fake relationship?" Sophia and my mom ask simultaneously as they walk in the door, obviously overhearing a part of our conversation I'd hoped would never happen. Even if Mason and I did end up together, I wasn't planning on telling them we faked it. It was easier that way. No fallout. No arguments. No drama.

Guess I can say goodbye to that sweet dream.

"Let it go," Char says. "Now's not the time. I'm too tired."

My dad comes in after our mothers and takes the baby from my arms. He whispers into my ear, "You might want to do some damage control. Your mother looks like she swallowed a cactus."

I stifle a laugh. "She does. Doesn't she?"

I make my way out of the room and continue down the hall. Sophia and my mom are on my heels.

"What is going on, Olive? Were you and Mason faking a relationship?" Mom asks. I begrudgingly turn to face them. My mom shakes her head; disappointment is written all over her face.

"I can't believe you both would lie to us." Sophia gasps, raising a hand to her chest.

Mason rounds the corner holding two steaming cups of coffee. His soft smile instantly shifts to a look of confusion. "What's going on here?" He sets the cups down on a table in the hall.

"You lied. Olive and you aren't together?" Sophia looks appalled.

Mason scoffs. "Enough. I've had it with the both of you."
Damn, Mason. Tell them how you really feel.

My mom pales. Sophia avoids eye contact from both of us.

Mason stands strong and continues to defend us. "I can't take it anymore. Yes, Olive and I pretended to date so we could enter the Cookie Chronicles. It was a stipulation. You had to be a couple to participate. We also pretended to date for the sake of enjoying the holiday. One where you'd stop your incessant nagging over me being single. Of us both being single. But you found other avenues anyway."

"Is that true?" Sophia asks.

"Yes," I confess. "We didn't want to lie to you, but it was becoming so draining arguing over people you wanted to set us up with. We just wanted to be left alone," I say this for both of us.

Sophia and Beth share a look. One full of regret. I think it's finally dawning on them.

"I'm sorry," Sophia says.

"Me too," Mom says.

Sophia looks remorseful as she says, "Please don't be mad at us. We were both so worried about you two ending up alone. We tried everything to get you set up with someone so you could both have a future and a family." His mom looks at the ground. "I messed up. You know how I get an idea in my head, and I run with it. I can't help it." She walks towards us and pulls us both into a bone crushing embrace. "We want you to be happy. It doesn't matter if you're forty and single. As long as you're happy, that's all that matters."

My face pales. *She had to add that one.* I hope I'm not forty and still single. But whatever life has in store, I will take. Even if it means living alone with my betta fish for years to come. As long as I have everyone I love in my life, including Mason, whether it be as a best friend or more, I will be happy.

"We were wrong. I see it now." My mom joins the hug and squeezes us all. "Sophia always gets me riled up and involved in her scheming."

Sophia steps back and points at my mom. "I don't know. Beth sure has a way of acting innocent when she's the one scheming all along."

"Don't start with me, Sophia. Two can play at this game. Do you want a fight? I'll give you something to fight over."

Mason looks at me, and we both start chuckling. Our moms were always the best of friends, but they constantly got into arguments over absolutely nothing important. I can't take it anymore. I turn away. Their arguing muffles into the background as we turn the corner.

"Wait, our coffee!" I run back to grab them, hightailing it out of the battle grounds.

I catch up to Mason, huffing and puffing from running away.

"Never a dull moment with our families, is it, Firefly?"

"And there never will be." I smile.

"So about earlier..." He takes a seat in the waiting room, and I sit beside him.

"When, today?" I ask, resting my elbow on the arm of the chair and my palm on my chin.

"No, I mean, technically speaking, yesterday, when you said you were afraid of loving someone because you didn't want to be weak."

"I—" I start, but he cuts me off.

I want to tell him my outlook has changed in a matter of hours. How crazy is it that my perspective differs so much in only a short amount of time?

"No. Please let me finish and say what I haven't got a chance to. Everything keeps happening every chance I get a moment alone with you." He scratches his head. I nod for him to continue. The determination in his gaze is enough for me to listen intently. "I looked up the definition of love and guess what came up?"

"Hmmm—weakness?" I guess out loud.

"Yep, you were right. Some people think love equals weakness. But to me, when you're with the right person your whole outlook on love changes. The right person won't inhibit you. You will only shine brighter. They won't make you weak or any less than who you are. They'll embrace every quirk and every little piece of you, cherishing everything that makes you unique." He smiles and the passion behind every word is captivating. "Love isn't similar to a category where someone puts it in a synonym section along the pages of a thesaurus. Or else no one would want to fall in love. I think when you find *the* person that makes your heart beat faster, you'll know it. They won't dull any part of your personality. You'll radiate with them. Your heart will melt. Your cheeks will blush. Your thoughts will be captivated by that person. So, no, I don't think love is a weakness."

He just poured his heart out to me, and all I can do in return is stare at him blankly. The words are on my tongue, but I don't say them. Every word that left his mouth was filled with devotion. I could almost feel them. He's absolutely right.

I know love isn't a weakness because I love you.

"I think you're—" I start to say.

"How did it go? I heard what happened back there. Our moms found out? On a scale of one to furious, how mad were they?" Jackie asks as she takes a seat next to us.

"Fire breathing, but everything is fine now," I say, although it's not. *Everything's not fine.* I almost told him how I feel. I have the worst timing. Why did I pause? If I didn't take a minute to think, I could have spit it out.

"They started interrogating us. Then they realized how ridiculous they were and started to argue with each other." Mason chuckles.

"Sounds like something they'd do. I'm glad because I'm sick of getting texts every day about wedding planning. So, you guys really aren't together?" she asks.

"No," Mason says, tipping his head down. He almost looks defeated. Which confirms my suspicions. There is something more than friendship between us.

Jackie leans back in her chair. "That's a shame because you two make a really good pair. I get why you did what you did. I would have done the same. I know I tease you sometimes, but I don't care what you do with your life. If you want to spend it alone, I'm all for it. If you want to be together, I'm all for that as well. Whatever passes by with the wind, I'll be there for both of you."

"Thank you," Mason says.

"Yeah, thank you, Jackie." I smile genuinely.

For my sake, I hope Mason and I spend it together.

Chapter 38

OLIVE

Mason opens the door to my apartment for me. Times like these make me so grateful to live in a small town, right across the street from everything. I don't have to travel far to get home. My legs ache, and my eyelids are heavy.

"I know you're exhausted. You shouldn't be driving with how tired you are. Will you stay with me?" I ask him. I also selfishly want him here with me. I feel comfortable in his company.

"You've gotta be too. I'll stay. I'm too tired to go anywhere, anyway." He shrugs his coat off onto the coat rack. The dark circles under his eyes are pigmented against his skin. "Dustin and Vivi picked up Moose last night. He's staying with them for the time being. So, we don't have to worry about him."

"What about the chickens?"

"I installed the automatic door. They'll be okay for one day. They can get in and out no problem now, and the chicks have plenty of food and water."

"Good," I whisper.

His eyes hover over me, blinking rapidly. His gaze is filled with what looks like longing. He takes my hand in his larger one, and he tilts his head, studying me.

This man has no clue I love him.

What if he doesn't love me? The idea that it may be one sided sends a pain shooting through my heart. What if all the signs I thought were saying *love* were actually ones of strong friendship? Maybe they're not what I was expecting at all.

"I have a confession to make." He breaks my thoughts.

A confession?

"Can I make one first?" I need to tell him I love him before he potentially ends our relationship. At least I'd known I told him. I wouldn't feel guilty about what should've been said at that moment. There's no time like the present. And I have to get it off my chest.

"Let me say it first. This is important." His eyebrows scrunch.

"No—Mason. Trust me. This is *very* important for me to say right now. I'm going to tackle you if you don't let me say what I need to say."

He grins. "How about we both say it at the same time. You know, we might as well toss all our eggs in one basket." A chicken pun right now. It's perfect. Vivi must be rubbing off on him. I laugh deliriously. Love makes one feel lighter. Or it could be the lack of sleep. My sanity is long gone at this point.

I count down slowly. "Say it in three, two, one."

"I love you!" we blurt into the silence at the same moment. Our eyes both widen. He looks as if he's going to pass out. I feel the same way.

He loves me!

"You love me? I heard that right?" He questions.

I am so happy. "Yes, I love you. You love me?"

"Well, of course I do. How could I not?" His expression is full of confusion.

How didn't I see it? "Why didn't you say anything?"

"Why didn't you?" His eyes widen.

"I just figured it out. Last night? This morning? Whatever day it was or is. I'm not entirely sure anymore."

"Oh, Olive. I've been waiting so long to hear you say those words. I had just about given up hope you ever would. I thought it was one sided." He wipes a shaky hand over his beard.

My eyes fill with unshed tears. "How long have you been in love with me?"

Mason pauses, gathering his words. He reaches out and grasps my hands in his. After a few beats he says, "Too long to tell you. I'm not exactly sure when the shift from like to love happened. I've known for years that I've loved you. You've been my every waking thought. You've taken over my dreams. My mind. My sanity. I've been hopelessly in love with you. Recklessly. Undoubtedly. I hid it from you for so long. I don't want to end anything between us. Our friendship will never die. I know that now. How could I ruin it? I would never ruin something between you and I." He interlaces our fingers. "I love the freckles dotting your nose and cheeks. I love how your nose turns red when you're frustrated. I also love you for what's on the inside. You have a heart of gold. You are full of compassion. I love your feistiness and willingness to fight for those you love and what you believe in. Your determination. I love that you take care of me when I have migraines. You're selfless. I love when you make blankets for shelter animals. And even when you pull hot sauce out of your purse, I can't imagine my life without you in it. I want to start a family with you. I want feisty little versions of us running around—red hair blowing in the wind. I love you, Firefly."

I smile, my eyes glisten as I soak in his words. My heart is so full right now. I never knew what I was missing... but now I see it as clear as day. I never let myself entertain the idea of us together. I feel free now that I've let him in and opened my eyes. "Listen to me, Knight. I love you. Not only for your heart of gold when it comes to protecting me. I love you for dropping everything to help me. For showing up every day to make me laugh. For listening to me ramble on and on about baking and crocheting and every random fixation I have. For coming to get coffee every day to see me. And for trying every pastry I bake. For taking care of me when I'm drunk and absolutely oblivious. I love you. I can't say it enough."

As Mason stares at me I melt under his gaze. He listens to every word intently. His eye-contact doesn't waver. He tilts his head as if he's thinking about something. After a few seconds he says, "Do you want to know what was said that night I brought you home?"

"Yes." I nod my head vehemently.

"It wasn't what you confessed. It was what I said. I didn't want you finding out. You asked if anyone ever told me I was handsome. I said, *not anyone that I wanted to mean it—until you.* It's always been you, Olive. There was no one else. It was only *you.*"

"Mason." My voice cracks. "I can't take it anymore. Kiss me already." I bite my lip, and my gaze locks onto his. He drags his thumb across my bottom lip and tugs. In an instant he crashes his lips against mine.

The last kiss we shared was remarkable, but this one puts it to shame. It's only our second kiss, but it's as if we've been sharing them for years. There's no awkward movements or hesitation.

I push him against the wall; he kisses me with fervor. Wanting crashes through my senses. My mind is laser focused, determined on experiencing this for what it is. His cologne is sharp; it wafts around the room with fragments of leather and smoke. He is intoxicating. I want to bottle up this feeling of desire and keep it close to my heart. This is a revelation that has been a long time coming.

I'm in love.

Chapter 39

MASON

When Olive begins to kiss me, my body aches with desire. The soft press of lips. Her lingering perfume—the fragrance of Glittery Snow. When we finally let our guards down there's no impending deadline. No end in sight for us. There's only fresh starts and new beginnings.

Love.

This is what true love should feel like.

I caress the side of her face with my thumb, tracing over the lines and edges of her features. Goosebumps form in the wake of my trailing finger, painting across her skin. I feel the pounding of my heart; it's loud and fast in my ears. She tugs at the bottom hem of my shirt, trailing cool fingertips across my abdomen. I soak in every little touch. She gasps when I rake my fingers over the hem of her pink crewneck. I lift it slowly. My eyes linger on her green ones, burning with heat, an unspoken question of, *is this okay*. She nods her head up and down in silent answer. I take it as my cue to continue dragging her shirt over her features. My fingers follow the path, up her hips, to her breasts, and over her head. I discard her T-shirt on the floor somewhere. I'm too engrossed in the present to worry about anything other than her. She slowly unclips the clasps on her bra. I gulp at the sight of her body exposed. All soft skin and curves. "Absolutely beautiful." My voice comes out grainy and thick with lust.

Her face heats. Her fingertips continue their torturous wander higher on my abdomen. My shirt falls to the floor in a heap with hers. Her gaze is locked with mine; it's filled with wanting. With love. Our pace continues with a slow rhythm. A dance. There's no need to rush. I've built up so much pent-up tension waiting for this moment. I want to take it slow. We both remove the rest of our clothing while continuing our way down the hall. Her breath hitches as we slowly inch to the edge of her bed.

My fingers map the hollow of her neck, tilting her chin to look at me. She melts under my touch, moaning against the soft caresses. She never once looks away. Confidence radiates off her; she's not shy in the least. It's what I'd expected. Olive does everything with the utmost certainty. I slowly lay her down on the mattress, and I tuck her hair behind her ear. Her breath is warm, hovering over my lips. I touch her arms and smooth my hands over her body. She moans my name against my lips.

"I'm on birth control and I've been tested. Everything's clear." Her breath comes out a rasp between her lips.

"I'm clear too." My voice is fuller and deeper with the words.

When her lips press against mine, it's as if there is an underlying hunger. With every gasp that leaves her lips, I know I will never be the same.

When we finally meet my nerve endings are on fire. My body reacts to hers. I'm taken to another world. Olive makes me delirious. The tension crackles between us. With each movement and soft caress, I begin to lose all traces of reality.

"I love you, Mason." She moans into my ear. She uses my name. Not any nicknames or terms of endearment or jokes. This moment is between *us*. Without any distractions.

"I love you too, Olive." My voice comes out a deep rumble.

We both find our releases and lie in a heap across her bed. All my limbs feel weak. I've never been so relaxed.

With her body still pressed against mine, I can feel the steady rhythm of her heartbeat. I feel the rise and fall of each breath. Her skin is slick with sweat. I twirl a few strands of her red locks. I look down at the woman that is *mine*. I roll off her and pull her into my arms. I kiss the temple of her head. After a few moments she begins to softly snore.

As I fall asleep, I realize this isn't a dream. This is real. *She loves me.*

I couldn't be any more content. With her safe in my arms, I'm so damn happy.

Chapter 40

OLIVE

The afternoon sun filters through the cracks in the blinds of my window. My feet are under Mason's legs, soaking up every ounce of heat he has to offer. His arm is draped around my side. My head rests on a soft pillow. I'm comfortable and warm. I've never woken so full of emotion. I'm really happy.

I stare at Mason in a new light. He's all gruff and hard edges and handsome. I can't believe I've missed this for so long. I brush my hand across the owl on his arm. His breath is even. He's still peacefully asleep. I look closely at his tattoo. I've never noticed all the details it hides. The design is intricate and shaded. Whoever his artist was did an exceptional job. I trace what looks to be a clock in the feathers. Then a little bug? I think that's what it is. A few trees. Every detail is precise and drawn with care.

"Why are there little objects hidden in his tattoo?" I wonder out loud.

"Because I asked the artist to design it that way. They're there purposely." I jump when his deep voice grumbles.

"Did I wake you?" I ask.

His voice is slightly groggy still. "No, I woke up a few minutes ago."

"Why didn't you say something?" I poke his chest and giggle.

His smile grows wider. "I wanted to see if you'd figure out what it means."

"I don't understand." I shake my head.

"Ask me then," he states.

"What does the clock mean?" I trace its intricate face with numeral numbers representing each hour. There's no hands marking it for time.

A smile tips the corners of his lips. "It represents time with no limits. And it also means time is irrelevant."

"Wow, very deep." I grin while teasing him.

"Keep asking what the others mean."

I trace over a few trees at the bottom of the owl. "What do the trees mean?"

Goosebumps form under my fingertips as I follow the trees. "They represent a place. They're like home. This town."

"And the bug?" I ask, touching the smallest details with the pad of my finger.

He grins. "It's not just any insect. It's a firefly."

"Oh—so what do they mean separately or together? It's something you're hinting at, right?"

"A clock representing time. Trees representing a place. And a firefly representing *you*. All hidden elements within the owl. Within itself representing the protector." He brushes his hand down my arm as he continues. "Through any place or time I will love you and protect you. There's no time limiting what I feel for you. There was never anyone else for me. It was you. Only you. It's always been you. My heart is yours. Whether you want to break it or keep it, it's up to you to do as you wish with it. I'm putting my heart in your hands."

My voice softens. Butterflies flutter in my chest. "You meant all of that when you got the tattoo?"

"Yes," he states. I can tell in his determined gaze that it's true.

My fingers continue to hover over his arm, and I lay my head on his chest, listening to his heartbeat. I whisper, "But you've had this tattoo for five years."

"I know. And I've felt it for longer. This was something permanent I chose to get to represent what I have felt in my heart."

"What if we never ended up together?" I can't help but ask as his chest rises and falls under me.

"Then I would've silently suffered watching you fall in love with someone else. But I would've been happy for you, nonetheless. I would've been grateful for your happiness. And grateful to have you in my life in any form." His voice cracks with emotion.

My eyes start to water. I hug him tightly. I don't ever want to let him go. I'm grateful for him, more than words can describe. He wraps his strong arms around my frame.

"One last thing," he murmurs in my ear. "It also means I've loved you from afar. Just like owls are patient and watch from a distance. I was waiting for the right time to tell you how I've been feeling. It just so happened the time panned out to be exactly when you wanted to tell me the same thing." I raise my head from his chest, and he kisses my forehead. He hovers over me, tracing my face with his gaze in the afternoon sun.

My room blurs as tears fall from my face in a steady flow cascading over my cheeks.

"Don't cry," he whispers, his thumb brushing a stray tear.

"I'm only crying because I'm so happy. I'm also mad at myself. Mad that I've only now realized what I had. If I would've opened my eyes sooner, I would've known what I needed was there all along." I sniffle.

"Don't be upset over something you can't change." He wipes a tear from my face. "It had to be the right moment. It had to happen on your own accord. Things worked out the way they're supposed to be. I wouldn't change a thing."

"You're right. It's worked out to be better than I ever imagined." I squint through water in my eyes at his blurry face.

He smiles charmingly. "Good. Let's enjoy every moment from here on after. Promise?"

"That's a promise I can keep." I smile through tears.

Chapter 49

OLIVE

About three months later

"A re you sure you're ready to handle everything on your own if I leave?" I ask Daisy.

"Yes! I have four days of training under my belt. I've got it covered," she says with confidence. "I'm no stranger to working under pressure."

I think she's ready to handle the shop on her own for a few hours while I'm gone. I hired Daisy on Monday, so she's had the week to learn. I think she's had enough of Joe's antics. She put in her one-day notice at The String Cheese, so I hired her when she asked for a job here. I could use the help, and I'd love to have more time to spend with Mason.

"Good. I think you're ready. If anyone gives you a hard time or if you have questions, call me. I'm a few shops away." I step back from the counter, walking backwards as I talk.

"Don't you worry about me. I'll be fine."

"I'll see you in a few hours." I wave to Daisy as I grab my purse and skip out the door. My phone pings with a notification. It's a new article from Constance.

Thornwood Valley Social
The Chicken Race is Tomorrow - Annual Spring Small Business Games

*This is your friendly reminder... if you haven't received my **many** emails. It's the time you've been waiting for! Tomorrow is the day of the first competition—The Chicken Race. The annual Thornwood Valley Spring Small Business games begin. The crowd favorite competition returns for another year. Don't forget to come prepared to watch or participate. I won't bore you with the rules. I'll announce them tomorrow before the race. There'll be food, drinks, laughter, games, and last, but certainly not least, chickens. Don't forget your team-colored sweatshirts, headbands, and shirts. You can pick them up at Chloe's Closet if you haven't had a chance. I promise it'll be a peck-tacular event you won't want to miss.*

Constance Williams – Thornwood Valley Gossip Mill Executive

I pocket my phone as I walk along the path behind the shops. I run towards Mason when I see him, meeting him halfway to the chicken coop. The sky is bright, backdropping the green buds on the trees. No more snow lingers on the ground. Spring is fast approaching. Dew lingers in the air, birds squawk, and squirrels jump from branches. Everything is so alive around me. It's just like me; I've felt so alive ever since Mason and I confessed our love for each other. The past three months have been a dream. I've never been so happy. It's all thanks to Mason. Speaking of him.

"Mason!" I call through gasps as I run.

"Olive! Why are we shouting" he yells back in reply.

"I don't know!"

"Stop shouting then!"

"You first!"

"Never!" He pauses for a beat before continuing. "Okay. I can't shout anymore. I'm going to lose my voice." It comes out raspy. If he continues it'll be gone.

"Thank goodness. I wasn't going to let up first—I have good news," I say, voice slightly hoarse from all the yelling.

He presses a quick kiss to my lips before wrapping me in a tight hug. I giggle in his embrace, and he asks, "What's the good news?"

"We are paired together for this year's small business games!" I clap my hands.

"Not this again." He sighs.

"Hey! It will be so much fun! We are paired together," I repeat and wink.

He sighs heavily. "I will do anything as long as you are by my side."

"Good, because Constance sent an email. And this year for the chicken race, we got Hennifer."

"We have a good chance. She's fast." He admits while poking my nose.

"She won last year's race too." I wiggle my eyebrows.

"You're up to something, Firefly. You have a devious look in your eyes. One that says you're up to no good. It's the same look you gave me when decorating for Christmas."

He's pretty good at reading me. "I was thinking—"

"You were thinking—"

I tap my chin. "What if we snuck Hennifer some extra treats today to give her a little boost for tomorrow?"

"Are you asking me to cheat?" He points to his chest, and his eyes widen with mock humor.

I look around. "Me? Never, Knight. I simply want to help her along. Give her a little shove. A tiny little advantage, you know? There's no speaking of cheating over here. Nope. None whatsoever. Besides, we always break a few rules together. It's nothing unheard of."

He leans down and whispers close to my ear. Goosebumps appear on my skin where his hot breath lingers. "I'll let you in on a little secret. Everyone does it. They train a couple days ahead of time and feed them all a pound of treats."

"What? You're kidding me!" I pull backward in shock.

"No. I'm not. It's not in the rules anywhere that you can't. Good job at being stealthy, though." He tips his head back and chuckles.

I slap his arm playfully. "I was trying so hard. I came prepared and everything. I even brought a bag of mealworms." I pull it out of my purse.

He starts to laugh some more; his voice is deep and breathy. "You—brought—mealworms—in your purse."

"Hey! Don't make fun of me! I was trying to sneak them around town. I didn't want the townies to see me with *the goods*."

"I'm not." He laughs some more. "You just look so cute when you're being conspiratorial."

I put my hands on my hips. "Do I really?"

"You do. Even more cute when your nose turns red because you're frustrated with me." He pokes my nose.

I strut towards the chicken coop, purse on one arm slapping against my leg with each step, and a bag of treats in the other. "Are you coming?" I look back over my shoulder. "We are going to feed Hennifer a whole bag of treats!" I yell it to the whole town.

Mason just grins. He runs up to me and picks me up by my legs and back. I yelp in protest. The bag of mealworms falls from my fingertips. It soars to the ground and dumps everywhere. "No!" I shout.

The automatic door decided it's going to make its grand debut. Right *now*. The door rises, and the chickens come running like a stampede. Filing one by one. Pushing and shoving each other to get to the treats. In no time, they're all pecking the ground, eating them in a frenzy.

"Get your filthy beaks out of Hennifer's treats!" I yell.

"They'll just have to share." Mason chuckles.

"They're being so greedy. Hennifer barely got a few." I pout, jutting out my lower lip.

He stares at my lips. "Then we'll just have to go get her some more." He kisses me softly while I dangle my feet in the air and wrap my arms around his neck.

When I pull away Mason smiles at me. I know he will get some more. He would do anything for me. It makes my heart pitter-patter. I am so in love with him.

Chapter 42

OLIVE

"I can't believe Marigold's here. She never shows up to the competitions." I nudge Vivi's arm and point across the field to the townies.

"Me neither." She cups her eyes, shielding the sun. "Yeah. It's her. I can tell by her pink overalls."

"I wonder why she came?" I scrunch my brows.

She shrugs. "Maybe for Dan? He's always running in and out of Fix-Its every day."

"I noticed that too, but he does need a lot of parts for cars, doesn't he?" I wonder.

"Maybe she's not here for him. I don't know. Maybe she's here to cheer on her dad?"

"We're just as bad as Constance right now." I groan at the idea of being compared to the town's gossip executive.

"Ugh. I know. But time will tell. I'm sure Constance is already working on something to get them together as we speak. Then we'll know." Vivi stretches her arms and yawns.

"I wouldn't doubt it for a second," I say.

As if on cue, Constance's voice booms over the field. "Please line up at the green and red lines. The race starts in five minutes. Don't forget your chickens. It's go time."

Mason strides from the walking path to the field where we're standing. "Hey." He laces his fingers with mine and kisses my cheek. "Are you ready?"

I nod, squeezing his hand. "I'm ready. Constance is already yelling at us. We better go." I wave to Vivi as we walk off.

"She's not all bad," he says while we continue walking, hands intertwined, to find Hennifer.

"What do you mean by that?"

He scratches the back of his head with his free hand. "We came to an understanding. I forgot to tell you what she really dragged me into my office about."

"I knew there was something you were leaving out." I remember how worked up he looked after she left his office that day. I felt bad, but didn't want to prod him.

"Yeah, sorry, but it was about you. So, I couldn't exactly say *Constance wanted to talk to me because she told me to tell you I love you*." He adjusts his glasses.

"You could've told me."

His eyebrows raise. "I was afraid of losing a lifetime of friendship. Remember?" He grabs Hennifer from the chicken tractor.

"It's starting to come back to me." I stick my tongue out. "She really told you that?"

Mason pushes his hair back. "I think it was her pushing me, and my talk with Dustin made me feel confident enough to say something. Her power of persuasion is unmatched, though."

I shake my head in disbelief. "Well, I guess I have her to thank, somewhat. I can't believe it."

"Me neither. You better hurry. She looks ready to announce the starting countdown. Go get 'em. Make sure you release her on the go." He kisses me softly on my cheek, and butterflies swarm in my stomach.

I laugh. "I have things handled."

Mason jogs to the other side of the field. I hold Hennifer close to my chest, whispering to her, "You got this girl."

Dustin had this all figured out two years ago. He made a spectacle of screaming positive affirmations. It was hilarious. Now all the townies think if you give the chickens positive encouragement they'll go faster. This obviously can't be true.

There's no way.

But after seeing Jane's powers of prediction, I'll take my chances. This town seems to have some kind of magical properties. Anything is possible. Nor do I care if anyone judges me. Everyone in our town is a little quirky anyway. Heck, I'm a little quirky myself. I fit right in. They probably think this is a daily occurrence. "Follow the plan," I tell Hennifer.

Constance announces the rules. I tune out the noise and focus on Mason. He stands on the opposite end of the field on the green line. His brown hair shines in the sunlight. His beard is longer now. I like the way it makes him look. A little rugged. Our relationship has been nothing but smooth sailing; it's been filled with laughter, drama-free family dinners (eighty percent of the time), and lots of time spent together when we're both not working. Not that we didn't already spend every free moment hanging out before we were in a romantic relationship. Nothing's changed other than him or I staying over at each other's place every single night.

I've never been so happy. Being in love has changed me as a person. It's opened me up to a world of possibilities. One full of vibrant colors. Where I'm free to be myself. As opposed to a world without love filled with mattes and neutrals. I understand what it's like to be truly myself.

I've found someone that doesn't dim my personality. He enhances it. Mason accepts me for me. He adores my mess. My flaws. My quirks. I love him even more for it.

Constance's voice breaks me out of my daydream.

"Three—two—one—go!"

I drop Hennifer. Everything becomes absolute mayhem. People shout encouraging words at their chickens. I opt for not saying anything. I don't want her to turn around and think she should come towards me. Hennifer decides today is the day she's not in the mood to run. She props one foot up and stands one legged. She has no desire to move.

Bluegrass music plays in the background, blasting through the portable speakers. It's fast-paced. Banjos, fiddles, and loud harmonizing adds to the intensity of the race. Another upgrade the gossip mill added to the festivities this year.

Mason yells, "Come here, Hennifer! Come get some food! Are you ready to eat? Here! Chicken! Chicken!" I break into a fit of laughter. Mason talking to a chicken will never get old. Hearing my boyfriend's voice hitch up an octave is enough to make me fall over. I'm going to pee myself if he doesn't quit.

"Do something, Olive! She's not moving!"

I can't do anything. I can't even see through the tears in my eyes.

This is better than any comedy show or sitcom. This needs to be recorded and televised. Aired on live television. The show would be called "A Cluckin' Mess," because it damn well is.

Hennifer remains glued to the ground. You would think I took a bottle of super glue and pressed her foot in place. She must need a rest. *I don't blame you, girl. I'd like to go home and take a nap too.*

"Hennifer! Olive! One of you, do—something. Nudge her my way!" He waves his arms. He looks like a green blob. Our shirts are both dark green. He has lines painted under his eyes and our team's name "Team Green" printed on his shirt. We look ridiculous.

Hennifer decides to lay down on both feet and rest her eyes. The rest of the chickens are already almost to the finish line. If I don't do something at this point we're getting last place. And that means we don't get to move on to any of the competitions next week or for the rest of the month. The prospect sounds promising to me. It sounds—refreshing.

I nudge her slightly with my foot. Chelsea (Constance's daughter) notices me, and her eyes go wide.

Oh crap. No one was supposed to witness that.

She doesn't say anything to my astonishment. But we couldn't get off scot-free. A grading voice from the other side of me yells, "They broke a rule! Cheaters! Olive is a cheater! Team Green should be eliminated! Olive pushed Hennifer!" *Damn, Joe. Really?*

That was personal.

"I thought we were friends." I scowl.

"We are. That was for Mason and the rest of the guys. They put MiraLAX in my coffee last week. That *shit* wasn't funny. No pun intended. I couldn't leave the bathroom the whole day. It wasn't your fault, though. Are we still friends?"

I put my hand out and shake his. "Friends. I won't hold it against you. That was very immature of Mason, Owen, Jamal and Ryder. They're thirty-year-old men. They need to learn that they're not teenagers anymore." The part I left out was when I laughed so hard after Mason told me. Joe also left out the part where he dumped salt in Masons beer last week after dumping salt in Mateo's water on Christmas. Can the guy think of any new pranks? It's getting a little redundant if you ask me.

Mason came back twofold. What can I say? It was impressive.

Joe doesn't realize we don't care. This is my favorite competition. The only one I enjoy participating in. The next one, the puzzle challenge, isn't my cup of tea.

"Team Green is disqualified." Constance's voice shouts (rather angrily) through the microphone.

Mason raises his eyebrows at me. I wiggle mine in reply. He has a shit-eating grin on his face. He shrugs as if it's no big deal. He knows why Joe ratted us out. He knew that by telling me to nudge the chicken, we would most likely be disqualified. Joe just helped us along. Constance continues to blab about prizes and other nonsense while Mason takes large strides across the field. He crushes into me and places a quick peck on my lips. Fireworks explode through my nerve endings every time.

"Our plan worked," he says.

"I told you it would."

"I love when you're feisty and devious." He lifts my chin to look into his eyes.

I gasp and giggle. "I love it when you help me pull off my carefully calculated plans. And help me break all of Constance's rules."

He kisses me again and sweeps me off my feet. It's like no one else is here with us. Only Mason and I. Oh, and Hennifer. She's still laying in front of us, taking a power nap. I think we fed her one too many treats to aid part of our plan. It worked better than I expected. But at least she looks happy.

He pulls away, but his hands fall to grip my waist. "Are you ready for our getaway tonight?"

"Yes." I snuggle my head against his chest. "I can't wait to hike the trails with Moose this time and spend the night in our cabin again." My voice is muffled against his shirt.

It's become our place now—ever since he came crashing through the door in the dead of winter, hell bent on making sure I was okay. Now looking back on it, that might have been when I started feeling things shift between us. From friendship to something more. I didn't let myself fully open up until the night Nova was born.

It's going to be so relaxing and refreshing to get away from the town's gossip. To spend some quality time together with no worries. No pressure from both of our businesses. Just the whispers of the forest and beautiful, sweet isolation.

Chapter 43

MASON

As Olive treads through the grass covered path in the woods, Moose runs after her carrying a stick, tail wagging. Pine, maple, and cherry trees light up the expanse with growing green buds. The air is damp with lingering dew and filled with an earthy fragrance.

My hands shake with nervous anticipation at my side. I'm more excited than anxious. I've been waiting patiently for this day. I want to start forever with her now.

When Olive reaches the top of the trail, she turns to look back at me. Her face is flushed against the morning breeze. Her freckles are distinct over crimson. Flowing curls drop from both sides of her face. I take in every aspect of her. I want to remember this moment for the rest of my life. I want to take a picture and frame it in the confines of my mind. That way, it'll remain a permanent fixture in my memories.

The sunrise behind her paints the sky carmine, a deep red and purple, with wispy clouds and strokes of orange. We're insignificant in the vastness of the woods surrounding us. It's a breathtaking view. But it all dulls in comparison to the woman I want to spend the rest of my life with. She smiles, a radiant full one, as if recalling months ago in this same spot. In a few months, so much has changed. The view has transcended from pure white to an array of colors. Just like the story of us.

I get down on one knee and call Moose to my side. I grab the ring box tied underneath his collar.

Her eyes widen and turn glossy. She covers her mouth with one hand, and I grasp her other one in mine. "Olive. I love you more than every tree in these woods. Every flake of snow that sits upon the ground in winter. I would go to the ends of the earth to keep you safe. There is no mountain I wouldn't climb. No river too wide or deep for me to swim through. For you, I would do anything and everything.

"We've spent a lifetime as friends. We know every little thing about each other. Like the scar on your right shoulder from falling off your bike when we were ten. And how much you love to fill your purse with everything because you never know when you're going to need something. We know the best way to annoy each other and laugh about it afterward. How we seem to finish each other's sentences. You're always the first person I think of when I wake up. And the one that fills my dreams at night. We've come up with so many nicknames for each other over the years. I've called you Sweetie Pie and Firefly, but the only one I want to call you now is my wife. Will you marry me?"

"Yes!" Tears flow in streams down her cheeks. I slide the ring on her finger. She crouches down and pulls me into her arms. She squeezes me tight. Moose tries to lick our faces. We both shake with laughter.

"I want to hold you and never let you go." She squeezes me tighter. "I love you, Mason."

"So don't." Tears cloud my vision. "I love you more, Olive."

Epilogue

MASON

Two months later

"Do you, Mason Cleary, take Olive Watson to be your lawfully wedded wife?" our officiant, Constance, says.

Turns out Constance was officiated and registered. She asked to do our wedding, and we agreed. Besides, she had a hand in getting us together in the first place. Why not?

Olive and I finish saying, "I do." And we share our vows with smiles and eager glances.

"You may now kiss the bride." Once the words leave Constance's mouth, I press my lips against Olive's, and I forget where we are completely. Every time we kiss it feels like the very first time all over again. I'm so in love with my *wife*. When we pull away the smile that paints her face is enough to bring me to tears. One trickles down my face. Her eyes well up, and she also starts crying. We end up a crying mess walking down the aisle, smiling wide for the camera.

At the small reception held at the pavilion behind the town shops, we feast on pizza from The String Cheese, courtesy of Joe. He felt guilty about one too many salt-in-drink pranks and wanted to cover all the food for our wedding. Everyone is here. The whole town. Both of our families. Olive changed into a smaller white dress that looks stunning. I smile in awe at my wife. I still can't believe she's my wife. I can't say it enough out loud or in my mind.

"Hey, husband." She blushes as she says the word, husband.

"Hey, wife." My heart pounds loudly against my chest as I say it back.

"Did you bring them?"

"Yes, they're right here in my pocket." I tap the pocket of the dress coat draped over my arm. The weather is too hot to wear it any longer. It's the first time I've worn anything other than my black T-shirt or black dress shirt. Olive was shocked to say the least, when she saw me wearing a suit.

"Let's go tell them the good news. Is now a good time?" she asks.

"Any time is a good time to spend with you."

She blushes. "You always know the right things to say."

"Of course I do. I'm your *husband*." I chuckle and follow her through the crowd of people.

Some congratulate us on our way to the picnic table at the far end. A few say, "We're so happy for you." Others smile and wave as we pass.

"Hi, Mom." I greet my mother sitting at the picnic table. "Hi, Beth," I say as Olive and I take a seat across from them. They smile eagerly and stop their somewhat heated looking conversation.

"What's wrong?" Olive asks, looking perplexed.

"Oh nothing," Beth says.

"Just tell them." My mom sighs.

"Sophia was griping over the fact you had light green tablecloths and Mason jars filled with flowers at each table. They're beautiful, but she was hoping for an ocean theme. With blues and seashells and sand and all the works." Beth sighs dreamily.

"You're a blue-faced liar, Beth. You were the one who said it, not me. Don't go trying to blame your crazy notions on me alone. As if you're the innocent one. Ridiculous." My mom shakes her head back and forth.

"Ladies. Calm down. Olive and I came up with the perfect solution," I say. Both of their eyes light up in wonder. Olive giggles at my side. Do they think we're going to redecorate right now for them?

Probably.

"We got you something to fill the ocean dream void. Four plane tickets for you. One for you, Sophia, and one for Liam." Olive smiles.

"And one for you, Beth, and one for Alex." I slide the tickets across the wooden table.

"Florida! Thank you!" Beth shoots from her seat and hugs Sophia. They jump up and down in place.

"Do you think that will satisfy them now? They'll finally get to go to the beach." Olive sighs.

"No, I don't. It'll only fill the ocean void temporarily. Long enough for us to enjoy our honeymoon at least."

"Thank, God." Olive smiles, and I pull her into my side, wrapping my arms around her.

"Can I have a word with you two?" Constance asks from the end of the table.

"Sure. We have a moment now that our moms are clearly preoccupied," I say.

"So, I thought you would like to know. Vivi and Dustin are together because I rigged the drawing for teams. Now that you two are together as well because I *baked* up a cookie competition, I'm working on something for Dan and Marigold. Let's just say they're going to get a nice *wrench* in their plans."

Olive and I look at each other and laugh.

Oh, no. I feel bad for Dan and Marigold.

"Should we warn them?" Olive whispers when Constance leaves.

"I don't know yet. It worked out for us, didn't it?"

"I guess it did." She smiles.

Three years later

Olive and I sit in rocking chairs on our back porch. Julian, our two-year-old son, runs through the backyard chasing chickens with Moose at his side. He giggles and picks up one of the Rhode Island Red's that he named Chicken Wing. He pets her feathers and smiles. The name he gave her is adorable. The warm summer heat prickles my arms with beads of sweat. Olive's smile glows as she places her hand on her growing stomach. Another boy. Funny, after my mom had three girls.

"What are you thinking?"

"I'm thinking about how lucky I am." I smile at my beautiful wife. Important moments flash through my mind. Pictures of memories we've shared. Our engagement. Our wedding. The birth of our first son. Another one on the way.

I reminisce more about our summer wedding. The wooden arch was decorated with flowers Vivi put together from the NSSG. The pink, purple, and yellow petals made for a stunning backdrop where we shared our vows. Olive wore the most beautiful crocheted white dress with colorful flowers sewed in. She made it herself. She was a sight for sore eyes. Her red curls flowed over her shoulders. Her face was covered by a sheer veil. When she lifted it and her eyes met mine... I knew I was the luckiest man alive. I could see the glow in her eyes. Our future was set in stone. I've never gotten rid of that feeling. Every time I see Olive, my heart beats faster to this day. I don't think it will ever go away.

The love we share is sempiternal.

"I'm lucky too." She puts her hand on mine. "This little life of ours is wonderful. I wouldn't trade it for anything."

"Me neither."

THE END

Acknowledgements

To you reader. This little dream of mine wouldn't be possible without you. Thank you for living in Thornwood Valley for a little while. I hope you enjoyed reading about Mason and Olive. I hope you fell in love with their story. And the quirky small-town atmosphere. I hope I made you laugh somewhere along the way too! After releasing my debut, A Fowl Match, I didn't know if I'd be able to write another one. There was so much support from everyone who read it. This story just flew from my fingers. Okay, maybe not literally. I don't write the story. My characters write their own story. Okay, maybe I'm physically typing the keys, but I never know how the plot's going to turn out in the end. When I get into my characters, they pretty much make their own rules and break them. Much like Mason and Olive did with Constance's rules. LOL.

To Andrea, Jimena, and Jordyn. Thank you for being the best beta readers EVER! Thank you for taking the time to read. Thank you for giving me your feedback. It made Olive and Mason's story even better. I can't say thank you enough.

To my proofreader/editor/rockstar, Haley. Thank you! This book would not be what it is without your help. You are amazing! P.S. I will be getting my chickens T-Rex arms. LOL. Thank you again.

To my ARC readers. Thank you for taking the time to read my second novel. And for shouting from the rooftops about my book on social media. For messaging me when you find something exciting. For making collages about my characters. You are the best!

To my editor, Ramona. Thank you for making my book flow nicely.

To my grandparents, Mom Mom and Pops. Thank you for being my alpha readers. For being the first eyes on my novel. Thank you for helping me with grammar, book name ideas, cover ideas, etc. I love you both so much for supporting my dreams.

To my husband, thank you for supporting all of my crazy dreams. For listening to me talk about ideas constantly. Like 24/7. For getting me a giant white board to plot my books. For listening to me read chapter after chapter. For helping me with funny ideas. And for showing me what a true friends to lovers trope looks like in real life. This one was inspired by our love story in a way.

About the Author

Sarah Madeline lives for small town romances and swoon worthy, tension filled moments. She fills her pages with laughter and happily ever afters. She resides in small town Pennsylvania with her husband, miniature dachshund, cat, and eighteen chickens. Hopefully adding some goats to her family soon. When she's not writing, you can find her reading in front of a warm fire, fishing, baking, or gardening.

Email: sarahmadelineauthor@gmail.com
Instagram: @sarahmadelineauthor
TikTok: @sarahmadelineauthor
Goodreads: goodreads.com/author/show/54572302.Sarah_Madeline

Also by

SARAH MADELINE

A Fowl Match is the first book in the Thornwood Valley Series.

www.ingramcontent.com/pod-product-compliance
Lightning Source LLC
Chambersburg PA
CBHW021956130726
47903CB00014B/1462